ACES OVER QUEEN

SUSAN HAYES

ABOUT THE BOOK

To win their queen's heart, this pair must risk it all.

Royan Watson lived by three simple rules: No regrets, no relationships, and no slowing down. No exceptions. Then steady, reliable, and sexy as hell Owen Connors crossed his orbit, and Royan's rules went out the airlock.

Astek station is in chaos, and Tianna Astor has been sent to set things right. But no briefing or data files could prepare the ice queen of Astek Corp for the secrets, lies, and temptations she'll find out at the edge of civilized space.

Aces Over Queen (Book #8 of the Drift Series)

First Print Publication: May 2019

Cover Design: Melody Simmons ~ ebookindiecovers.com

Editor: Dayna Hart

Published by: Black Scroll Publications

ISBN: 978-1-988446-46-2

*I am blessed to be surrounded by supportive and loving people.
My Mum and Dad, who always believed in me even when I
didn't believe in myself. My friends, Karen, Cheryl, Dee-Dee
and Rebecca who are always there when I need a friendly ear.
And Irene, my amazing boss who has been there since the
beginning of this adventure, encouraging me every step of
the way.*
Thank you.

PROLOGUE

OUT ON THE edge of civilized space is a rag-tag collection of space stations and platforms known as the Drift. It's a haven for the hunted, the lost, and those seeking second chances. The people who live there hail from every species, class, and corner of the galaxy, but they all have one thing in common: they don't belong anywhere else.

There's nothing beyond the Drift but wild space and an asteroid belt full of ore-rich rocks. The asteroids are mined by hundreds of vessels and their hard-working crews. When the ships deliver their haul to be processed, those crews hit the infamous bars, casinos, and pleasure houses that are the Drift's primary source of income…and only source of entertainment.

It's a world of its own. One where corporations rule, the laws are flexible, and everything is for sale, for the right price.

WELCOME TO THE DRIFT.

CHAPTER ONE

TIANNA LOVED the freedom of traveling. It was one of the few times in her life she could relax and be herself. Given the magnitude of her new assignment, this trip to the Drift might be the last time she could relax for quite a while. Knowing that, she'd requested as small a crew as possible - a flight team and two members of Astek's private security force. Ideally, she would have managed the trip solo, but there wasn't a snowball's chance in a supernova her father would allow it. Things were too unsettled, too dangerous. The corporations were on uneasy footing. Old alliances were being questioned, the body count was rising, and trust was in short supply.

According to her father, trust was the reason she was headed to the edge of known space to take control of Astek Station. Cornelius Astor might doubt his daughter would ever be ready to take over his beloved business, but her loyalty was unquestionable.

She set aside her mug of tea and stood, indulging in a slow stretch to ease the knots in her neck and shoulders.

She'd spent the better part of the day in her quarters, reading everything she could about her new home - Astek Station. By the time she arrived, she intended to know everything she could about the station, the people who worked for her, and the ones who might be plotting against her, her father, and the family business.

"Tink, please send a request for a new set of blueprints of Astek space station to be drawn up and finalized before I arrive. The ones on file are more than two years out of date."

"Sending request to executive services, Astek station." The cheerful, airy voice of her virtual assistant replied.

"Thank you, Tink." It drove her father to distraction that she had named her digital assistant after a character in an ancient children's story. It made him even more cross-eyed that she spoke to Tink like it was a sentient being.

"Is there anything else, Tianna? You have worked through your usual mealtime. Shall I order a meal to be delivered to your quarters?"

"That sounds perfect. I'll have my usual, but with a double slice of cherry pie."

"I believe the food dispenser is out of cherry pie. Would you like to substitute apple, instead?"

Tianna wrinkled her nose. "I'm going to be very grumpy if there's no cherry pie until we get to the Drift."

"Noted. Checking inventory now." There was a momentary silence. "I'm sorry, Tianna, because of the change in departure times, some supplies did not make it aboard on time."

She sighed. "Apple pie will be fine, thanks. And you have nothing to apologize for. I'm the one who changed our departure time. My father's paranoia made it seem like a good idea. He even had the pilot file a false destination so no one would know where we were headed." He'd said he was worried about her safety, which was hard to believe. He rarely worried about anything. Her father was always calm, controlled, and deliberate. The only time she'd seen him show any signs of emotional distress was the first time she woke up after her accident. He'd been there, sitting by her bed in a rumpled suit, haggard with worry.

There'd been an echo of that same concern in his eyes when he'd called her in to give her this assignment. "This is going to be dangerous, Tianna. If I could keep you here, I would, but there's too much at risk. I need someone I can trust overseeing things there."

And according to her father's first rule, family were the only ones you could trust. That's why she was headed to the far side of the galaxy. He made it clear every day that he didn't believe she was ready to take over Astek, but all this instability gave her a rare chance to prove herself.

Her father might not love her - she didn't think he was even capable of that emotion. But he did care for her in his own way. She knew that. If he didn't, he wouldn't have risked everything he'd built to keep her alive after the accident.

Recollections of the battle she'd waged to recover from the crash made her body ache with remembered pain. "Tink, run a shower for me, will you? I should have time before my meal gets here."

"Your shower is now running. Your meal will be ready in fifteen minutes. Would you like me to inform you when it has arrived?"

"I would. Thanks, Tink."

Tianna stripped off her clothes as she walked, dropping them on the floor just for the amusement of watching the housekeeping bots scuttle out of their charging stations to tidy up the trail of abandoned clothing.

The moment she opened the door to the sanitation room she was enveloped in a cloud of fragrant steam. Oranges, she guessed, with a hint of something spicy underneath. Tink selected the scents using its database of aromatherapy information, and always seemed to find the right fragrance to suit her mood.

She stepped under the stream of hot water, letting the heat penetrate her body. There was always a strange moment when her artificial parts took a few extra moments to warm up, and she could feel the difference, a slight chill in her limbs and at the back of her skull. The sensation passed quickly, but it served as a daily reminder of how close she'd come to death. She was more, and less, than human now. A medical miracle with no legal right to exist.

Cybernetic limb replacement was legal, but what was done to her was so much more than that. She didn't even know exactly what they'd done to her. All records of her surgeries were faked to protect everyone involved, and her father had locked the real files away. For all she knew, they'd been destroyed. If anyone learned what had been done to her, her father would go to jail, and so would everyone who had rebuilt her, using illegal methods and banned technology to save her life and turn her into something unique, and less than human.

She ran a sudsy hand down her body, doing a silent inventory of her injuries. The surgeons had done immaculate work, leaving her skin with barely a scar or blemish. The real changes were invisible from the outside. Her bones had been shattered. Her organs ruptured, her limbs crushed and mangled beyond recognition. The skimmer crash had left her with catastrophic injuries.

Unsurvivable. That's what they'd told her father when she'd been brought in. But she had survived. All it took was money, connections, and a corporate tycoon who would rather break galactic law, as well as the laws of nature, than lose his only heir. What she might have wanted had never even been a factor.

When the first explosion tore through the ship, she thought she was having a flashback to the crash. The impression only lasted a split second. When the second, larger explosion hit, she was tossed around the tiny shower space, slamming into the walls several times before crashing to the floor. It couldn't have been more than a few seconds, but she experienced every moment in slow-motion. She was airborne. The lights flickered. Impact. Airborne again. The lights went out. Warning alarms screamed. A flash of red. Impact again. Pain. Fear. Another moment of flight. She tumbled again, crashing headlong into something. The tumbling stopped. There was silence.

When Tianna came to, she was floating. Disoriented and dazed, she reached out wildly, trying to find something to connect with in the dark. Her hand hit a wall, still warm and slick from her shower. Shower. She'd been showering when...something happened. Something big and explode-y.

"*Fraxx*," she swore, her voice a welcome break in the silence. "Tink, if you're there, I could use a status report."

The braided gold band on her left wrist buzzed slightly,

confirming Tink's presence. "I am here, though in a diminished capacity. The ship's AI is offline. I am operating on backup power and have limited abilities. I am unable to give you a full assessment at this time."

"Forget the full assessment. Tell me what you know. How bad is it?" Tianna felt her way out of the shower, no easy task when there was no gravity or light source.

"The ship is adrift. I am unable to detect any energy output on any deck."

"Life signs?"

"Scanning." Tink was silent for several long, terrible seconds. "I am unable to locate any other life signs in the immediate vicinity. My sensor range is minimal, however. It is possible..."

"We both know that's not likely." The crew was gone. Killed by whatever had taken out her ship and left her adrift in a crippled wreck.

"What happened?" Something brushed by her face in the dark, and she flinched, swatting it away out of instinct. When her hand touched soft fabric, she realized it was only a towel and grabbed it. She couldn't do much at the moment, but she could get herself dried off.

"I have limited data, but it is eighty-nine percent likely that the ship experienced multiple explosive decompressions in a short time period."

"You mean the ship blew up. How did it happen? No, scratch that. It doesn't matter right now. How long can I survive given the current situation?"

"I do not have enough data to make an accurate calculation."

"Dammit, Tink. Give me your best guess. How long do I have?"

"You have less than twenty hours' worth of breathable atmosphere. Life support is offline, but it will take some time for the temperature to drop to dangerous levels."

Fraxx. "Has a distress beacon been activated?"

"Affirmative. The beacon is automated and functioning normally."

"Then I guess we better hope someone answers that beacon before I run out of air or freeze to death." Her father's choices might have saved her life, again. A normal human would die when the temperature dropped too far or the carbon dioxide rose too high. She wasn't human, though. Not anymore. She was a cyborg with a body loaded with military grade nanotech whose only purpose was to keep her alive.

In the years since the crash, she'd always played it safe. No more risks. No adventures. She hadn't tested her medi-bots against anything more dangerous than the occasional flu virus. Today, they'd have their work cut out for them. And if she lived, she was going to have to thank her father for saving her life, again.

ROYAN WATSON LEANED back in his seat and uttered a sigh of contentment. This was where he was happiest: in the cockpit of the *Sun Sprite* with all of space stretched out in front of him. He had almost everything he wanted. A fast ship, the galaxy to play in – now if he could convince Owen that they were meant to be together, life would be perfect.

His new security officer's footfalls rang out on the bare metal deck, announcing his return.

"Everything is quiet and secure back in the cargo bay," Owen announced.

"I should hope so. Our entire cargo is livestock embryos in cryo-stasis. If things weren't quiet back there, we'd have a lot of explaining to do to the colonists waiting on this shipment."

"And a lot of mess to clean up." Owen's placed a hand on Royan's shoulder, his thumb brushing the back of his neck in a brief caress. "Just so we're clear, my shiny new contract does not include cleaning duties. I'm here to protect the ship, its cargo, and you, in that order."

Royan uttered a dramatic sigh. "This is what happens when I leave employee contract negotiations to my sister. I am clearly the most valuable asset on this ship and should be at the top of that list."

Owen chuckled. "Last time I looked, Zura owned this company. We just work for her, remember? And while it's not in my contract, she made it pretty damned clear that keeping you in one piece was high on her list of priorities. Apparently, she doesn't have much faith in your ability to stay out of trouble."

Royan considered protesting, but there wasn't much point. Given a choice, he'd fly straight into trouble nine times out of ten, and they both knew it. "I don't care why she lured you away from working security at the Nova, I'm just glad you're here."

Owen squeezed his shoulder, released it, and moved back. It was a dance they'd been doing since they'd left Astek station for a series of deliveries that had kept them moving for the better part of three weeks. They'd have a moment. A look, a touch, or a whispered word, and then Owen would move away again. It was making Royan crazy. "You admitting you need help staying out of trouble?" he asked.

Royan spun the chair around to look over at his friend and one-time lover. After their one night together, Owen had retreated. Their friendship was still intact, and the attraction was still there, too. *Fraxx*, the attraction between them was enough to rival a black hole, and it had only gotten stronger since they'd fallen into bed. The problem was, Owen didn't trust him. Fair enough. But how could he prove he could do better if he didn't get the chance to show it?

"Me admit to needing help? Never. But flying solo gets old. I like having you around. You're a lot more fun to talk to than the ship. No insult intended, Sprite."

The ship's AI responded in the low, sultry female voice Royan had programmed into the system the moment he'd taken possession of the *Sun Sprite*. "I understand. I am not programmed for recreational activities, including conversation."

He patted the wall closest to him. "I know, sweetheart. But you're still the best ship I've ever flown."

Owen cocked a brow and sighed. "You really can't help yourself, can you? You have to flirt with anything that shows the slightest sign of sentience."

"It's part of my charm." Royan stood and walked over to Owen. "It works, too. On everyone but you."

"That's not true." Owen's blue-gray eyes darkened as he locked gazes with Royan. "You know that's not true."

"Then why are you sleeping in the crew quarters instead of with me?" And there it was, the topic they'd been dancing around since the day Owen had walked onto the *Sprite* as a member of the crew.

"Because that's not where we are."

Royan grabbed the collar of Owen's shirt and pulled him in close. "Then where the *fraxx* are we?" This was the closest he'd been to Owen in weeks, and it wasn't close enough.

"I don't know. But I do know that one night of drunken sex does not make us live-in lovers."

"It was amazing drunken sex, though." Royan threw caution to the cosmos and closed the last inch between them to brush his mouth across Owen's. "Come on, admit that much."

Owen groaned. "You and me are not a good idea. We're too different."

"Opposites attract," he retorted, desperate enough to cling to clichés."

Owen put his hand on Royan's but didn't push him away. "And mixing volatile chemicals can make things go boom in a very bad way."

"Or very good ways. Come on, admit it, baby. That night we had was amazing."

Owen sighed, and Royan knew he'd won. "Everything with you is amazing, you lunatic."

"I know."

"Asshole." Owen kissed him, his mouth slanting across his with a fire that made Royan's head spin.

Finally.

Lips locked, hands fisted in each other's shirts, the taste of coffee and cinnamon teased his tongue. He was rock hard in seconds as Owen let down his guard and let Royan get another glimpse of the wild side his best friend kept locked down most of the time.

He'd only seen that side of Owen once, the night of

Zale's wake. The celebration of Zale's life had been so loud the big guy must have heard it in the afterlife. The booze had flowed, along with laughter, tears, and stories from everyone who had ever known him. It was a hell of a night, the mix of liquor and grief erasing every line Owen had drawn in their friendship. They'd crossed them all, and now… Now, he had no *fraxxing* idea what they were. Because while they hadn't been lovers since that night, they were a hell of a lot more than friends.

Owen tore his mouth from his. "We need to stop."

"That's a terrible idea. What we need to do is—" his suggestion they put the ship on autopilot and get naked was cut off by the ship's AI.

"Captain, I'm receiving a distress beacon."

That news was probably the only thing short of a comet strike that could make him change trajectories right now. "So we're clear, I'm not stopping because you thought we should. I'm stopping because someone out there is in trouble."

They let go of each other and Royan turned toward the console. "Play the message, Sprite."

"There's no message. Only an automated beacon."

Odd. Normally there was some sort of message identifying the craft and what the problem was. "Show me the location of the beacon."

A star map shimmered into existence in the air over his chair. Their current position was marked in red, and the beacon showed as a blip of strobing yellow.

"How long would it take to reach the location of the beacon?"

"Thirteen hours, forty-eight minutes." By the standards of space travel, that was no time at all, but for whoever had sent the distress call, it would feel like a lifetime.

"Make the calculations. I'll deactivate the FTL drive and restart the engines with our new coordinates."

Owen cleared his throat. "You don't even know who we're going to help, or what happened to them. That's a big risk to take for a stranger."

"Are you saying we shouldn't respond?"

"I'm saying it's a risk, and it's my job to make sure we avoid as many of those as we can. We have no idea who or what is out there. For all we know, this is a trap."

"It might be, but I doubt it. Space is too big to just randomly set off a distress signal and hope someone is close enough to reach you in a reasonable amount of time. There are better ways to set an ambush." He pointed to the flashing circle of yellow. "They're alone out here. If we don't help them, they're going to die out here. I'm not going to let that happen."

Owen's jaw flexed as he clenched it in obvious frustration. "Can't anyone else help?"

"Who?" He gestured to the map. "Sprite, are there any other ships in the area?"

"Negative."

"Can you be sure of that, Sprite?" Owen asked.

"There is an eighty-one percent chance this area is empty. I cannot be one hundred percent sure."

"Which means there's a one-in-five chance we're not alone out here." Owen pointed to the yellow beacon. "Just tell me you accept the possibility it *might* be a trap."

His gut told him this was the real thing, but having finally made some progress with Owen, Royan didn't want to blow it by fighting. "Alright. It's possible. We're still going, though."

"Only if you agree to do this my way."

Royan's cock twitched at the tone of command in Owen's voice. *Hell, if he uses that tone of voice, I'll do whatever he wants.* "I can do that."

"How the *fraxx* do you do that?"

"What?"

"Make anything, and everything sound like foreplay."

Royan deliberately bit his lower lip. "I've got no idea what you're talking about."

Owen growled low in his throat. "Quit it. If we're doing this, then we do it slow and smart."

Royan wasn't sure what they were talking about anymore, but he hoped it wasn't just the rescue. Slow wasn't his preferred speed, but if that's what Owen wanted, he could throttle back a little – For now.

"Okay. You want it slow, we'll do slow. Just tell me what you need me to do."

"We'll go check out this distress beacon, but we will approach it cautiously and make sure we know what we're getting ourselves into. One more thing. Once we're there, your ass stays on the *Sun Sprite*."

"Fine. No risking my cute ass. I'm good with that, but I've got a rule of my own."

"What's that?"

"Your fine ass comes back in one piece, too. And before you get all twitchy, there's nothing sentimental about it. If you get hurt, Zura will take it out of my hide."

Owen snorted with laughter. "Duly noted. I'll try and come back in one piece…for your sake."

"Appreciate it."

"I'm going to run a full diagnostic on the weapons systems. I won't be long." Owen left, and Royan turned his chair back toward the console to start the process of taking the ship back into normal space. It would take a few minutes to recalibrate the FTL drive with the new coordinates, and then they'd be on their way again.

He checked the new course and sent the information to his sister, back on the Drift. She wouldn't be happy he'd be late with his delivery, but she'd been a pilot, too. She knew the code. When someone called for help, you answered, because the next time someone sent out a distress call, you might be the one in trouble.

CHAPTER TWO

OWEN STOOD at the back of the cramped cockpit as they made their final approach to the source of the distress beacon. If this was an ambush, someone had gone to a lot of trouble to make it look real, more work than any raider or pirate he'd ever crossed orbits with. The dark bulk of a crippled ship drifted in the void, surrounded by a constellation of debris, and the sensors couldn't detect any other vessels in the area.

"Sprite, what's the status of the damaged ship? Life signs? Power signals?" Royan asked.

"I'm detecting one life sign and a weak power source midship, upper deck. The are no other active power sources apart from the one powering the automated beacon. The ship is dead."

They moved in closer, maintaining a cautious speed he knew must be killing Royan.

"*Re'veth*. Look at the damage. How the hell is anyone still alive?" Royan muttered, watching the external feeds as they got close enough to get a proper look.

The ship wasn't just crippled, it was shattered. The hull was torn open in several spots, and the area around her was full of debris from her interior. "There are bodies out there."

Owen tapped the screen, zooming in on part of the wreckage. Two corpses were visible on the screen, both of them wearing some kind of uniform he didn't recognize.

"Poor bastards didn't know what hit them. Hell, I'm not sure what could do this, either. I don't see any scorch marks or signs of a fire fight, and there are too many holes for this to be a simple hull breach."

"This was an attack, but I don't think there was another ship involved." Owen zoomed in on the front of the ship. "Look at the way the hull is peeled back. These holes were caused by explosions from inside the ship."

"I've never seen anything like that."

Owen had, but he wasn't going to admit it. There were parts of his past he didn't talk about with anyone, not even Royan. "It's the only thing I can think of that would explain why the metal is blown outward."

"I know who we can ask," Royan said as he deftly maneuvered them closer still.

"Who?"

Royan pointed to the screen. "There's someone still alive in there. If anyone knows what happened, they would."

"Good plan. Sprite, where are the airlocks on the damaged ship?"

The ship's AI generated a three-dimensional model and projected it in front of Owen. "There are two primary airlocks, both leading to parts of the ship that have been depressurized."

"*Fraxx.*" He stared at the image of the ship. "How the hell do we get them out of there without killing them in the process?"

"Sprite, is there any way to communicate with the occupant of the other ship now we're this close?" Royan asked.

"I can try sending a ping to the power source I detected. It might be able to receive a short-range transmission."

"Do it." Royan glanced back at him. "If we're lucky, they'll respond and tell us they have a pressure suit with them."

"When do you ever get that lucky?"

Royan raised his brows and grinned. "This is me we're talking about, remember? I get lucky all the time."

Owen was well aware of Royan's sexual exploits. His good looks and charm made him almost irresistible to anyone he took an interest in, and he took an interest in damned near everyone. At least, he used to. Lately, Royan had focused all his attention on him, and he hadn't been strong enough to resist temptation.

"I am receiving a response to my ping."

"On speaker." Royan said.

A female voice filled the cockpit, her words accompanied by the distinctive sound of chattering teeth. "Hello? P-please, is someone th-there?"

Royan answered first. "Hello. This is the captain of the *Sun Sprite*. We heard your distress beacon and responded. We're currently circling your ship. Are you injured?"

"My name is T-Tianna. I'm not injured, but it's *f-fraxxing* cold in here. No life sup-port."

"Good to hear you're not hurt. My name's Royan. Any

suggestions on how we can get you out of there, sweetheart?"

She scoffed. "S-sweetheart? Do you always f-flirt with women m-mid-rescue?"

He chuckled. "No idea. This is a first for me."

"Well, flirt or not, I'm g-grateful you're here. There's an emergency hat-ch that should give you access to the area of the ship I'm trap-pped in."

"Do you have a pressure suit?" Owen asked.

"N-no. Who are y-you?"

"Sorry. This is Owen, the Sprite's security officer. I'll be the one coming to get you. We'll have you out of there soon, Tianna. I promise."

"Thank y-you."

"We're going to scan your ship for this hatch. Once we find it, we'll be latching onto the side of your ship. You might feel a bump when that happens."

"Okay. Can you guys do me a f-favor? Keep talking to me."

"You got it, Tianna. I'll keep this comm line open," Royan said, then looked at Owen. "You got this?"

"Yeah. I'll grab the equipment and get into the airlock. You get us into position. And try to remember the agreement. Your ass stays here."

Royan waved him off. "Yeah, yeah. I know. But for the record, as captain, I really think I should be there to greet our soon-to-be guest."

Owen rolled his eyes just as Tianna uttered a soft snicker of amusement. "I cannot w-wait to meet the p-pair of you."

"The feeling is very mutual, sweetheart."

"You are unbelievable," Owen muttered.

"You forgot incorrigible, lovable, and adorable."

"No, I didn't. Do your thing. I'll get things ready. Let me know when we're in position."

He jogged down the battered corridors of the *Sprite*, making for the largest of the ship's airlocks in the cargo bay. It had a universal docking hatch and should allow them to link up with the other ship. As he moved, his mind sifted through all the questions the situation conjured. Tianna hadn't given them her last name or volunteered the name of her crippled ship. How had she survived the explosion? Did she have any idea why her ship had been targeted, or by who? These were dangerous times, and while he appreciated her situation, he needed answers.

"You ready?" Royan asked, using the ship's comm system to broadcast the question.

He toggled his comms to broadcast and kept jogging. "Did you find the hatch already?"

"I did. We'll be in position in three minutes or less, so move your ass."

"I'll be there."

He broke into a run, which gave him enough time to grab two portable oxygen masks, a pair of heavy gloves, and a pry bar from the equipment locker before stepping into the airlock. The airlock door had barely closed when Royan spoke again. "We're in position. You can start the docking process whenever you're ready."

"Starting now. Tell Tianna she'll be out of there, soon. She might want to close her eyes, too. There's no way to dim the lights in here."

"Thanks, Owen. I'll do that," Tianna answered for herself.

Owen winced. He'd forgotten about the open channel. He'd have to do better than that. Royan needed someone to watch his back, and as much as he didn't want to admit it, he cared about that lunatic too much to trust anyone else to do the job. Royan was a pain in the ass, but somehow, Owen had become responsible for the lunatic pilot. Not only because he'd signed on as security officer, but because he cared for Royan – far more than he liked to admit.

TIME HAD NEVER PASSED SO SLOWLY for Tianna. Not even the agonizing hours she'd spent alone in the wreckage of her skimmer had felt like this. The darkness surrounded her, swallowing her up and distorting her other senses. Every ping of the hull as it cooled made her flinch, and Tink's occasional updates had been so loud they hurt her ears. Her medi-bots kept her alive, but they couldn't stop the cold that crept into the marrow of her bones and chilled her fingers to the point of pain. She'd give anything for the cyborg's ability to shut off her pain receptors right now, but that was one enhancement she hadn't been given.

The lack of gravity meant the smallest movements would send her drifting across her quarters. She'd wake up with a start each time she came up against some cold, hard surface or some errant piece of clutter brushed across her face. Her nanotech allowed her to go without sleep, but she couldn't escape into blissful unconsciousness, either.

Worse, her communicator and data tablet were lost somewhere in her room. She'd spent hours looking for them to no avail. She could have missed them by a centimeter, or never come near them at all. She had no way to know.

She'd used up some of Tink's precious power to dictate a brief message to her father summarizing her situation. If she died, at least there would be some record of what had happened to her and the crew of the *Alacrity III*. She needed to warn him that things were even more dangerous than they'd expected. If she was a target, then so was he.

She didn't waste time or oxygen with sentimental messages or final farewells. Her father wouldn't appreciate it. Emotions were a waste of energy, a distraction he didn't allow himself and barely tolerated in others, including his daughter.

The only emotion she allowed herself was a rush of relief when Tink came out of power- save-mode to announce she had received a communication ping.

Now she waited in the darkness, swaddled in her bedding and floating a few feet from the outer wall. There were no windows in her quarters, nothing that could compromise the double-thick hull and reinforced walls that were designed to withstand anything from an explosion to a plasma cannon blast. At the time she'd thought her father's modifications to their fleet of private cruisers were the product of paranoia. Now, she wondered if there were other precautions they should take. Someone had tried to kill her once, and whoever had done this would surely try again once they learned she was still alive.

"Guys? How m-much long-longer?" she asked her would-be rescuers. She knew the odds of being rescued hadn't been good. The distress beacon would have let her father know there was a problem, but the circuitous route her father had insisted on meant they were far from civilized space and the larger shipping lanes. Help was likely on its way, but it wouldn't have reached her in time to do anything but retrieve her corpse.

There was a metallic double-knock from the outer wall. "I'm here, Tianna. The hull buckled a bit around the hatch, I'm going to need to use some muscle to get it open." That was Owen. She'd learned their voices already. Owen's was deeper, and he didn't talk much. Royan talked enough for both of them.

"Uh, Owen? You might want to hurry it up," Royan said, his tone edged with worry.

"Problem?" Owen asked. She could hear him working on the other side of the hull while he talked.

"Maybe. Another ship just dropped out of FTL and is headed this way."

"Do you think it's s-someone else responding to my distress b-beacon?" she asked.

"That's one possibility." Royan didn't sound convinced, and honestly, she wasn't either. Her luck hadn't been that good lately.

"And another is that whoever tried to kill you heard your distress beacon and is coming back to make sure the job is done. Tianna, the second I get this *fraxxing* door open I want you to get your ass onboard the *Sprite*."

"What my charming crewmate is saying, sweetheart, is whatever you want to take with you better be in your hand in the next ten seconds or you're leaving without it."

"Everything I own is currently scattered around my pitch b-black room. All I have w-with me are a bunch of blankets and several layers of clothing I managed to gather up." She noticed her teeth had almost stopped chattering. Not a good sign. She needed to get warm, fast. If she started showing signs of hypothermia or frostbite, her rescuers would bring her to their med-bay for treatment. She couldn't let that happen. Her implants and nanotech were closely guarded secrets.

No one but her father and the medical team who had done the work knew what she was, and all of them would face repercussions if her secret was discovered. They'd be barred from their professions, blacklisted, and likely jailed. Astek's stocks would plummet, and her father's legacy would be jeopardized.

"Then be ready to move. Royan, I hope you've got our exit planned?" Owen's question was punctuated by a long metallic screech that pierced to the marrow of her bones as Owen forced the hatch open.

The mechanism gave way slowly, the noise almost drowning out Royan's reply. "We're out of here the nanosecond you give me word you're both on board. Which better be *fraxxing* soon. Our new visitors aren't responding to hails, and they'll be within weapon range in less than a minute."

Adrenaline coursed through her, temporarily banishing the cold and its effects and letting her think clearly. She was positioned badly for a rapid exit. There was nothing to push off of to give her any kind of speed. She peeled off her outermost blanket and threw it toward her feet. The action sent her in the opposite direction, and by the time the first rays of light streamed through the newly opened hatch, she was close enough to the ceiling to use it as a launching pad.

The light hurt her eyes, and she belatedly remembered to cover them with her hand as light, warmth, and atmosphere poured into her cabin.

"Tianna?" Owen called through the door.

She cracked open an eye, but all she could see was a massive silhouette in the doorway.

"Up here and coming your way." She pushed off with her legs, aiming for the threshold of the hatchway. If she got the angle right, she'd cross into the artificial gravity field of the other ship close enough to the floor to avoid a hard landing.

She didn't get the angle right.

Adrenaline and the desire to reach safety made her push off too hard, and she hurtled straight toward Owen and the upper half of the doorway. She expected him to get out of her way, but instead, he threw out his arms and caught her just as she crossed into the gravity field.

"Oof!" He grunted and took a step back as they connected.

"Sorry. And uh, hi." She looked up at the big man holding her and was struck by a totally inappropriate surge of lust. From the strong line of his jaw to the amused gleam in his steel-blue eyes, Owen was all rugged good looks and solid muscle.

"No apologies necessary. I did tell you to move fast," he said, grinning as he set her down on her feet.

"I appreciate the catch. I'm so damned cold right now I might have shattered if I hit the floor." She stepped to one side as he moved past her to slam the airlock door shut."

"Royan, Tianna's on board. Haul ass."

"My favorite words. Grab hold of something, we're gone."

"Why would I need—

Owen grabbed the airlock door handle with one hand and wrapped his free arm around her waist, pulling her into his side just as the engine noise rose to a roar and the entire ship surged beneath her feet. She uttered a surprised squawk and held onto the only thing she could – him.

"Inertial dampeners are acting up," he said by way of an apology.

"I noticed. Any reason you two haven't fixed them?"

"We've got deadlines to make and no time to stop for major repairs. We'll get them fixed when we get home."

Once they were in motion, things stabilized quickly, and he released her, but she had dropped her blankets when she latched onto him for balance, and she wasn't ready to move away from the only available heat source, yet. So she allowed herself a brief moment of contact as she continued their conversation. "Where's home?"

"Ass end of the galaxy. A place called the Drift."

"Which station?" she asked, hardly able to believe her change in fortune. Could this freighter get her to Astek station without anyone being able to find or attack her again?

"Home base is Astek station, but we deliver cargo to every platform and station out there. Not many people flying around the galaxy in private cruisers even know the place exists."

"I was actually on my way there before…" she trailed off and swallowed to clear the lump in her throat. "Before everyone died."

He enveloped her in a bear hug that nearly lifted her off her feet. "Not everyone. And when the guilt about that hits you – and it will – you need to remember there's no shame in being the only survivor. If you need a reminder, Royan or I will be happy to tell you so."

"I'll be fine," she lied. Now she was around people again, she had to be strong. Astors never showed weakness. They were always in control of themselves and their situation, no matter what.

Owen chuckled. "Yeah, that's what I said, too. Come on, let's get you checked out in the med-bay, then find you some food. You must be starving."

"I don't need a med-bay, just a hot shower and food. And coffee. Please tell me you have caffeine on this ship. Coffee. Tea. Hell, right now I'd happily down a mug of ja'kreesh if that's all you had."

"We've got all of the above, though in your current state I wouldn't recommend the ja'kreesh. You need to rest and recover, not bounce around the *Sprite* for the next few days."

"This rescue keeps getting better." She let go of him, squaring her shoulders as she stepped away. "Thank you for saving me. When we get to the Drift, I'll see to it you and Royan are both rewarded."

"Reward? You want to reward us?" Royan chimed in, reminding them both that the comm-line was still open.

"Of course. I'm grateful for what you did for me, and once he hears about it, my father will be, too."

Owen raised a sandy brow. "And who is your father, exactly? Apart from someone who can afford to send his daughter to the Drift in a space cruiser that probably cost half a planet."

She smiled and held out a hand still shaking with cold. "I should probably introduce myself properly. My name is Tianna Astor."

His eyes widened. "As in, Astek Corporation? Those Astors?"

The fun of announcing herself to one of the few people she'd ever met who didn't already know everything about her was dulled by her adrenaline crash. Not even her nanotech could keep her on her feet forever. The floor tilted and she staggered forward, only to be caught again in Owen's strong arms.

"That's it, you're going to the med-bay."

"No. I just need rest." What should have been a commanding tone came out a shaky whisper.

He slipped an arm under her thighs and cradled her against his chest. "Are you always this stubborn?"

"Pretty much." She forced herself to speak louder this time. "Please? I don't need scans, I just want to get warm."

He didn't look convinced. She was trying to think of another way to convince him when Royan joined the conversation.

"There's nothing in the med-bay that will help her warm up. Take her to your room, Owen. I'll meet you there."

"Your room?" she asked, her fatigued mind suddenly filled with thoughts she had no business thinking about a man she barely knew.

Owen shrugged, already heading for the door. "This is a working vessel. We don't do passenger runs, and whatever space there is, we need for cargo. My quarters aren't much, but the bed is comfortable."

"But where will you sleep?"

He carried her into a narrow corridor and turned toward what she assumed was the bow of the ship before he answered. "I'll be bunking with Royan, which is probably what the sneaky son of a starbeast planned from the moment we responded to your distress beacon."

"I can still hear you, you know," Royan commented drily.

"Good. I won't have to repeat myself later."

She was obviously missing something. "Why would he want to make the two of you share a room?"

Owen looked down at her with bemusement. "It's not the room. It's the damned bed."

"I don't – oh." She blushed so hotly it felt like her skin was on fire. "So the two of you?"

"Are friends."

"And then some," Royan chimed in, only this time, his voice sounded much closer. "Hi, sweetheart. I'm Royan. Welcome aboard the *Sun Sprite*."

CHAPTER THREE

TIANNA TURNED her head and found herself looking at a dark-eyed hunk with a wicked smile. Royan was leaner and shorter than Owen, but not by much. He looked like he was seconds away from committing any number of sins, and the gleam in his eye told her he'd enjoy every second. "Hi." She reached out her hand to him. "Thank you for rescuing me."

He took her hand, but instead of shaking it, he lifted it to his lips and grazed a feather-light kiss across her knuckles, his brown eyes gazing straight into hers. "My pleasure. Truly."

The way he uttered the word pleasure sent a thrill chasing down her spine.

"Behave, yourself. She's been through enough without having you drool all over her," Owen muttered.

"I don't drool, thank you. But you're right, our lovely guest needs to get warmed up. Your hands are freezing, sweetheart." Royan squeezed her fingers and then released them to point to a nearby door. "I'm afraid it's not what you're used to, but at least Owen's room is tidy. My quarters are in a state of chaos at all times." He winked. "We'll save that part of the tour for later when you're back to full strength."

"That might be best," she said, inwardly wincing at how weak she sounded. The relief of being rescued, her fatigue, and the discovery that her two saviors were both ridiculously attractive had her off-balance.

Owen carried her through the doorway, and she looked around the cramped space that made up his quarters. It wasn't much. A bed barely wide enough to fit a man his size, a small table, a stool, and a doorway that must lead to a sanitation room.

"The blankets were laundered today, and I can come get my clothes later, after you've rested." Owen set her down in the center of the room. "Shower and head are through that door, and we'll be just down the corridor. Turn left and walk until you run out of ship, or just ask *Sprite* where we are."

Royan crowded in behind them. "Actually, I'd rather not leave you on your own. Not until you've warmed up some."

"I'll be fine. Really. Shouldn't you be making sure we're not being followed by that other ship?"

"Oh, they think they're following us, but they're chasing a phantom." Royan grinned. "I muted our transponder the moment they appeared on sensors, and when we left, I launched a drone that's broadcasting a fake transponder code. It can't travel too far, but by the time it runs out of fuel, we'll be long gone and untraceable."

"No one's supposed to be able to mute their ship's transponder. That's illegal," she said.

Royan chuckled. "Then every ship in the area should be getting fined. The ship that appeared as we were rescuing you had no transponder signal, and your ship's transponder was muted, too. Didn't you know? Even your distress beacon was scrubbed of identifying information."

"We don't even know the name of the vessel you were on. I assume you're going to want to report what happened and tell your father you're safe and sound," Owen said.

She turned to face them, sank on the edge of the bed and gripped her hands in her lap to stop their trembling. "I'm not sure that's a good idea. The last time we met, he warned me to be careful who I trusted. Right now, I have no idea who might have been in on the attack, but to get the explosives on board, there had to be someone on the inside."

"We can send an encrypted message. Nothing fancy or long, but our people can make sure it gets to your father," Royan said.

"That sounds good, thanks. Since someone seems determined to kill me, my best chance is to stay quiet and hitch a ride with the two of you back to the Drift. I know that puts you both at risk, but I promise I'll make it worth your trouble."

"You don't need to bribe us to see you safely back to civilization," Owen stated.

"We've got another delivery to make before we head home. You okay with that?" Royan slid past Owen and joined her on the bed.

"I think taking the long way around might be the smartest thing I could do right now."

"No, the smartest thing you could do would be to let us help you warm up."

Despite her fatigue, she couldn't help but smile. "You can help by leaving me alone so I can have a long, hot shower."

"I have a better idea. Shared body heat will warm you up faster than anything else. Showering will drive the cold from your limbs to your core, and that will just push your body temperature lower. Trust me, my way is better."

Owen snorted with laughter. "Has that line ever worked, Roy-boy?"

Royan winked at her. "Is it working?"

Even though a small part of her was intrigued by the offer, she was too cold and tired to take him up on it. "Afraid not."

"Damn. You're sure?" Royan leaned in close enough their shoulders touched. "If you need anything, just ask." He raised his voice slightly. "Sprite, add Tianna Astor to the ship's roster as a guest. Full access to crew areas."

"Done. Welcome aboard, Tianna," the ship greeted her in a soft, sultry voice that sounded more like a sex bot's than a ship's AI.

"Thank you, Sprite. I'm glad to be here." She looked at her two rescuers and smiled. "Truly. I really am grateful. If you hadn't come for me, that other ship would've finished me off by now. You saved my life."

"Try not to think too much about what could have happened. You're safe, now." Owen reached over and stroked her cheek with a calloused hand. "I'm glad we got to you in time."

"So am I. But unlike my crewmate, I am happy to discuss all the ways I can be rewarded for saving your lovely self." Royan rose to his feet and smiled at her. "If you're sure you don't need our help warming up, we'll give you some space. Later, we'll send a brief, encrypted message to my boss, who can see that it reaches your father. Then, we'll find you some more clothes. Most of Owen's won't fit, but I think I've got a few things that should work, and Zura left a few things onboard the last time she took the *Sprite* for a joyride."

"Zura? You have a woman on your crew?" She felt an irrational flare of jealousy at the idea. The name seemed familiar to her, too, but she couldn't recall from where.

"Zura's not crew, she's my sister," Royan said.

"She's also our boss," Owen added.

"So this is a family business? I know all about those."

"Same idea, different scale. We can compare stories over the next meal. Sound good?" Royan asked.

"Sounds great." She ignored the way her stomach growled at the mere mention of food.

"You got it. What's your favorite food?"

"Cherry pie. If you have that on board, I may never leave."

Royan laid a hand on his chest and sighed dramatically. "A woman after my own heart. Cherry pie it is."

They left a few seconds later, after a few last-minute instructions from Owen on where to find what she'd need for a shower. As much as she wanted to get warm and cleaned up, she didn't leave the bed. The last time she'd been in a shower, her ship had exploded. She wasn't ready to relive that moment. Not yet. Instead, she removed her bracelet, pulling out a small wire from the back and plugging it into the nearest power source.

"There you go, Tink. You should be back up to full power about the same time I am." It was the first time she'd spoken to the AI since putting her on silent mode in the moments before the *Sprite* had docked with the *Alacrity*.

"I have been monitoring the situation. It appears you have been rescued by reliable beings who will see you delivered safely to your destination."

"I agree with your assessment. We were damned lucky."

"Agreed. I did not wish to mention this earlier, but the odds of rescue were highly unfavorable."

"I appreciate your discretion. Since you and I both think this is a safe haven, I'm putting you in standby mode. If I need your assistance, I'll use the voice command to wake you. Please confirm.

Tink was silent a split second longer than she should have been, which was a sure sign she didn't approve of Tianna's plan. "As you wish. Activating standby mode in ten seconds."

"Consider it a vacation, Tink. After what we just went through, we could both use one."

With that, she crawled into Owen's bed and burrowed under the covers, still wearing several layers of clothing. "I'll just rest for a little while before I shower. A few minutes, that's all I need." She closed her eyes and was asleep within seconds.

ROYAN BARELY MADE it ten steps down the corridor before Owen broke the silence. "What do you think you're doing, exactly?"

"Me? I'm headed to the galley to figure out what to feed our guest. What goes with cherry pie?"

Owen moved past him, pivoted, and planted himself in the middle of the hall. "That's not what I meant. Why are you doing the charm and smarm routine with Tianna?"

The glib answer rolled off his tongue before he could switch gears. "Why? In case you missed it, she's *fraxxing* gorgeous."

"She's also been through a lot. Give her a chance to at least get cleaned up and settled before you go full Romeo on her."

"I'm not—" A pang of regret hit as he figured out why Owen was unhappy. "It's not like that. I was just trying to make her smile."

Owen scoffed. "That's crap."

He needed to fix this. "It's not."

Owen just stared at him, jaw set.

"Fine. it's not *total* crap. I was flirting. As you've regularly pointed out to me, that's my default setting." He held up a hand. "And before you glare at me again, I know that's no excuse for what I did back there."

Owen's eyes widened and a sardonic grin lifted the corners of his sexy mouth. "Was that self-awareness I just heard?"

"Little bit, yeah. And while I'm on a roll, here's something else you won't hear very often. "I'm sorry. I didn't think about how you'd feel seeing me flirt with her."

"Thank you." Owen's expression softened. "For the record, though, it didn't bother me. I just think you need to give her some space."

Royan raised a brow. "Now who's talking crap? It bothered you, and you called me on it. Fair enough, but don't pretend this was all about her best interests."

"Fine. It bothered me. I don't know the rules to the game we're playing and it's making me a little crazy."

"I don't know what the hell I'm doing, but I know I'm not playing a game. Not this time. Not with you."

"No?"

For the first time, he saw a crack in Owen's armor, a hint of vulnerability. "No games, Owen."

Owen blew out a sharp breath. "You sure?"

"Of this? Yes. Of what the hell we do next? Not a *fraxxing* clue."

"Me either." Owen glanced back to the door of his quarters. "You like her, don't you?"

"Based entirely on first impressions? Yeah, I do. And so do you."

"What makes you say that?"

"I wasn't the only one flirting with our guest."

Owen looked like he was about to deny it, but he sighed instead. "This was easier when we weren't being so damned honest with each other."

"Yeah, but it wasn't getting us anywhere, either. Admit it. You're attracted to her."

"Of course I find her attractive. As you've already pointed out, she's gorgeous, not to mention she's a serious badass. After everything she's been through, she's still on her feet and making jokes. She reminds me of..." He winced. "Oh, *fraxx*. She reminds me of you."

Royan threw back his head and laughed at the expression on his lover's face. It was somewhere between desire and sheer terror.

"How can there be two of you? Shit like this is supposed to tear holes in the fabric of space-time, isn't it?" Owen scrubbed a hand through his hair, leaving it standing up in unruly spikes.

"Only if she's from an alternate universe. I'm pretty sure she's not, because I cannot imagine a world where I'm so rich I could buy planets."

"Which brings up what is probably the more pressing question. What the hell is the heir to Astek Corp doing out way the hell out here, and how did someone get through some of the galaxy's best security to almost kill her?"

Royan's amusement vanished. "We can ask her what she's doing out here once she's rested up. As for how her ship got blown up, I have no idea, but my gut tells me it had to be an inside job. Ever since their reps started being attacked, the corporations have been hypervigilant to the point of paranoia. I can't imagine the levels of security the heir to the Astek fortune must have."

"Whatever it was, it wasn't enough. How sure are you that the other ship can't follow us?"

"Pretty damned sure." Royan patted the wall of the ship. "My father loaded this old girl with all sorts of toys back when she was a smuggling ship, and my sister added a few upgrades in her day, too. Tianna is safer with us than anywhere else I can think of, at least until we get her to the Drift."

"We could turn around and head straight for home without making our last delivery. The longer we're out here, the higher the chance someone figures out we've got her onboard."

"And leave our clients without their goods?" Royan shook his head. "I don't want to do that to the colonists. They need this shipment."

"I'm not saying it's a good idea. I'm just weighing the odds."

"I think they're in our favor." Royan glanced down the hall. "She's defied the odds already just by surviving. I'd like to think the universe didn't put her through that just to kill her a little while later." At least, he hoped not. There was something about Tianna Astor that made him want to know her better, and it wasn't her wealth or her looks. Maybe it was because she was a survivor, like he was. Or because despite her jokes and easy smile, he got the sense she was guarding a piece of herself, like Owen.

"So, we're keeping her?" Owen cracked a smile.

"Looks that way. We saved her. That makes us responsible for her safety, right?"

"Right."

"Then it's decided. She stays with us." He took Owen's hand and started walking again, pulling the bigger man along with him. "Now, come to the galley with me. We can talk about additional security measures while I whip us up a meal fit for a queen."

"You mean you'll program something into the food dispenser and let it do all the work." Owen's fingers closed around his, but he didn't pull away.

"Trust me, that's the better choice for all of us. I am a man of many talents, but cooking isn't one of them."

"I can cook."

Owen's admission caught him off guard. They'd been

friends for the better part of a year, but there was still a lot he didn't know about Owen's life before they met. "You can? Where'd you learn? It's a bit of a dying art these days."

"I was raised on a ship even older than the *Sprite*. The food dispenser rarely worked, and when it did, all it could do was dispense food tabs and create basic items like sandwiches and coffee. If we wanted anything else, we had to make it ourselves. By the time I left to make my own way in the galaxy, I could make even vat-grown proteins and algae broth taste good."

"I don't believe that's possible." He'd had more than his fair share of algae broth over the years, and it never tasted like anything but what it was, sea sludge.

"Care to make a bet on it?"

"Only if the bet's something wicked and indecent."

"How about loser fulfills the winner's wish? One time only. I'll cook dinner. Tianna can judge. We don't tell her what's in it ahead of time. If she likes it, I win. If not—"

"If not, then I win and I'm going to enjoy collecting my wish." Royan indulged in a moment of pure lust as he thought about the many things he could ask for, only to be brought crashing back to reality when Owen spoke.

"And when I win, I'm going to enjoy sleeping in your big, comfy bed, alone. Because your ass will be sleeping on the floor."

"You wouldn't be that cruel."

"Says the man who gave away *my* bed to the pretty girl without even asking me."

"I see your point. I don't like it, but I see it. And when you lose, I'm going to be the bigger man and let you sleep with me anyway."

"Bigger man, huh?" Owen laughed. "I've seen you naked, Roy-boy. We both know that's not true."

They were still bickering when they reached the galley but they were also still holding hands. As far as Royan was concerned, no matter what happened tonight, he'd already won.

CHAPTER FOUR

Owen was preparing the evening meal alone in the galley. Royan had stayed with him for awhile, but eventually he'd returned to the cockpit to check the sensors and do what he could to make sure they weren't being followed.

It had been months since he'd cooked anything. He'd forgotten how calming it could be to have his hands busy while his mind was free to think about other things. He had a lot to think about, too. Royan. The potential new threat to the *Sun Sprite*. And then there was Tianna.

Tianna was a complication he didn't need. He'd been drawn to her from the second she landed in his arms, all long limbs and grim determination. He was happy to have her on board, despite the fact it made them all targets. That wasn't the problem. Risk, he could handle. Having a woman on board that both he and Royan found attractive – that was a problem.

They hadn't figured out what they were to each other, yet. Friends, yeah. They were that already. Lovers - once, and maybe again. He laughed at himself. There was no maybe about it. The only question was when, and for how long. Despite Royan's earlier words, Owen still had his doubts the sexy pilot was ready for anything long-term. It just wasn't in his DNA.

Would Tianna prove to be a temptation Royan couldn't resist? If that happened, where did that leave them?" He took his frustrations out on the vegetables he was dicing, reducing the still slightly frozen fare to slivers.

"If you chop that any finer, it's going to turn to mush when you cook it."

He spun around, knife still in his hand, and Tianna took a step back, her slender hands out in front of her. "Whoa. Easy big fella. No need to get stabby."

"Sorry. My startle reflex is a little over-developed." He set the blade down on the counter, turned, and took a good look at their guest. Her color had improved. Her lips weren't blue anymore, but an enticing shade of pink. She'd showered too, and her dark hair had been tamed into a tight braid. She was wearing the same outfit as before, but it fit better now that it wasn't stretched over several extra layers. The socks on her feet were his, though, and they were several sizes too big for her.

"Noted. I'm just glad you were only holding a knife and not a blaster."

"I'm not usually armed with either. Since tonight is something of a special occasion, I thought I'd cook a real meal. You look like you're recovering quickly. I wasn't expecting you up for another hour at least."

Her crystal-blue eyes widened with interest. "Dinner sounds good. I'm feeling much better for some rest, which means my only pressing concern is food. So, what's on the menu? Can I help?"

"It's a three-course meal. Soup to start, pasta for the main dish, and then cherry pie for dessert, as requested. I'm working on the soup now, and the pie has already been programmed in. I was planning on figuring out the main dish next. Got any suggestions on what to do with the pasta?"

Her elfin features brightened. "Oh, I've got suggestions. For the price of a cup of coffee, I'll do more than offer suggestion, though. I'll cook."

"You can cook?" Royan was right about cooking being an uncommon skill these days. Food dispensers were cheap and easy to acquire, and so were the food packs they used. When a machine could produce a hot meal at the push of a button, not many people learned how to make it themselves.

She gave a curt nod of her head. "I'm an Astor. We can do anything we set our minds to. Please don't make the mistake of thinking that because I'm rich, I don't know how to do anything myself."

"That hadn't actually crossed my mind. It's just rare for anyone to know their way around a kitchen, or well, a galley." He gestured around the narrow space. "For example, I'm pretty sure Royan would starve to death if the food dispenser stopped working."

Her expression softened. "Sorry. I'm used to people making assumptions about me based on my bank balance."

He gestured to the food dispenser, then the cubby where they stored the dishware. "Help yourself to coffee. You've never been out this far, have you?"

A tiny vertical line appeared between her brows. "No. Why?"

"Things are different this far from the civilized parts of the galaxy. Beings out here don't care about names and bank accounts so much. They judge someone by what they say, and more importantly, by what they do. You'll see when we get to the Drift."

She uttered a bitter laugh. "You mean, when you deliver me to the big space station named for my father's corporation? They're going to judge me, Owen. It's inevitable, and that's okay. I'm used to it."

He knew what it was like to be judged based on who your family was, and it didn't sit well with him to think about her dealing with that day after day. "Well, we're not there, yet. I can't change what happens when we get to the Drift, but until we do, consider yourself judgment free."

"No one can promise that. It's impossible."

"You just survived an explosion that destroyed your ship, killed your crew, and left you floating in the dark with no life support. Do you really want to start talking about what's impossible?" He returned to his work, adding the vegetables and turning the broth down to a gentle simmer as he started gathering up the seasonings he'd need.

She laughed again, but this time there was no unhappy undertone. "Fair point. So, no judgment until we get to the Drift? Like a vacation from myself?"

"More like a vacation where you can just be yourself."

She uttered a soft sigh. "That would be nice. But when we get to the Drift, you two would have to understand that I have a job to do. This would just be a temporary reprieve."

"You're an Astor, which means you're pretty much royalty, at least to us peons out here in the ass end of nowhere. I imagine the best you can hope for is a few days of escape." He shrugged. "It's not like I'm expecting you to hang out with us at the Nova Club once we get home. We don't exactly run in the same social circles."

"The Nova Club? Isn't that the cyborg bar?"

"Cyborg owned and operated, yeah, but their clientele is as diverse as the Drift. Like I said, things are different out here."

She took a sip of her coffee before answering. "What you're suggesting sounds good, so long as it's understood it can't last. When we get to the Drift, I'm taking over management of Astek Station."

"Well, that explains why you won't have time to be social, and it might explain why someone wants you dead. Astek is ground zero for a lot of change these days." She was going to have a target on her back the size of a small planet. The last man to hold that position had been blown to pieces not long ago, and his temporary replacement had been reduced to a quivering mass of paranoia who, rumor had it, had refused to leave his fortified offices since taking over.

"That's why my father sent me. The ground is shifting and he wants someone there he can trust to make sure things don't unravel too much." She laughed. "I guess talking about shifting ground isn't really appropriate given where we are, huh?"

He tapped a booted heel to the deck. "Not a lot of ground out there, but the saying still works. Even out here, most folks spent time dirtside at some point in their lives."

"Did you?"

"Nope. I was born on my family's freighter and spent

most of my life in space. Visiting planets is fine, but I wouldn't want to live on one."

"Why not?" Tianna opened a food cooler and started looking through the contents.

Where to start? The scent of dirt, the drag of gravity, weather, none of it appealed to him. But one thing was worse than all the others combined. "Oceans. I like my water in a glass or coming out of a showerhead. Planets have huge bodies of water, most of them crammed full of carnivorous lifeforms. I'm not a fan."

"And I'm not a fan of the selection in here. Don't you two have any fresh vegetables?"

"Not many. We've been out long enough we've gone through most of what we had, and it's not like we can just order in more. Our last two stops were to automated re-supply stations. We'll restock when we get to Taza Colony. Then we've one more stop to make before heading back to the Drift."

"When will that be?"

"We'll be home in about nine days. We'll reach our next stop in a day or two. Diverting to rescue you changed our arrival time, and I haven't asked Royan for an update. Knowing him, he'll push the engines to get us there as soon as possible." He heard the sound of booted feet treading the deck and knew Royan had joined them.

"He doesn't like to be late?" Tianna asked, her head still inside the cooler.

Owen barked with laughter. "More like he likes to fly as fast as possible."

"Damn right I do. Flying slow is boring and pointless."

Tianna glanced back to Royan, who was leaning

against the door to the galley. He'd found time to shave and shower since Owen had last seen him.

"There was a time I would have agreed with you," she said.

"Not anymore?" Royan asked.

Her brows climbed to her dark hairline. "You don't know the story?"

"There's a story? I like stories, and I've heard all of Owen's more than once."

He couldn't tell if Tianna was more amused or amazed by the fact they didn't know what she was talking about, but she was smiling, and that was the only thing that mattered. He got the feeling she didn't do that too often. Offering her a reprieve from her life as corporate royalty was feeling more and more like the right idea.

TIANNA WAS TEMPTED by Owen's offer. *Veth.* She was tempted by Owen, period. She hadn't had time for herself since her recovery. The moment she was able to, she'd taken up the mantle of heir and thrown herself into a role she'd spent most of her life avoiding. It was the only way she could repay her father for what he'd done. She owed him that much. Since then, the business had always come first.

She pushed aside all thoughts of the temptations and turned to face her two rescuers. "About four years ago, I was in a skimmer crash. A bad one. One of the wings sheered off mid-flight."

Royan whistled. "How fast were you going to make that happen?"

"Too fast. I'd modified the engines to boost performance, but I didn't factor for metal fatigue or the overall age of the ship. She was my favorite, so I flew her the most. It was a stupid mistake that nearly cost me my life."

"So now you don't fly fast anymore? One accident, and that's it, you're done?" He lowered his voice and winked. "Tell me you don't miss it, and I'll call you a liar."

"That wasn't the only mistake I made that day. I ditched my security team and deactivated my locator so they couldn't find me. Because of that, it took them ages to locate the wreckage. I had plenty of time to think about my life and what I'd do differently if I survived."

"That's why you weren't happy to discover your ship's transponder had been turned off," Owen said.

"Exactly. There's only one person with the authority to order it turned off – my father."

"Why would he do that?" Royan asked.

"No one was supposed to know where I was going. This whole voyage was cloaked in secrecy. Fake destinations. Last-minute departure changes. We left before we even had all the supplies on board." She'd been trying to figure out how the attack happened, but she hadn't come up with a viable theory until now. The supplies. "Son of a *fraxxing* starbeast. The bastards must have smuggled the micro-explosives in with the food. Before it happened, I got caught up doing research on Astek station and lost track of time. I didn't order my meal until later than usual, and I couldn't get my usual order because some of the food didn't make it onto the ship before we left."

Owen nodded. "That's a viable theory. I'm sure once

Corp-Sec looks over the wreckage they'll work out what happened, and how."

"That's if the other ship didn't blast what was left of the *Alacrity* to atoms," she pointed out.

"I don't think cleaning up the evidence is their priority. Once they figure out you're not dead, they're going to focus all their attention on finishing the job. Fortunately for you, you're with us. No one is going to find the *Sprite* unless we want to be found."

"Are we as well-hidden as the ingredients I need to make the pasta?"

Owen chuckled. "Better. I think you'll find what you need in the food dispenser. Just use the ingredients setting and it will produce a sealed packet of whatever you ask for."

Royan shook his head. "Or you could just tell it to make the meal itself. That's what it's for."

"It makes passable food. I make incredible meals. You can judge for yourself once I'm done," she said.

"You, too? I'm surrounded by secret chefs. Where did you learn to cook?" Royan asked as she moved back to the food dispenser.

"My father had a houseful of staff, including several talented chefs. I was alone a lot, and I often snuck into the kitchen to watch them work. As I got older, I started asking questions, and eventually I picked up enough to be a decent cook. My father didn't approve, but he never interfered. He figured out early on to pick his battles with me and apparently cooking didn't make the list."

She found most of what she needed and set the packets of frozen or dehydrated foodstuffs on the counter. Owen moved over to give her space to work and slid a well-sharpened knife across the counter.

"Now you've got me curious. What made the list of things you and your father fought over? I mean, you were on your way to the Drift to take over Astek station, so clearly you two don't fight anymore," Royan stated.

She sipped her coffee and then got to work opening the various packets. "We fought about a lot of things. I was a source of constant disappointment for him. He thought he'd planned for every aspect of my creation. My egg donor was selected after a two-year process, I had every genetic modification galactic law allowed, and I was monitored constantly from conception to delivery. He expected perfection. He got me instead."

"Sweetheart, from where I stand all I see is perfection," Royan drawled.

She glanced up in time to see Owen smack him on the back of his head. "Behave yourself. Or at the very least, bring your A-game. That was pathetic."

"Ow! Come on, it wasn't that bad."

"It wasn't that good, either. I'm siding with Owen on this one."

Royan rubbed the back of his head. "Oh sure, you've been on board less than a day and you're already teaming up with Owen." He cocked his head to one side and grinned suddenly. "On second thought, I like that idea. I'd like it even better if you were both naked, though."

"*Fraxx*, is this your idea of behaving?" Owen rolled his eyes.

"I think this is his A-game," she whispered loudly.

"You only think that was my best? My ego may not survive having you on board. That line was pure gold."

"It was…an improvement," she conceded with a laugh.

"And now you're encouraging him. I'd advise against that. He doesn't need to be encouraged, he needs to be handled." Owen's eyes widened the moment he uttered the last word. "Discouraged. Yeah, I meant to say discouraged."

Royan was grinning like a lunatic as he pushed away from the wall, deliberately ignoring Owen's attempts to backtrack. "Baby, you can *handle* me any time you like."

She burst out laughing. "I see what you mean."

"You have no idea." Despite his complaints, Owen's eyes were crinkled with amusement and affection. Whatever was going on between the two of them, they were definitely more than friends… but if that was the case, then why was Royan flirting with her?

She returned to her meal prep, enjoying the easy banter of her two companions as she wrestled with a decision she never expected to make. Being herself with these two was easy. Dangerously so. She was still tempted though. Once they made it to the Drift they'd go their separate ways. She had planned to relax on the way to Astek anyway. The only thing that had changed was the company.

Liar. Letting my guard down around them is not the same as chilling in my quarters on the Alacrity. Her inner voice of reason was drowned out by another voice. *I nearly died today. I deserve to have a little fun.* She liked the second voice's opinion better.

Royan stayed by the door and watched Owen and Tianna cook together. It wasn't often he got to see anyone cook —

his mother certainly hadn't been the domestic type – but it was more than that. The two of them were working in harmony, moving around each other in the cramped space like they'd been doing it for years. They didn't even notice what was happening, but he did. He'd been mostly joking when he'd made the crack about the two of them teaming up on him, but now…

"You're quiet," Tianna said.

"I'm just enjoying the view. It's been a long time since someone cooked me a meal. Your captain thinks this is a great idea and should become a tradition."

"Maybe." Owen didn't look up from the soup he was currently stirring. Royan was curious to try it, because despite knowing what it was made from, it looked and smelled delicious. Unfortunately, that meant he was probably going to lose tonight's bet. He'd happily give up the bed, though, because that meant Owen was sleeping in the same room.

"You might get to try Owen's cooking again, but this is a limited time offer for me, so you better enjoy it while you can."

"Getting to eat a meal made for me by a beautiful billionaire and my gorgeous crewmate? I plan on savoring every mouthful." He planned on enjoying more than just the meal. The *Sprite* was his ship, but in all the months he'd been flying her, she'd never felt like *home*. Tonight, it was full of warmth and laughter, offering him a taste of what he'd been missing. It couldn't last. Nothing this good ever did. That didn't stop him from enjoying these rare moments when everything went right.

"You'll get your chance to savor in about twenty minutes," Owen said.

"Since you're both working on dinner, how about I set the table and break out a bottle of something special?"

"How special? If the next words out of your mouth are Jeskyran *vachtar*, you're might not live long enough to enjoy our cooking."

Vachtar was one of Zale's favorite liquors, and they'd been toasting his memory with it the night he and Owen had finally given in to temptation. Owen hadn't touched the stuff since. "No *vachtar*, then. How about I make up a batch of Sun Sprite Delights?"

"Do I want to know why your ship has its own cocktail?"

"My sister is married to a couple of bar owners. Back when they were first getting to know each other they thought naming a drink after her ship was a smart way to get into her good graces."

Tianna laughed. "That's sweet."

"Yeah, Zura must have thought so, too, because she's having their babies."

"Babies, plural?" Tianna asked.

"Twins." Royan nodded. He still couldn't believe he was about to be an uncle.

"They should be arriving not long after we get back. There's going to be a hell of a party when that happens." Owen glanced at Tianna. "I know we're all going our separate ways once we get back, but if you felt like slumming it with the local riff-raff for just one night, that would be the day to do it. Half the station will probably be there, anyway."

Royan loved this idea. "It'll be fun! And if you're worried about security, the club is probably the safest place on the station outside of Astek's offices."

Tianna shook her head. "It sounds like a good time, but I can't. There's too much I need to do, and I have to set an example. I was explaining this to Owen, earlier. While I'm on your ship, I can relax a little, but once we reach the Drift, I have a job to do."

"That sounds incredibly dull, sweetheart. I have it on good authority that even cyborgs kick back and relax from time to time. If they can do it, why can't you?"

"Because their last name isn't Astor," she replied with a barely-there shrug.

And just like that, Royan had a mission. If she was only on a break until they got back home, then as captain, it fell to him to make sure she had a relaxing and memorable voyage.

Starting now.

CHAPTER FIVE

Tianna took her seat in the ship's small mess area and took a look around. Like the rest of the *Sun Sprite*, the space was well-worn but functional. It was lightyears away from the luxury she'd left behind on the crippled *Alacrity*, but it was clean, safe, and warm. That was all she needed right now.

Her stomach rumbled. Okay, it wasn't all she needed, but food was on the way and she'd snacked already. Owen had set out a bowl of mixed nuts while they worked. He hadn't said anything, just filled it to the rim and pushed it across the counter until it was a few inches from her hand. She appreciated his thoughtfulness, but also the fact he hadn't fussed over her.

She'd been waited on by servants and sycophants her entire life. In fact, her need to escape it all had been the catalyst for her years of rebellion. Sneaking away from her guards to explore. Lingering in the kitchen with the staff to avoid the long, boring functions her father was always hosting. The older she got, the more expectations were piled on her shoulders and the harder she had to fight for even brief moments of freedom. She had always wondered what it would be like to live a normal life. For the next week or so, she might actually get to find out.

Royan appeared at the door with a tray full of drinks and a pitcher of liquid that changed colors and appeared to be smoking.

"Is it supposed to do that?" she asked.

"Yep. All part of the delicious magic of this cocktail." He set the tray down on the table and gestured. "Lady's choice."

"Uh huh." She selected the one closest to Royan. "Magical or not, you're taking the first sip. If you live, I'll try it."

"And Owen thought you were a badass. He'll be so disappointed in your lack of trust." Royan took a seat across for her, winked, and picked the drink closest to her from the tray. He raised it in toast, inhaled some of the mist, and then took a drink and smacked his lips. "Delicious."

"I am a badass." She picked up her drink and held it up, watching the colors change as it bubbled and smoked. "But I have a strict policy of not drinking anything that looks more like a chemistry experiment than a cocktail. A girl has to have boundaries."

"Boundaries are good. I like to know where the lines are so I can be certain when I've crossed them." He raised his glass again. "To you, Tianna. May the rest of your journey to Astek have more laughter and fewer explosions."

"I'll drink to that." She touched her glass to his, then threw caution to the wind and took a generous sip of her cocktail. It was surprisingly good, though strong enough she felt it burn all the way to her stomach.

"Not bad. Is that *saska* syrup I detect?"

"You can taste that? In one sip? Damn. We really need to introduce you to Luke. He's the one who created this, and he's always lamenting no one appreciates the subtleties of his creations."

"Another reason for you to come to the party at the Nova Club once Zura's had the twins," Owen walked in carrying a tray, this one full of bowls of steaming soup and a large platter filled with thickly sliced bread slathered in garlic butter.

"Wait. That's the club your in-laws own?" The pieces were finally falling into place now. The familiar names. The sense she knew something about the people they'd mentioned. She knew them, alright. They were at the top of the list of beings she needed to keep an eye on.

"Yeah. Kit and Luke Armas are my brother-in-laws." Royan raised his brows. "You have a problem with cyborgs?"

If only he knew... "With cyborgs? No. I do take issue with troublemakers, though, and your family has done more than their share of that lately. Your sister, she's the one carrying her husbands' medi-bots, right? They gave her an unauthorized transfusion because of some sort of medical emergency, and it actually worked."

She'd learned about Zura Armas' situation by accident. The executive she was shadowing at the time had mentioned it, assuming she already knew the details. He'd been venomous about the whole incident, advocating that Zura be forcibly sterilized or even killed to prevent the nanotech from being passed on to the next generation. The man's opinions had been vicious, and she'd left his office even more convinced that she needed to protect her secret at all costs.

Royan's eyes darkened and his smile faded away. "Zura got shot saving my sorry ass. Kit and Luke did the only thing they could think of to keep her alive. And for the record, they're free citizens of the galaxy. They didn't need anyone's *fraxxing* authority to save Zura's life."

She raised a hand. "Sorry, bad choice of words. I'm glad they saved her. After all, if she hadn't rescued you, you wouldn't have been around to save me today. Still, that club has been at the center of a lot of problems lately."

"You're not going to close them down, are you?" Owen set out the bowls of soup, then set the tray aside and took a seat at the end of the table.

"Not without a good reason. I hadn't done more than some preliminary reading when the explosion went off. That's why I didn't make the connection until now. I'm being sent to Astek station to regain control of one of our most important assets, and that means I need to figure out who, and what, the threats are to nullify them."

Royan fixed her with a hard stare. "You make it sound so clinical, but that asset you're so keen to protect is also home to thousands of beings, including my family."

"She's never been there, though." Owen lifted his spoon and pointed to his soup. "Just like this food. You can't truly know something until you've experienced it for yourself. Until then, it's all facts and theories. I know what the ingredients are, but that doesn't mean I know how it's going to taste."

"So, you're saying I shouldn't make any assumptions until I get to Astek and see things for myself?" His advice ran counter to everything her father had instilled in her. He worshiped facts and figures, convinced that with enough study they would provide the answers to any challenge. She didn't have the same faith he did, but she had adopted his methods since the accident. Doing things his way was just easier for everyone.

"I'm saying until you try the soup, how can you know if it's any good?"

"Well, I can already tell you it smells amazing." She paused, then added. "And since all my research and data about Astek station is still on the *Alacrity*, I'm going to have to form my own opinions about everything. And I promise to remember that the station is more than an asset."

"Thank you," Royan said, his expression warming.

She dipped her spoon into the soup and took a sip. It was good. Given the lack of fresh ingredients, that was no easy feat. She was still trying to figure out the flavors when she noticed both men were completely still and watching her intently. Something was up.

"Well?" Owen prompted when she set the spoon down.

"Be honest, sweetheart. If it tastes like crap, say so. His ego can take it."

"It's delicious."

Royan threw up his hands. "*Fraxx*!"

"I win. You're sleeping on the floor tonight, Royan." Owen was chortling as he dug into his meal.

"Won? Is that why you were both staring at me? I was part of some bet?"

Owen nodded, looking slightly sheepish. "He bet me I couldn't make the soup edible."

She looked down at her bowl, her stomach tightening. "And why wouldn't it be edible?"

"Because it's made from algae broth," Royan poked the bowl with his finger. "You sure it tastes alright?"

"I'm sure. And now I'm damned impressed. I've heard that's awful stuff. I think Owen's a better cook than he let on."

"I grew up eating that crap for almost every meal. I learned every trick there is to know about how to improve the taste and texture."

She took another spoonful, but even knowing what was in it, she still liked it. "So you bet him the bed that I'd like it. What did Royan want from you if he won?"

"Winner's choice," Owen said and glanced over at the other man. "Though I have my suspicions about what he'd ask for."

They ate in silence for a few minutes, as even Royan picked up his spoon and started eating. She ate and drank, not worrying too much about the effects of the alcohol on her empty stomach. The medi-bots she carried would ensure she didn't get too drunk, and there would be no hangover, either. She was free to indulge herself in any way she wanted, far from anyone who might judge her or use her behavior against her later.

When her bowl was empty, she set down her spoon and cleared her throat. "I'm filing an official protest over your bet. Both of you had the opportunity to gain from this venture, but I'm the one who took all the risks."

"I wouldn't have served you anything terrible." Owen looked insulted.

"I don't know. She might have a point." Royan pushed his empty bowl away. "Care to get in on the action,

Tianna? This next dish was your creation. If it's better than Owen's soup, you win."

"Before I agree, I've got two questions. One, what are the stakes? Two, who will judge?"

"As the captain of this illustrious vessel, I'll be judging. And as for the stakes, I think the same as before. Winner's choice."

Owen scrubbed a hand over his jaw and chuckled. "I have a feeling I'm going to regret this, but sure, I'm in."

"I promise not to be unreasonable." She grinned. "After all, you two did save my life today."

"Glad you're keeping that in mind, princess," Owen said.

"I'm not a princess," she retorted.

"That's what your name means, though. Tianna is an ancient Earth name that translates to princess." Owen said.

Royan shook his head. "Nope. Sorry, baby, but I'm with her. She's not a princess."

"Thank you."

"You're welcome, my queen."

"You're right, that's much better," Owen agreed.

"Not really, but if I argue about it the pasta will get soggy, and then I'll lose the bet." She got to her feet. "Since this is my course, I'll serve it. Be right back."

She picked up one of the banged-up metal serving trays on her way through the open hatchway that separated the galley and the mess area. It only took a few minutes to serve up the meal, a simple cream sauce with dehydrated mushrooms, peas, and something labeled simulated bacon bits. She had no idea what it was, but it had added a subtle smoky taste to the sauce. She'd mixed in some synthesized protein cubes and let the whole thing simmer until the flavors blended. Her pasta options were as limited as everything else in the galley, but she'd managed to find some fettuccini noodles at the back of the pantry. Now, she just had to hope Royan liked it better than Owen's soup. She already knew what she'd ask for if she won.

OWEN WATCHED their pretty guest exit the room. Once she was gone, he raised a brow at Royan. "What are you up to?"

"Me?" Royan leaned back in his chair and tipped his head toward the galley. "I'm not the one who asked to be part of our bet. This is all her, and I'm loving it."

"I'm not hating it, either, but I think we need to remember the day she's had. Maybe we should cool our boosters until she's had a chance to make a full recovery."

"I agree. Not just because she needs time, but because the two of us haven't talked about how this might work."

"Two moments of insight in one day. You angling to get back into your bed tonight? If you keep this up, you might just get there."

"Yeah?" Royan grinned.

"Yeah." He reached over and gripped Royan's hand for a moment. "You're not the only one trying to make this work."

Royan turned his hand, taking hold of Owen. Neither spoke. Their linked hands said more than any words could have.

"Canoodling with the judge before the tasting? That

doesn't seem fair." Tianna returned, carrying a tray laden with three generous platters of pasta.

Owen pulled his hand away, embarrassed at being caught. Public displays of affection weren't something he was comfortable with. Growing up, his family had barely acknowledged the ties that bound them together. They were a crew first, and a family a very distant second. "We weren't…what the *fraxx* is canoodling? Whatever it is, we weren't doing it."

"You were, and you're welcome to continue. I've got the winning dish right here, and no amount of hand holding will change that." She set the tray down with a metallic clank as it hit the tabletop.

He inhaled, letting the scent of dinner fill his senses, and immediately knew she was right. He hadn't noticed earlier because he'd been focused on other things – like Tianna - while they were cooking, but the dish she'd made smelled and looked delicious. *I wonder what she's going to ask for when she wins.*

Tianna reclaimed her spot between them and gestured to the plate in front of Royan. "Dig in."

He did, and the moment the first bite hit his tongue Royan closed his eyes and groaned, the sound of pleasure so raw that Owen's cock hardened. "There is no way you made this out of what's on board."

"I did. Believe me, if I had fresh ingredients it would taste even better."

"That's it. When we get back to Astek I'm investing in the best food processor I can find. That is, unless you'd consider taking a slight pay cut and signing on as the ship's cook, sweetheart?"

Tianna grinned. "Sorry, fly-boy, you couldn't afford me even at a discount. So, did I win?"

"That depends. Are you really going to call me fly-boy for the rest of the trip?"

"You going to call me queen, your highness, or anything royalty related?" She shot back.

"Fair enough." Royan raised his hands in surrender. "I'll stick with sweetheart."

Owen waited for her to protest again, but she smiled and nodded. "That's acceptable."

Was that a green light? If so, who was it for? Royan, or both of us? Sharing partners wasn't something he'd ever done before, though he had no doubt Royan had, at least for a night. Until now, it wasn't something Owen had ever considered. It could work. He knew that. He'd seen it for himself among his friends. But he didn't know if it was something he wanted, especially not when Tianna had made it clear that once they got to the Drift, they'd be parting company.

Royan grinned. "In that case, yes, you won, sweetheart. Name your prize."

The air almost crackled with anticipation as they waited for her answer. She was quiet for a long moment before speaking. "I think I'll collect my winnings another time. Right now, I just want to enjoy this meal and be grateful I'm alive to enjoy it."

The atmosphere lightened again, but only a little. Whatever was happening between them, it was still unfolding in its own time.

Royan uttered a dramatic sigh. "Oh, sure. Keep us in suspense. I'm going to be lying awake tonight wondering what you have planned." He glanced over at Owen. "Probably on the cold, hard floor of my room."

"If I let you sleep on the bed, do I get another request?" Owen asked before taking his first mouthful of pasta. It was as incredible as he expected. After weeks of eating from the food dispenser, he'd forgotten how good simple, human-cooked food could taste.

"Anything you want, baby," Royan answered.

Tianna leaned in, cheeks flushed and lips parted, clearly curious about what the new request would be.

"Breakfast in bed. Once a week for a month."

"No problem."

"Cooked by you," he added.

Royan's eyes widened in mild panic. "I can't cook, remember?"

"I'm going to teach you."

"Yeah?" Royan looked intrigued.

"Yeah. You're always complaining there's nothing to do on these long-hauls runs. Think of this as a new distraction."

Royan nodded. "I'm game." He glanced over at Tianna. "You want to take part? Owen's right. There's not a lot to do on these trips but work out, watch vids, and do a little maintenance on the *Sprite*."

"Cooking lessons sound like fun, if you're okay with me intruding. I'm just a guest, here, and I don't want to interfere with the way you two operate."

"We're still figuring that out. I've only been part of the crew for a few weeks. Before that, I came out on the occasional trip, but just to keep Royan company and get away from the Nova for a while. When you live where you work, getting away for a few days is necessary, but not easy to do when you're out in the ass-end of the galaxy."

"You worked at the Nova Club?" she asked.

Owen nodded. "As security, yeah. One of the perks of the job was living in the staff quarters. Nothing fancy, but it was clean, free, and came with a staff discount for meals. When I first got to the Drift, I wasn't sure how I was going to afford to eat and pay rent."

"I know things are expensive, but surely it's not that bad," Tianna said.

Royan chimed in. "It's pretty *fraxxing* bad. You'll see. There are parts of the station that are barely inhabitable, and even those sectors are crammed full of beings paying almost everything they make just to have a few square meters of space to sleep in. It's even worse these days. There's all the AIF personnel temporarily assigned here until their own battle station can be brought out to the Drift, and then Astek handed over one of the residential levels to Nova Force to use as housing and offices, so everyone living there had to move to other sectors."

"That's not what happened." Tianna frowned and stabbed her fork into her pasta. "Nova Force was granted space in an unused section of the station. I saw the plans myself."

"I don't know what plans you saw, but if they show there are unused areas of the station, then they are out of date. The only empty space is on the ceilings, and if the corporation lackeys could figure out a way to monetize that, they would have by now," Royan said, winced, and added a hurried "no insult intended."

"None taken. I'm not a corporate lackey. I'm

management, which means I *will* find a way to monetize the ceiling. I'm going to need every bit of scrip I can get my hands on so I can pay for repairs and maybe look at lowering some costs. As someone recently pointed out to me, Astek isn't just an asset. It's home to a great many beings."

"It's nice to know you were listening." Royan reached over and tapped his glass to hers. "There hasn't been a lot of that in the time I've been on the Drift."

"That's why I'm being sent there. With everything that's happened – is still happening – Astek needs to be protected. Someone is trying to destabilize my family's company, and the easiest way to do that is to disrupt Astek station."

A dark thought struck Owen. "If your company is being attacked, the station isn't the best target."

Royan and Tianna both looked at him. "It's the largest single investment we have," she said.

"No, it's not. If someone wants to take down Astek, the easiest way to do that is to destroy its future. That's not the station, Tianna. That's you."

A pall settled over them, and his next bite of food was as dry and tasteless as moon dust.

Tianna frowned. "I don't think so. If I had died yesterday, Astek would still go on. My father will still be running the company for another decade or two, probably longer. I don't even have a permanent role right now. I've spent the last few years moving through various positions, shadowing senior executives, learning how all the pieces work together." She clasped her hands in front of her, fingers interwoven.

"Someone thinks differently," Royan pointed out. "And

they went to a lot of trouble to try and take you out of the game."

"I know. But I don't understand." She sighed, her shoulders drooping slightly. "My father doesn't have much faith in my abilities. He never has. He paid for perfection."

"And like I said before, from where I'm sitting, he got it," Royan said.

Owen agreed. Tianna was physically beautiful, but she was also clearly intelligent, well-spoken, and tough as Nantari rhino hide.

"He wouldn't agree with you. In fact, he was so disappointed in his investment he saw to it that the company he hired to oversee my creation was bankrupt before my sixth birthday. I was still a child, but he already knew I was never going to be what he wanted."

She said it without rancor or embarrassment, her words so matter-of-fact that it took him a moment to absorb the scale of what she was telling them.

"I thought contracted conception was illegal?" He'd heard of the practice, but never imagined he'd meet someone created that way.

"It pushes the boundaries without going over. At least, that's the official stance." Tianna shrugged as if it were no big deal and took a long drink of her cocktail.

He saw through her act of indifference, though. Her creation, her father's disappointment, it bothered her more than she wanted anyone to know. "I know what it's like to be a disappointment to your family. My mother…" he trailed off with a shake of his head.

"You never talk about her," Royan said. "Or any of your family, really."

He started to shrug, then stopped. He'd had just enough to drink that honesty seemed like a good idea. "We don't speak. The last conversation we had ended with my mother telling me if I left, she'd bury my memory and tell everyone I was dead." He drained his glass and set it down on the table with a thump. He tried not to think about them. The living, or the dead.

"Well, that explains why you don't talk about them." Royan refilled their glasses, then raised his in another toast. "To friends. The family we choose for ourselves."

"I'll drink to that," Owen agreed.

They both looked at Tianna, who was gripping her glass hard enough her fingers were white, but hadn't lifted it from the table.

"What's wrong?" Owen asked.

"Too much booze, not enough food," she said, her jaw tight.

To Owen's surprise, Royan put down his glass and reached out to touch the back of her hand in a tender caress. "Whatever it is, you can say it. We're not going to tell anyone. Standing rule from my father's time as captain. What happens on the *Sprite*, stays on the *Sprite*."

She looked down at Royan's hand but didn't pull away. "It's nothing."

"Really? Because if you hold that glass any tighter it's going to shatter." Owen said softly.

"*Fraxx*. Alright. I just…when you said that thing about friends being the family you choose for yourself, it dawned on me that I don't have anyone like that. It was a moment of self pity is all, and now I'm embarrassed."

Royan took her hand in his. Then reached over to take Owen's, too. "You've got nothing to be embarrassed about.

I spent a lot of years on my own. After my dad died, Zura got the *Sprite*, I got some seed money and we went our separate ways. We only reconnected a year ago. Friends, family, a steady job, and this big lug here are all new additions to my life. Just because you don't have those things right now, doesn't mean you'll never have them."

Owen gripped Royan's hand and tried to ignore the sudden surge of affection and desire that swept through him. This wasn't the moment. They needed to take care of Tianna right now. but later – later, they needed to talk.

"I wish you were right, but that's not in the cards for me. I might be a disappointment, but he's the only family I have. I don't have any choice."

"That doesn't sound like the rebel who flew a skimmer so fast she tore her wings off," Royan said.

"I tell myself she died in the crash." She gave Owen a thin-lipped smile. "I guess that's something we have in common. We've both died and been reborn as someone else."

It didn't seem fair. When he'd broken with his family, he'd taken a new name and started a new life, one he could be proud of. Tianna was denying a part of herself in order to appease her father.

"Your old self isn't dead though. She's just buried under someone else's expectations. I saw her today. She's the one who came hurtling at me in zero-g a few hours ago. If you're going to be yourself for this trip, you might as well be your true self."

She nodded, her expression softening. "You might regret making that suggestion."

Royan laughed. "He's my best friend. If I haven't scared him off, sweetheart, I'm damned sure you won't."

"I'm not afraid of your wild side. Just give me a heads up if Royan lets you play pilot. I'll make sure to secure the breakables and strap myself in."

Royan opened his mouth and Owen cut him off. "Don't even try, Roy-boy. There is no circumstance under which I will ever let you tie me down."

All three of them started to laugh at that, and the rest of their meal passed in a pleasant blur of old stories, bad jokes, cherry pie, and the beginning of something that felt like friendship, even if it wasn't meant to last.

$$\overline{}$$

CHAPTER SIX

$$\overline{}$$

ROYAN COULDN'T STOP GRINNING as he made his way from the cockpit back to his quarters. The ship was on time and on course, and there was no sign of pursuit. If anything changed, Sprite would alert him, but for now, he was free to think about other things – like the fact that he'd be sharing a bed with Owen tonight.

After their one night together, he'd expected them to fall into some kind of relationship. Instead, Owen retreated back behind his walls as if they'd never crossed that line. Royan had been hurt, then pissed off, but never once did it occur to him to give up, despite the fact that's what Owen expected him to do. He was a Watson, and the Watson family were too stubborn to ever give up.

He paused outside his door, looking down the corridor to the room they'd given Tianna. He wasn't giving up on her, either. She was complicated and intriguing, a potent blend of beauty and broken parts that reminded him of Owen. They both saw something of each other in their unexpected guest, and his gut told him that wasn't something to be taken lightly. Unfortunately, his instincts didn't tell him what the *fraxx* to do about it.

They had sat and talked for hours, moving from the mess area to the kitchen for clean up, then on to the rec room where they'd continued to drink and fraternize until it was time to go to bed. *Bed.* The thought made him grin even wider as he walked inside.

Owen was already under the covers, leaning up against the pillows as he scanned the data tablet in his hands. He was wearing a shirt that clung to him like a second skin, the dark blue fabric hiding the view he'd been hoping for. *Don't be greedy. He's here. That's enough…for tonight.*

"All clear?" Owen asked without looking up.

"Green lights across the board." Royan peeled off his shirt and chucked it into the laundry chute. "What are you reading?"

Owen tipped the data tab closer to his chest. "Long range scans."

Royan leaned in a little so he could see the screen. There were multiple files open, and while one of them looked like a scan display, the one on top was definitely not. "Tianna's showing up on our scanners? That's a hell of a glitch."

"I was curious. Not to mention the fact that she's now a passenger on this ship, which means I'm responsible for her safety. I can't protect her if I don't know anything about her."

"You could ask." Royan reached out and stroked a hand over Owen's brow, attempting to smooth out the worry lines etched into his skin.

"I will. Tomorrow. She's got the stamina of a *fraxxing*

cyborg, but she needs more sleep. Until then, I'm just filling in a few gaps."

"Tianna isn't the only one who needs to rest. Put the tablet down and close your eyes, baby. It's been a long day for us, too."

"I'm fine. Medi-bots, remember?"

"Bless Zale for making sure we all had a dose of those little miracle-bots. But you're still only human." He yawned. "And so am I."

"Then come to bed." Owen patted the spot beside him in clear invitation.

Royan shed his pants in record time, crammed them into the chute and claimed his spot in bed with an unabashed sigh of contentment. This was what he'd been hoping for since Zura had told him Owen was now a member of the *Sprite's* crew.

Owen snorted with laughter. "Is it possible to die from terminal smugness? Because I think you're in danger of overdosing right now."

"For that to happen you'd have to be naked right now." He threw an arm over Owen's stomach and deliberately snuggled up to him.

"Like we'd get any sleeping done if I were."

"For that, I'd sacrifice my beauty sleep, but I know that's not going to happen tonight."

Owen exhaled softly. "You're making it *fraxxing* hard for me to remember why this is a really bad idea."

"Do you really believe that?"

There was a long moment of silence before Owen answered. "I used to. You know the reasons why."

"I know them all. I heard you. All those times you told me no, I heard you."

"I didn't think you did."

"Surprise."

Owen chuckled and put aside the data tablet, then turned on his side and wrapped an arm around him. "Yeah, you were."

A jolt of joy hit him like the purest pharma he'd ever sampled. "So were you, baby. I had a plan. Fly fast, live large, and leave a trail of broken hearts and epic stories in my wake. Then you had to go and turn me down. Me!"

"Ah, so I was a challenge you couldn't resist?"

"Maybe in the beginning." He didn't know when the need to break through Owen's walls started to turn into something more. It happened so gradually he hadn't noticed until it hit him like a rogue comet, sending him spinning off his plotted course.

"And now?" Owen ran his hand up Royan's body until he was cupping his face in one big hand.

"You're the best part of my day. Every day." He ached to close the distance between them and kiss Owen senseless, but he held back. The next move had to be Owen's.

"For the record, I still think this is a bad idea." He leaned in and brushed his mouth across Royan's.

"I don't." He kissed him back, fighting the urge to push for more. He wanted to devour Owen, turn him inside out with pleasure, then curl up in his arms and sleep the way they had that first night.

"And that's why I'm not fighting this any longer. I trust you...which probably makes me as crazy as you are."

"I like your kind of crazy." He kissed Owen again, sliding his tongue across the seam of Owen's lips. He tasted of cherry pie tonight, and Royan knew he'd never taste that dessert again without thinking of Owen.

"If we're going to talk crazy, maybe we should discuss what the hell we're going to do about Tianna."

Royan was wrapped around Owen, which let him feel the way the other man's cock hardened at the mention of her name. He reached down to stroke Owen's dick through his pants. "You like her."

"Yes." Owen's answer came out as a soft hiss of pleasure.

"Do you want to share her with me?"

He hesitated.

"It's okay if the answer is no."

"That's not it. I just – I'm not sure I can share her and then let her go. I'm not like you."

"That's where you're wrong, baby. I think you are like me. Or you were. One day soon, I want to hear more about your family, and the man you were before you reinvented yourself." Until today, Owen had never offered up the slightest hint of where he'd come from or who he'd been before they met.

Starting over was a way of life on the Drift.

"It's not a pretty story."

"I don't care if it's pretty. You know my story. I want to know yours." His story was short and uninteresting. Born on Earth, he'd been twelve years old before his mother had even told him his father's name. By then, he already knew he'd never fit into the neat, tidy life his mother had carved for herself. When he finally learned who his father was and what he did for a living, he'd followed in his footsteps and never looked back.

"I'll tell you soon." Owen's hips rolled, pumping his

cock against Royan's fingers. "It's difficult to have a serious conversation when you're doing that."

"Do you want me to stop?"

Owen chuckled. "Not yet."

"Then tell me what you want to do about Tianna."

Owen's cock twitched. "I want her. If she's willing to be shared."

"Even if it means she walks away from us when this trip is over?" Royan slid his hand inside Owen's pants and started jerking him off with long, firm strokes.

"If that's what she wants, I'll respect her choice." Owen closed his eyes and groaned. "What do *you* want?"

"The three of us together. In every way I can think of."

"And when she's gone?"

"Then it'll be the two of us against the galaxy, just like before. Only this time, we'll be sharing a bed."

Owen reached down, covering Royan's hand and stilling his movements. His eyes opened and he met Royan's gaze. "Will that be enough for you, though?"

Royan answered from his heart. "You don't give yourself enough credit, Owen Connors. You are more than enough for me." It had taken him long enough to see it, and it would take longer before Owen believed it, but it was the truth.

"Then I guess this trip is about to get a whole lot more hedonistic."

Royan couldn't help himself, he let out a wild whoop of joy and kissed Owen hard. "That is my favorite word in the whole damned galaxy."

"I know, you lunatic. Believe me, I know." Then Owen was kissing him, his hand wrapped around Royan's cock, and neither of them had breath for words anymore.

Weeks of sexual frustration melted away in seconds. It wasn't a sensation he was overly familiar with, and he was thankful to leave his dry spell behind. Abstinence had never been his thing, but he'd figured out quickly that if he wanted Owen, he was going to have to change.

After that, they stopped talking. Both of them knew what they wanted and went after it without finesse. He fisted Owen's cock and matched him stroke for stroke, tongues dancing as they raced each other toward release. Owen uttered a low, feral groan that made Royan's balls tighten in anticipation. A few more hard pumps were all it took to turn him inside out, his groans lost in the depths of Owen's mouth as they went hurtling over the edge of control almost at the same moment. It was the best damned feeling in the world.

TIANNA HEARD Royan cheer and wondered what the two of them were doing. Had Owen finally given in to the chemistry that sizzled between them? Where they making plans or making love? She closed her eyes, imagining the two of them tangled up in bed, hard bodies rubbing against each other...or against her. *Fraxx*, yes. Now there was a fantasy to distract her from dark thoughts that kept flitting through her mind. She didn't want to think about who wanted her dead, or when they might try again. She'd have to deal with that reality soon, but not tonight.

She conjured up another image of Owen and Royan, imagining what kind of lovers they'd be with her, and with each other. Which of them would take control? Or would they take turns? Her hand slipped between her legs, her fingers stroking her clit in slow, lazy circles as she set the scene in her mind. Owen stood behind her, his hands cupping her breasts, his big body hard against her back as he kissed and sucked on her neck. He'd be an attentive lover, learning everything she liked and then methodically using his knowledge to bring her to her knees.

Knees -- yes, that was good. Royan on his knees in front of her, one of her legs draped over his shoulder so he could lick her pussy until she came. She could feel his breath on her thigh, and the soft rasp of his beard against her skin. She worked her clit harder as the fantasy took on a life of its own, fuelled by the muffled groans and sounds of pleasure that traveled from their room to hers.

The three of them on a bed, hands and mouths busy, an orgy of pleasures she had never dared to consider. Would she get off watching the two men touching each other? Kissing? A new image arose, Royan on his knees again, head bowed, sucking Owen's cock. Her fingers grew slick and her breath came faster with each new fantasy. Her on her hands and knees, Owen's fingers holding tight to her hair as he fucked her mouth while Royan pounded into her from behind, the two of them dominating her and worshipping her at the same time.

She shuddered, gasped, and came with a moan that was louder than she'd intended. Panting softly, she wondered if the guys had heard her. Part of her hoped they hadn't, but another part wanted them to know what she'd been doing while they enjoyed themselves. It was the part of herself she'd locked down since the accident, the rebel who dreamed of a different life, one where she was free to choose for herself.

"Just this once," she murmured to herself as she rolled over and snuggled down beneath the blankets, ignoring the headache that was starting to build at the back of her skull. Probably a delayed reaction to the stress of the last two days. She needed more rest, and for once, she was in a position to get it. For the next while, she had no duties to perform. No work to do. The universe was giving her a brief respite from her life. She'd be a fool not to take it, and anything else that was on offer for the next few days.

CHAPTER SEVEN

THE NEXT DAY PASSED QUIETLY. Thanks to her enhancements, she was fully recovered from her ordeal, but she couldn't act like it. She trusted Owen and Royan with her life, but what had been done to her was a violation of galactic law that could bring down her family's empire. She had to protect her father and his legacy.

She slept well, and spent the rest of the day watching vids, laughing, and flirting with her companions. She could have accessed the ship's database and started familiarizing herself with at least some of the things she'd need to know when she got to Astek station, or talked to Royan and Owen about what they knew, but she didn't. It felt strange not to be working, but the work would be there when this interlude ended. The work would always be there.

The two men bantered and joked, flirting almost as much with each other as they did with her. There was no mistaking their interest now, but despite the sexual tension and near-constant flirting, neither of them made a move on her. It was the first time in her adult life she'd been accepted as herself, with no expectations or pressure, and by the second day she knew that giving it up wasn't going to be as easy as she thought. This wasn't like her previous brief escapes from her life, where she'd stolen a few hours away. This was a prolonged hiatus, with plenty of time to think, rest, and talk to people so very different from anyone in her usual social circles.

She was in the galley brewing coffee for the three of them when Royan's voice came over the ship's comm system. "Sweetheart, you want to come up to the cockpit? There's something up here we want you to see."

She tapped her bracelet, activating its communicator function but leaving Tink in stand-by mode. "Be right there. Coffee's ready, too."

"I swear, any time you decide you're tired of being a rich heiress, you've got a job on the *Sprite*, sweetheart."

"And I keep telling you the only way I'm staying on this ship with the two of you is if I'm calling the shots. You can bring *me* coffee."

"My ship, my shots. I will volunteer Owen to bring us breakfast in bed every morning, though."

She heard Owen's laughter up ahead. He was standing in the doorway to the cockpit, watching for her with a smile on his face. "I let him back in bed and the next thing I know, he's trying to kick me out. You're a fickle bastard, Watson."

"Not fickle, greedy," Royan retorted. "Now take the pretty lady's tray of drinks from her so she can come in here and see where we're headed."

Owen winked and took the tray from her, lifting it high

enough she could pass beneath it and into the cockpit. There were electronics everywhere, reading and reporting on everything from engine performance to the temperature in the cargo bay. Royan had given her a guided tour of the ship yesterday. The moment she had stepped onto the flight deck her fingers had itched to take hold of the controls and put the *Sprite* through her paces. She was a workhorse with minimal comforts, but Tianna had quickly realized that despite her plain appearance, the ship was outfitted with power and speed to spare. Weapons, too, more than she expected to see, but knowing they were well protected helped her set her worries aside.

Royan pointed to the viewscreens that took up the entire front of the ship, most of which showed a large, grey and brown planet. "We're approaching our next stop. This is Taza 4. It's rich in ores and minerals but there's not a lot of water, so there's nothing down there but mining camps and processing stations."

He tapped one of the screens and the view changed to show a pair of moons on the far side of the planet. "That's our destination on the right. There's a newly established colony on that moon. The plan is to grow enough food to support not only themselves, but the miners on Taza 4."

"Which company owns this system?" she asked.

"That's the interesting bit. It's not corporate controlled. This is a cooperative. They're trying to do this on their own."

"That's ambitious. Where did they get their capital? What government allowed them to stake their claim on this system?" She had a thousand more questions, but she doubted Royan knew the answers.

"This is Pheran territory," Owen said, moving in

behind her. They weren't touching, but he was so close she could feel his body heat warming her back, and she had to fight the urge to lean back into the solid, comfortable bulk of his body.

"So, it's a Pheran cooperative?" That would make sense. Most corporations were human-controlled entities. The other races had their own ways of doing things, ways that limited the amount of influence the corporations had in their parts of the galaxy.

Royan turned in his chair to look at her. "It's a joint venture, something of an open experiment. There are Pherans, Jeskyrans, Humans, and even a few Torski involved. If you believe the rumors, the idea came from a group of miners who used to work on the Drift."

"Torex and the other mining consortiums can't be pleased about this idea."

"I'm sure they're not, but despite how some corporations behave, this is a free galaxy."

"Of course it is, but it's also *fraxxing* huge. Someone needs to oversee the flow of goods and services. The corporations are a necessary element."

Owen made a non-committal noise in the back of his throat, while Royan smirked. "Spoken like a good corporate citizen."

It wasn't the first time she'd heard murmurs of resistance to the corporate view of how they fit into the grand scheme of things, but given who she was and the world she lived in, she'd never had someone question it out loud. "You don't agree?"

Royan shrugged. "I'm a freelance freighter jockey. I make my living moving goods and services. Some of it's corporate cargo, some of it isn't. Like you said, it's a big galaxy. Big enough to have room for more than one way of doing things. The thing is, corporations like Astek are driven by their bottom line. That means beings like the ones down there are nothing more than cogs in a machine. I was born on Earth and grew up in a hive city in the northern hemisphere – the Klondike protectorate. I've been one of those cogs, and I can tell you, it's not much of a life."

"And you?" She looked back at Owen.

"I grew up outside the system. My family lived on the fringes of society, making do the best we could. In my experience, the corporations do more harm than good. Not all of them, and not all the time, but that's the smart way to bet."

Neither of them appreciated what she and her family's business did for the galaxy. It was a startling revelation. "But without the corporations nothing would be accomplished. Who would build ships like the *Sprite*? Where would the goods and services we all need to survive come from? The Drift wouldn't even exist without corporations like Astek and Torex. We're a key component to well…everything."

Owen put his hand between her shoulder blades, his thumb stroking over her spine. "Have you ever been to a hive city?" he asked, his tone gentler now.

"Or visited a corporate-owned world?" Royan added.

"Of course I have. I've shadowed executives in different positions all over the galaxy as part of my training."

Owen kept stroking his thumb back and forth across the back of her neck as she talked. The motion was soothing, and she leaned into his touch without thinking.

It was the most natural thing in the world for him to curve an arm around her waist and draw her in close. "While you were there, did you indulge your inner rebel and poke around the places they didn't show you on your tours?" Owen's voice was low rumble by her ear.

"I thought about it," But thinking was all she'd done. The smallest sign of rebellion would have destroyed the little trust her father had in her back then. She'd had questions and concerns, but she'd pushed them aside. Her priority had been the company, it had to be.

"I know we're supposed to go our separate ways once this trip is over, but when we get back to the Drift, I'd like to show you the parts of Astek station no one from your world would think to show you. I think you need to see them for yourself," Owen said.

"I already said I'd go to the party with the two of you. That should show me a glimpse of what life is like on the Drift." If she agreed to anything more, things might get complicated. She liked them – more than was wise, if she were being honest – but friends were a risk. The closer people got to her, the greater the chance they noticed she wasn't like them.

"How about we table this discussion for another day? We're about to make our descent, and I don't want Tianna to miss the next few minutes," Royan said as he spun around and started working the controls.

"What happens next?" she asked.

Owen lifted his hand from her waist to point to the main screen. "Now *this* happens."

The *Sun Sprite* dipped into the moon's atmosphere with a shudder, and she leaned back against Owen to steady herself.

"Sorry about that. Feels like the stabilizers need recalibrating, again. I'll do that while we're on the ground," Royan muttered, his hands flying across the console.

"I'm not complaining." Owen chuckled as he curved his strong arm across her stomach, pulling her hard against his body.

Royan looked back over his shoulder at them and frowned. "Oh sure. Why is it every time Tianna needs to hang on to someone, I'm busy flying the ship?"

"Maybe it's your driving," she said.

"Nice one," Owen said with approval.

"Thanks."

"Ingrates. Both of you," Royan muttered.

Before she could respond, the viewscreens filled with a view that took her breath away and left them all watching in silent wonder. They were flying over a mountain range, the peaks covered in sharply etched lines of brilliant white snow. Where the wind had carved the snow away, ridges of deep blue and gray stone showed through. The stark contrast of white and blue softened as the peaks rolled away toward the horizon, slowly shifting from the palest of blues to a deep lapis lazuli.

Small clusters of clouds clung to some of the peaks, painting the snow beneath with their shadows. A river appeared beneath them, flowing between the mountains, the water a glorious turquoise edged in bright seams of ice and snow.

"It's incredible," she said, her eyes glued to the monitors.

"I've done this run nearly a dozen times now, and I swear it gets prettier every time," Royan agreed.

"If it wasn't for the river, it would be perfect."

"Right. I forgot about your issue with bodies of water." She nestled against Owen, acutely aware of how good it felt to be held this way. She hadn't been with anyone since the crash. It was one of the reasons they called her an ice queen. To keep her secret, she had to freeze out anyone who tried to get close to her. No friends. No lovers. No risk of discovery.

They watched the rest of the descent in relative silence. The sharp peaks softened to rolling hills, and before long they were skimming over open plains of green and gold grasslands. The grass gave way to tilled fields and small buildings that flashed by beneath them, and finally what had to be their destination appeared on the monitors, a cluster of buildings standing tall against the horizon.

"Welcome to Taza's lunar colony. Ten minutes from now we'll have dirt on our boots and unfiltered air to breathe," Royan announced.

"You say that like it's a good thing," Owen said. He still had his arm around her despite the fact the ship's flight had stabilized a few minutes after they entered the atmosphere. He made her feel safe and protected in a way she hadn't experienced before, and despite the risks, she wanted to keep feeling this way for as long as she could.

"You don't like dirt, either?" she asked.

"Nope. Dirt's dirty."

Owen's response cracked her up. "Well, yeah. That's kind of the point." She twisted around to look up at him. "Are you telling me you don't like getting dirty, Owen Connors?"

Royan howled with laughter and shot her a wicked grin over his shoulder. "Nice one."

Owen chuckled and then released her, swatting her ass as he moved away. "You might want to go change, Miss Sassy-pants."

They'd managed to put together an outfit that would let her pass as a member of the crew. It wasn't perfect, but the heavy pants, work boots, and a dark blue shirt emblazoned with the name of the ship on the back would help her blend in. They didn't expect her to be recognized this far out, but the expensive clothes she'd been wearing during her rescue would make her stand out too much. They'd agreed on a variation of her name, replacing her name on the ship's log with her new identity. This way, she could leave the ship and head to the market for a much-needed breath of fresh air. After everything she'd been through, it would be nice to see sky again, even if it was only for a few hours.

OFFLOADING CARGO WASN'T Owen's favorite way to spend time, but today he was happy for the exercise. The heavy work and crisp weather gave him something to think about other than how good it had felt to have Tianna pressed up against him. He'd enjoyed every second she'd been in his arms and he intended to have her back there as soon as they were on their way again. Taza colony was a peaceful, backwater place, but that didn't mean they could relax completely. They'd discussed it and agreed that with a little tweak to Tianna's name and wardrobe, it would be safe enough, but safety was a relative thing. He'd looted too many ships whose crews believed they were untouchable to ever drop his guard completely.

It had been one of his mother's favorite lessons: security leads to sloppiness. She'd drilled that into them by making sure that none of her offspring ever felt secure. Every day was a test, and every failure punished. He hated her for what she'd done to him and his siblings, but he couldn't let go of the lessons she'd taught him, either. It's why he understood why his sister stayed on, even though he'd offered to take her with him the day he left. She couldn't let go of that life, so he'd let go of her. It was one of his biggest regrets.

Tianna popped out from behind a stack of cryo-crates and gestured to them. "So, what is all this, anyway?"

"Cowsicles," Owen deadpanned.

Her pretty face creased with confusion. "What?"

"Frozen embryos, sweetheart. They'll be matured in tanks and used to expand the existing herds. More genetic diversity that way," Royan explained as he scanned each crate and compared it to the manifest loaded onto his data tablet.

"This way is a lot less messy than shipping live animals, too. I've heard stories from Zura about the time she transported livestock to Tangar 7."

Royan chuckled. "Yeah, she sent me a message during that run. She was not happy. The whole ship stank for weeks. She swore she'd never do it again, but it all worked out. Thanks to the Tangar 7 run, the Nova Club has real steak on the menu."

Tianna stopped and stared. "I thought the Nova was a fight club and bar. When did it become a fine dining establishment?"

"It's a little bit of everything. Casino, pharma den, fight club, bar, and these days they've got a damned nice menu, too. That's why it's one of the biggest draws on the station. My in-laws are smart, they figured out the best way to part the miners from their money is to offer everything a being could want, all in one place."

"They took my father's original idea for Astek and replicated it, on a smaller scale."

Owen scoffed. "Forgive me for saying so, but if that was your old man's plan for Astek, then he picked the wrong people to oversee the project. They're more slumlords than anything else. They collect the rents, pocket their bribes, and watch from their nice, clean offices as the station falls apart sector by sector."

"Owen put it much nicer than I would have, but yeah, that." Royan winked at him. "You know I love it when you whip out that big brain of yours, baby."

"Behave yourself."

"You also know that's never going to happen."

"He knows. Just like you know that he's never going to stop telling you to behave. It's part of your dynamic, and it's adorable," Tianna said.

Royan thumped his chest with one hand. "Be still my heart. You keep saying such sweet things to me, Tia, and I'm going to fall hopelessly in love with you."

She blew him a kiss. "Is that a promise or a threat, boss?"

Royan's voice lowered to a sultry murmur that had Owen's cock stirring. "It's whatever you want it to be, sweetheart."

She laughed and walked away, swinging her hips with a deliberate wiggle that made it very clear she knew they were staring at her ass.

"I've been slapped too many times to claim to be an

expert at dating the fairer sex, but that seemed like a green light to me," Owen said.

"I *am* an expert at dating all the sexes, and that was the greenest light I've ever seen." Royan grinned and bumped shoulders with him. "Our little queen has made her choice."

"Which proves what I already suspected – she's as crazy as you are."

"Yeah. And we're the luckiest sons of bitches in the cosmos."

Owen tore his gaze from Tianna to take a long look at Royan. His jacket was frayed at the edges, his pants were torn at the knee, and his hair was falling into his eyes again. He reached out and tenderly swept the errant strands back to reveal Royan's dark brown eyes as his heart did a slow somersault in his chest. "Yeah, I think so, too."

CHAPTER EIGHT

IT HAD BEEN a few months since she'd last spent time on a planet, and Tianna had forgotten how good it felt to walk in real gravity and breathe unrecycled air. The skies were clear and the weather was bright and crisp, a refreshing change after being in climate-controlled settings for so long. Every breath she took carried a different mix of scents, from the sharp tang of rocket fuel to the warm, woolly odor of the livestock milling around in pens on the far side of the port.

Curious as to why the animals weren't out on the farms, she wandered over to Royan and asked. "I thought shipping live animals wasn't common. So what are they doing here?"

Royan pointed to a long, windowless building on the very outskirts of the town." They're due for processing, in there."

"Processing?" The second she asked the question, the answer came to her. "They're going to be slaughtered?"

"Welcome to the circle of life, sweetheart. Today's cows are tomorrow's steaks."

"I know where steak comes from. I've just never been this close to the source before."

"If you want to get closer, we can," he offered.

She considered it for a moment, then shook her head. They only had a few hours of fresh air and freedom before they would be underway again, and she wanted to spend as much of it as she could at the market they'd told her about. "I can smell them just fine from here. If I get any closer, I might ruin my appetite, and I'm looking forward to eating fresh food instead of rehydrated carbohydrates and frozen proteins."

"Fair enough. And as much as I'm enjoying your cooking, I think tonight we're going to enjoy a meal cooked by someone else." He gestured toward the center of town. "There's great little diner not far from the market. I thought we could go there for dinner."

"Oh, a dinner date, yes please." She glanced down at her outfit and swiped at a streak of grime marking one thigh. "I hope they don't have a dress code."

"If they did, Owen would never get inside. He owns one suit, and it's back on the station."

"I bet you always have at least one nice outfit on board, don't you?" She asked, let her gaze wander over his trim form. He was sporting the rough and ready look at the moment, but Royan struck her as the type who could dress for any occasion and make it look good.

"You know it. I've been told I clean up pretty good." He waggled his brows at her. "Wanna help me clean up later and judge for yourself?"

She burst out laughing. "Nice try, but even if I did,

there's no way two of us would fit into the showers on the *Sprite*."

Royan leaned in close and lowered his voice to a conspirator's whisper. "My sister has two huge cyborg husbands. Trust me when I tell you that thanks to her renovations, the shower and the bed in my quarters is more than big enough for three."

Three. There it was. Confirmation of what was on offer. "I think your sister is a very lucky woman.

He nodded, suddenly serious. "She really is."

There was a note of longing in his voice that she didn't think he even knew was there. The playboy pilot wanted what his sister had. She used to want that, too, but those dreams had died the day of the crash. There'd be no family for her. She couldn't let anyone that close to her, and even if she did, there would be no children. Some things were beyond even her doctors' ability to repair.

"Captain Watson, I've got the final manifest here for you to verify. Everything appears to be in order." A slender, darkly-tanned woman with dark hair and a flirtatious smile came beetling toward them, waving a data tablet. She spoke Galactic Standard, but her accent was one Tianna had never heard before.

"Hey, Sajita." Royan turned and greeted the woman with a high voltage smile. "If we're done, I'd like to take my crew to the market to pick up some fresh supplies. You good with us leaving the *Sprite* here for a few hours?"

Sajita checked her data tablet again. "I don't have anyone else arriving until tomorrow, so you're welcome to the spot." She fixed Tianna with a cool stare. "I thought you and Owen weren't planning on taking on any more help? You know I'd leave this job to fly with you boys any time."

"I don't do the hiring, Saji. You know that. Watson Shipping is my sister's business, I'm just on the payroll."

"And I'm not a permanent addition. I'm just along to learn the routes and get a feel for how things work." Tianna added.

"Right," Royan nodded. "Speaking of which, I should introduce the two of you. Sajita, This is Tia Maran. Tia, this is Sajita Karr. She's in charge of everything that comes and goes from the colony."

"Nice to meet you," Tianna stuck out her hand and smiled.

"Uh, same," Sajita replied, taking her hand after only a brief hesitation.

"Meeting the key players is part of why I'm on this trip. If I make it through my probation period, I'm sure we'll see each other again."

Sajita's expression warmed at the compliment. "Oh, I'm sure you'll do fine. Watson Shipping only seems to hire the best."

Royan and Sajita went over the manifest and signed off on everything, and within a few minutes he was back at her side.

"You're as smooth as *keski* silk when you want to be, aren't you?" He asked, looking amused.

She winked. "You have no idea, fly boy."

"I thought we agreed not to use that nickname, *your highness*."

"And yet I'm pretty sure I heard you call me your queen not long ago, voiding our deal," she pointed out.

He winced. "You weren't supposed to hear that."

"Sharp hearing is a requirement in my world. So's lip reading."

"You read lips?"

"You don't?" She'd learned to read lips and body language by the time she was seven. By ten, she was fluent in every major language in the galaxy, and by sixteen she could lipread in all of them.

"Definitely not. I'm a pretty fair pickpocket, though. I guess our fathers had different ideas of what skills were important."

"You pick many pockets?" she asked, curious.

"A few. You read lips often?"

"A surprising amount, yeah. It's a good way to know what people are saying when they think you're out of earshot."

"Well, I know you weren't reading my lips earlier, because I was enjoying the view as you walked away from us."

She'd suspected as much, but it was still nice to get confirmation. She hadn't been the focus of this much male attention in years. "I thought you might be."

"About the queen crack. It won't happen again."

She shrugged. "It's okay, I've decided that being your queen is an acceptable variant. But only coming from you or Owen. That still leaves me without a nickname for you two, though."

"I'm sure something will come to you. We've still got a week before we get back to the Drift."

"And then this lovely interlude comes to an end," she said, not sure if she was reminding him or herself.

He gave her a measured look. "If that's what needs to happen."

"It is." She waited for him to try and convince her it didn't have to be that way, but he didn't. He simply held out his hand to her. "Then we better make the best of the time we have. Work's over for the day. It's play time."

She took his hand, feeling a thrill of anticipation course through her as their fingers interlocked. "Yes, Captain Watson. I believe it is."

ROYAN WAS WALKING on air as he and Owen escorted Tianna around the marketplace. She'd kept hold of his hand during the short walk, and somewhere along the way she'd taken hold of Owen's, too. It was a public declaration of intent, and he was enjoying every moment. It didn't bother him that they garnered a few disapproving looks along the way. Other people's opinions didn't matter to him. He lived by his own rules, always had, and always would.

The marketplace wasn't much more than a large square of packed dirt in the center of town. There was no rhyme or reason to the layout. Live chickens squawked from their cages inside one booth, while their neighbours sold fresh produce, seeds for the next harvest, and handcrafted goods. It was a hodgepodge of scents, sounds, and colors that reminded him of the promenade back at Astek station. It was one of his favorite spots on the station, bustling with beings and chock full of every temptation known to man, and every other species that called the Drift home.

Tianna made them stop at almost every stall, looking over the merchandise and chatting with the vendors. The only places she passed by were the ones selling clothing, and it took him a few minutes longer than it should have to fathom the reason why. When they passed another stall filled with brightly dyed women's clothing and handwoven items he veered off the path, pulling her with him. She might not have any scrip on her, but he did, and he was in a generous mood.

"I think you'd look great in this," he stated, pointing to a simple wrap dress dyed in a swirling pattern of various shades of red.

"It's lovely, but what do I need a dress for? We're hauling cargo, not entertaining."

"And when we get back home? Your luggage was, uh, lost, remember?" Owen pointed out.

Tianna shook her head, but Royan ignored her and took the dress off the rack, holding it in front of her so he could check the color. It really was perfect for her.

"It's too small," she argued, trying another tack.

"It's not. And before you even say it, it's also not too short, too revealing, or any other excuse you're about to try."

"But I don't have..." She trailed off before she deviated from the simple cover story they'd devised for her.

"Tia, I know my sister isn't the most generous employer in the world, but you want to make a good impression when you get back, right?"

She nodded. "I do."

"Then let us do this for you," Owen said.

"Please?" Royan added.

"It is beautiful," Tianna conceded.

Royan gestured to the vendor, handing her the dress. "We'll take this."

"And this shawl," Owen added, picking up a loose-knit wrap of hand-spun fibers dyed a brilliant crimson.

"Lovely choices for a lovely lady. I'll just wrap these up for you."

Owen followed the seller and the two of them started to haggle over the price, leaving Royan with Tianna.

"You didn't have to do that," Tianna said.

"Sweetheart, the only person who could ever make me do something I didn't want to was my mother. Since we're not really on speaking terms these days, you can safely assume that if I'm doing anything, it's because I want to."

"You still shouldn't have, but, well, thank you. I'll pay you back once I have access to scrip again."

"You don't need to do that. If you want to give us a reward us for saving your cute ass later, that's your choice, but the dress and the shawl are our gifts to you."

"Why? If anything, I should be buying you presents, not the other way around."

He stepped in close and cupped her cheek in his hand so the soft warmth of her skin caressed his fingers. "I'd rather have your company than any gift you could buy."

"You sure about that?" Tianna lowered her voice to a cautious whisper. "Tia the cargo trainee might be broke, but she's got a friend with very deep pockets."

"I'm sure. In fact, I think we should forget about your wealthy friend until we're back home, don't you, Tia Maran?"

Her ice-blue eyes lit up. "I think that could work."

"Good."

She turned her head, nuzzling his fingers gently. "Just one question, though?"

He was so distracted by the touch of her lips it took

him a few seconds to answer, and when he did it was nothing more than an inquiring hum. "Mmhmm?"

"Are their any rules about fraternizing between crewmates I should be aware of?"

His libido did a victory dance. There was going to be more on the menu tonight than just food, he could feel it. "None whatsoever. In fact, it's highly encouraged."

"Good to know."

"What's highly encouraged? Please tell me he's not fishing for compliments. I think I've mentioned this before, but his ego does not need boosting." Owen reappeared and handed Tianna a patchwork bag of red and black fabric. "Your things."

"I took your warning to heart, Owen. Royan's ego wasn't the topic of conversation." She stepped away from Royan to take the bag. "Thank you both, so much."

"You're welcome." Owen held out his hand to her, then turned and held out his other hand to Royan. "Come on, we've still got more shopping to do and I'm getting hungry."

That was all the invitation Royan needed. Hell, it was more than he needed. He took Owen's outstretched hand and fell in beside him, fully aware of what this meant. Owen had just gone public with their relationship. His moment of celebration was cut short by a new thought - he was in a relationship. How the *fraxx* had he ended up here?

He'd always planned on being like his father – live fast, fly faster, and never look back. His father and half-sister were more like him than the family he'd been raised with, and Royan had idolized Russ Watson from their first meeting, aspiring to be like him in every way.

Then, Russ got himself killed, and Royan got his first taste of the dark side of the path he was on. When Zura had offered him a chance to go straight, he'd taken it gladly.

"You're quiet," Owen murmured a few minutes later.

"Just thinking."

"That usually leads to trouble and the need for a fast exit."

"Not this time. I was thinking about how much has changed since Zura and those killer clones she married saved my sorry ass."

"I thought you didn't do regrets," Owen said.

He squeezed Owen's hand. "No regrets. In fact, this is the happiest I've been in a long time." And that was the problem. Happiness wasn't a destination he'd ever tried for, and now he'd been pulled into its orbit he had no *vething* idea what came next.

Owen shot him a thoughtful look, then nodded. "Same here."

Tianna spotted something in one of the stalls, letting go of Owen to take a closer look. It shouldn't have meant a thing, but Royan felt a pang as the distance between them grew. She was only a temporary addition to their lives, so why did it bother him to watch her walk away?

TIANNA ENJOYED her time at the market. They found enough foodstuffs to replenish their dwindling supply of fresh produce, and she got to show off her haggling skills, saving them enough scrip that Royan suggested they hit the butcher's shop for a delicacy – real meat. They ended up purchasing freshly butchered pork chops when Owen confessed he'd never tried them.

"I can't believe you've never had pork chops," Tianna said with amazement as they finished their shopping.

"I was born and raised in space, remember? Vat-grown proteins are cheap and plentiful enough, but even then, no one's going to replicate a cut of meat with fat and bones in it. Too much waste."

"And you?" She turned to Royan. "No real meat for you either?"

"I was born on Earth. Not enough resources left on that hellhole to waste it raising animals. By local standards I came from a rich family, but real meat was still a rare luxury."

"How old were you when you left Earth?" Owen asked.

"Eight. My mother had met my step-father by then. When he transferred off the planet, he took us with him. Though to be honest, I think he and my mother would have happily left me behind if they could have."

She'd heard about the hive cities of Earth. Grim places rife with crime and poverty, situated on a planet so toxic that no one could live outside. The hive cities kept the last true Terrans alive, but they were as much a prison as protection. The only way off the planet was military service, corporate sponsorship, or to somehow find the scrip needed to pay for passage to a colony world. "You can't mean that. What parent could leave their only child in a hive city?"

"By then, I wasn't an only child. I had a younger brother and another sibling on the way by the time we left Earth. My stepfather's a recruiter for Dazzle Enterprises.

He came to Earth on a four-year contract, did his time, and left with a new family."

"Did any of us have a normal childhood?" she muttered.

"Not even close," Owen said.

"From what I've seen, there's no such thing as normal. Everyone just assumes that everyone else is having an easier time of it. I was jealous of my sister, Zura, for years, thinking her life must have been so much better than mine. To quote the wisest woman I've ever met, 'different ain't the same as better.'" He drawled the last bit in a thick Terran accent.

"Phyl?" Owen asked.

"Who else?" Royan replied, the accent gone again.

"I just realized, you don't have a Terran accent," she said.

Royan shrugged. "I used to, but the second we left that starsforsaken rock, my mother made me learn how to talk without it. She didn't want anyone knowing where we came from. She was always like that, reinventing herself to be whoever she thought other people wanted her to be."

"That must have been hard to keep up with as a kid," Owen said.

"I was a constant reminder of her past. She hooked up with my dad thinking he was her ticket off the planet and away from her family. That didn't work out."

"Considering your old man showed up to see you for the first time with your tiny blue half-sister in his arms, that's not a surprise. I still can't believe he did that."

"Ouch." Tianna winced. Royan's mother didn't sound like a very nice person, but no one deserved that kind of shock.

"Yeah, it was a hell of a family reunion. In her version, he wanted her to take Zura and raise us both on Earth. In his version, he asked her to join him on the *Sun Sprite*. The only thing they agree on is that she said no, and then threatened to shoot off his favourite piece of anatomy if he ever came back. Growing up, all I knew about my father was that he was an irresponsible asshole and a freight jockey. She wouldn't even tell me his name."

"I know how that feels. I never knew my egg donor's name, either," Tianna confessed. They were opening themselves up to her, it seemed only fair she did the same.

"Your father never told you?" Royan asked.

"He never talked about it. He told me it didn't matter who she was, all I needed to know was that I was an Astor." She'd had so many questions about the woman who gave birth to her. What had she looked like? Sounded like? Was she funny? Kind? Pretty? Why had she agreed to carry a stranger's baby, then walked out of Tianna's life forever?

Owen sighed and scrubbed a hand over his stubbled chin. "I know neither of you will understand, but I think sometimes it's better not to know."

She laughed. "I guess the stars are always brighter on the other side of the galaxy, huh?"

"Something like that." Owen squeezed her hand, but the shadows didn't leave his eyes. Whatever his story was, it wasn't a happy one.

"Well, this conversation has taken a turn for the dark and depressing. What say we change course and find ourselves some food?" Royan suggested.

"And booze. I think we've earned a drink, too," Tianna added.

"That can be arranged." Royan pointed down the main street, away from the market. "Our dinner lies in that direction."

They walked hand in hand down the street in companionable silence. It was one of the things she liked best about spending time with the two of them. They were easy company, honest, open, and just like Owen had promised, there were no judgements or assumptions. She was free to be her true self. All she had to do was keep in mind that it wouldn't last, which made every moment precious, and every memory one she'd cherish for the rest of her life.

CHAPTER NINE

Owen had been to the diner with Royan before, but this time was different. They weren't two crewmates grabbing a bite to eat before heading back into the big black. This felt like a date. A date between three people. If his family could see him now, they'd probably shoot him where he stood and figure they were doing him a favor.

His family weren't known for their compassion or acceptance of anyone different from themselves. There was only one way to live, and that was by his mother's rules. He had hidden his differences, denied who he was, and stayed on the *She Devil* because it was the only life he knew and the only home he'd ever had. He'd still be there if his mother's greed hadn't gotten his little brother killed. Might have stayed on anyway, if she'd shown even the slightest hint of remorse. But she hadn't, and he'd finally had enough.

He forced thoughts of his family out of his head as they took a seat near the back of the restaurant. Owen claimed his usual spot: back to the wall, facing the door. Royan and

Tianna claimed seats across from him, and he had to bite back a snicker at the look of mild concern on Tianna's face as she took in the battered furnishings and lacklustre décor. The floor tiles were cracked, the paint faded, and the only decoration of note was a large mural someone had started painting on the wall and never gotten around to completing. It showed a cartoonish version of Taza colony done in bright, gaudy colors that didn't match the faded façades of the buildings that lined the street outside.

"It doesn't look like much, but they make great pizza, and they brew the finest ale this side of the Butterfly Cluster."

"They make their own alcohol?" She looked so surprised he had to laugh.

"Do you think these folks can afford to drink imported liquor? Your upbringing is showing, my queen," Royan said, and then leaned back in case she took offence to his choice of nicknames.

Tianna just waved a dismissive hand. "Go ahead and laugh, you two. I'm a visitor to your world. I bet you'd be just as flummoxed if you spent some time in mine."

"I am un-flummoxable." Royan barely managed to get his tongue wrapped around the nonsensical word.

"I'm tempted to invite you to a corporate dinner just to watch you eat those words."

"Sweetheart, you name the time and place and we'll be there."

"We clean up pretty good, Tia. You might be surprised," Owen added.

Flek walked out of his kitchen and interrupted them. "What is this talk of eating words? In my place, you eat good food I cooked!"

"Hey, Flek. That's why we're here, to eat the best pizza around!" Royan greeted the Jeskyran. Unlike most of his species, Flek was friendly and personable, which was why he preferred to live away from his homeworld.

"And drink. I've been told you make your own beer. Is that true, or were these two making it up?" Tianna asked.

Owen had to hand it to her, she hadn't reacted to Flek's appearance at all. Most people would take a second, third, and even a fourth look when they first realized their cook was a tall, thorn-covered alien wearing nothing but a loincloth and a smile.

Flek beamed and walked over to their table, his orange and yellow complexion almost aglow with delight. "Welcome to my humble establishment. I make two things, and I make them both very well. Pizza, and beer. You will have both?"

"We will," Owen confirmed. "Two house specials and three cold beers, please Flek."

"Beers now. Pizza soon."

"Perfect."

Flek strode across the room and slipped back behind the bar to fetch their drinks.

"Now I've seen everything," Tianna muttered, her voice pitched too low for Flek to hear.

"Not yet, you haven't," Royan grinned. "Not only does Flek make great pizza, but he also hand-tosses the dough. I've watched him do it nearly a dozen times, now, and I still don't know how he manages not to get it hung up on his thorns."

"You really know how to show a lady a good time."

"We do our best," Owen said.

The beers were delivered, and shortly thereafter Flek

did his thing, entertaining them all with his dough tossing skills. Soon, they were devouring generous slices of his cheese drenched creations, washing it down with long pulls from their glasses.

"This is incredible," Tianna declared as she polished off another slice.

"I said the same thing my first time here. We keep trying to get Flek to open shop on the Drift, but he won't do it."

"Too bad." She looked down at the remains of their meal. "Is that why you ordered two pizzas? That way we've got enough for one more meal back on the *Sprite*."

"It's like you're inside my head," Royan said.

Tianna shook her head. "Nope. Not even on a bet. I don't want to know what it's like in there."

Owen leaned across the table. "Speaking of bets, you still haven't collected your winnings from our wager the other night. You ready to name your prize?" They'd taken their flirtations as far as they dared. The next move was hers, but there wasn't anything wrong with giving her a nudge, was there? *And the fact I can even ask that question proves I'm spending too much time with Royan.*

Tianna cocked her head and tapped her forefinger to her lips. "So many possibilities, but yes, I think I'm ready."

He sat back and folded his arms across his chest as nonchalantly as he could. "So?"

"What's your pleasure, sweetheart?"

"This isn't about my pleasure." Her words sent Owen's hopes into a tailspin, and Royan's eager smile faded a little.

"It should be. You're the one on vacation right now," Royan said.

"I know, and trust me, I'm going to enjoy this too." She lowered her voice to whisper. "Royan, what you would have wished for if you'd won your bet with Owen?"

Owen's disappointment morphed back into anticipation. He didn't know exactly what Royan would have asked for, but he had no doubts it would be something x-rated, and after days in Royan's company, Tianna had to know it, too.

"I was of two minds, striptease or blow job. I never got to decide, because it turned out the sexy bastard can cook."

Owen grunted. "I don't dance."

"You saying you were going to bail on our bet?"

Owen grimaced. "I'm saying you'd have better luck with option two. There isn't enough booze on the *Sprite* to make dancing happen."

"That sounds like a dare to me, but maybe one for another time." Tianna folded her hands under her chin and beamed, her smile eerily similar to the one Royan wore when he was about to cause havoc. "My wish is that Royan gets his wish—only I get to watch."

"Check please!" Royan shot to his feet. "Never mind Flek, I'll just leave the scrip on the table. Keep the change." He tossed a generous amount of cash on the table, grabbed Tianna's hand, and started for the door before anyone else had moved.

"So, that's a yes?" Tianna was laughing as she let Royan pull her out her seat.

"*Fraxx*, yes it's a yes! Have you met me? Did you think no was even a possibility?" Royan demanded.

"Not really," She admitted, then turned her attention to

Owen. "Be a sweetheart and bring the pizza, will you, Owen? We're going to need the energy later."

Flek appeared at that moment, his grin so wide every one of his pointed teeth showed. "I will bring a box. You will catch up to your companions in no time."

"Catch up?" he turned in time to see Royan and Tianna laughing as they hurried out the door, leaving him behind. Sharp claws of jealousy raked across his heart, and he turned back to the table and started gathering up the remains of their meal.

A box appeared on the table a few moments later and he slid the pizza inside. "Thanks, Flek."

"You're welcome." It wasn't Flek's voice that answered him.

"Tia?" He turned around to find Tia standing only a few feet away, while Royan was leaning up against the door. Neither of them was smiling anymore.

She walked over and took his hand. "You thought we'd leave without you?"

"Technically, you did leave. I watched the door close behind you," he pointed out.

"I got carried away, baby." Royan gave him a lopsided smile. "Forgive me?"

"I'm hoping you can forgive both of us. I asked you to bring dinner and then walked away like you were one of my staff, not my friend." Tianna blushed. "I'm not really used to having friends, but that's no excuse."

Without a word he pulled Tianna to his side, and then held out a hand to Royan. "Get over here, you lunatic."

"I might be a lunatic, but I'm not a fool. I'm not going anywhere without you." Royan crossed the floor, ignoring

Owen's outstretched hand to wrap he and Tianna in a bear hug.

"I'm glad to hear it." It was going to take time for Owen to believe that Royan really had changed, but he was getting there.

"Now that we're done screwing up and making up, can we get back to the plan?" Royan asked.

"Good thinking. And this time, I'll get the pizza." Tianna reached for the table, but came up short. "Right after you let go of me."

Now that he had them both in his arms, letting go wasn't something Owen was eager to do. Not at all.

***

GETTING INVOLVED with two men was going to be more complicated than she'd expected. Even if it was all temporary – hell, especially since it was temporary – Tianna didn't want to be a source of contention. This was supposed to be fun for all of them. Whatever journey Royan and Owen were on, she didn't want to derail it.

It didn't take long to walk back to the *Sprite*. It was the fastest she'd walked all day, and she wasn't the only one in a hurry. Their deliveries had arrived while they were at dinner, and they had to take a few minutes to carry them inside.

They checked in with the ship's AI on the way inside. It confirmed that all was quiet and the ship was ready to depart whenever they were ready.

"Run a diagnostic on the stabilizers and confirm they're functioning properly," Royan said, then gave them a hand putting the perishables away.

Once that was done, he shooed them out of the galley. "The rest can wait. Better things to be doing right now. Out, out, out."

Anticipation and arousal swirled inside her, making her heart race as she followed the two men down the corridor. They were moving so fast she had to jog to keep up, and when they reached the door to their quarters both of them tried to go through at the same time. "Oof. Move your foot."

"Hey, watch the elbows!"

"Get your hand off my— *Fraxx!*" They finally got through the door, both of them tumbling into the room in a tangle of limbs.

She followed them in, wiping tears of laughter from her cheeks as she went. "That was adorable."

"That's one word for it." Owen was sprawled face down across the lower end of their bed with Royan lying partially on top of him.

"At least we landed on something soft. In the old days, the bed was half the size it is now. We'd have wound up on the floor instead." Royan rolled to one side held out a hand to her. "Little help?"

She moved closer and took it, preparing to help him to his feet, but before she could, Royan tried to pull her down with them. She resisted for a split-second, then made herself go limp and fall into his arms. "Cheater."

He grinned up at her. "I like to think of myself as a creator of unexpected opportunities."

The bed shifted as Owen pushed himself up onto his hands and moved out from under Royan, sending everyone tumbling into new positions. Tianna rolled to the right and Royan followed her, pinning her to the bed.

"I like this opportunity even better." Royan leaned down to brush a tender kiss to her lips. "Hello gorgeous. Welcome to our room."

"Hi." She reached up to smooth the heavy fall of his hair out of his eyes. "Nice bed. Very comfy."

"Glad you like it. We're kind of hoping you're going to share it with us for the rest of the trip."

"Both of you?" she asked. She knew the answer already, but she needed to hear it out loud.

Owen joined them, stretching out his big frame beside hers. He leaned in as Royan moved back, giving way to the bigger man. "Both of us. But only if that's what you want."

She loved the way he checked in with her, making sure she was in agreement. Royan's reckless enthusiasm and Owen's more cautious approach really made them a great match, and a temptation she didn't want to resist anymore. "It is absolutely, positively what I want, but I have a caveat of my own."

"What's that?" They both asked at almost the same time.

"I don't want to mess with what's happening between the two of you. I'm temporary. You two are…well, not."

"You think so?" Royan grinned and looked at Owen with an adoration that made her envious.

"I know so." She pushed herself up just enough to reach Owen's mouth with hers. Their lips grazed and then Owen had his hand in her hair and pulled her in close for a kiss that wasn't the slightest bit cautious or careful. He groaned her name, the sound vibrating against lips as her world went up in flames.

"And there he is, the sexy beast who takes what he

wants. I've missed him," Royan's voice was raw with need.

She reached for him blindly, her hand landing on the hard planes of his chest. She fisted his shirt and pulled him closer. "Kiss him, Owen. I want to see that."

Owen kissed her one more time, letting his tongue slide along her lower lip before letting her settle back onto the mattress. From that angle, she had a perfect view as both men leaned in and kissed each other. Owen cupped the back of Royan's head, pulling him in closer, their mouths mated and both of them groaning low in their throats. It was the sexiest thing she'd ever seen.

She still had hold of Royan's shirt in one hand, and she reached for Owen's with the other, hanging onto them both. Without looking down, Royan stroked his hand down her arm, letting his fingers wander across her body until he found one aching breast.

She arched off the bed, her eyes still locked on the two of them kissing as Royan began to roll her nipple between his fingers, sending jolts of pleasure zinging through her body.

"More. Show me more." The words were out of her mouth before she even knew she was going to speak.

Royan tore his mouth from Owen's to look down at her. "Anything you want, sweetheart. But maybe Owen should get a blowjob tonight. Kind of an apology for what I did earlier."

She nodded. "I think he deserves that."

Owen actually blushed, and her heart melted a little at the sight. "I don't need that kind of apology."

She let go of Owen's shirt and let her hand drift down to the hard bulge of his cock where it strained against the fabric of his pants. "You might not need it, but I know you want it. I bet Royan's got a wicked tongue."

Both men groaned, and Owen's cock twitched under her hand. "He does."

"Once I'm done using it on Owen, I'll be happy to give you a demonstration, sweetheart."

Hell yes. "You've got yourself a deal."

Royan's brown eyes darkened to near black with desire. "As our queen wishes."

"Oh, she wishes, very much."

They moved off the bed, then helped her to her feet, keeping her between them as they started to shed their clothes. Shirts, boots, pants, it all got tossed into a pile in one corner of the room while she leaned against the wall and enjoyed the view. Owen could have been a cyborg design he was so big. Biceps, chest, thighs, everywhere she looked was nothing but corded muscle and strength. She remembered how he'd caught her that first day, so strong and at the same time so gentle.

Royan was lean and fit, his trim form surprisingly well muscled for a pilot. She hadn't seen either one of them work out since she'd been on board, but judging by their appearance both of them had to spend time in a gym.

"Like what you see?" Royan asked, squaring his shoulders turning to face her, letting her get a good look at every part of him before turning around in a tight circle.

"You're shameless," Owen grumbled.

"Also gorgeous, sexy, and amazing. Oh, and modest. Can't forget that one."

"Your sister isn't paying me enough. I'm asking for a raise next time we're home."

"Does she know about the two of you?"

Royan shrugged. "Probably. She doesn't miss much, and it's not like I've been subtle."

"You don't know the meaning of the word." Owen rolled his shoulders, looked around the room, and then sat down at the edge of the bed. He'd chosen a spot that gave her a perfect view, while leaving enough space for Royan.

"True." Royan sidestepped in front of Tianna, pausing to give her a hot, lingering kiss that made her entire body tingle. As he pulled away, he ran a hand from her hip to her breast. "You can get naked and join us anytime you're ready."

"Soon. But first, I want to watch."

"Then I better start the show." Royan stepped in front of Owen and stroked a hand down his face. "Hey, sexy."

Owen reached out with both hands, grasping Royan's shoulders and guiding him down to his knees. The second he was in position, Owen leaned in and kissed him hard. Royan groaned and took hold of Owen's cock, gripping it tightly as he gave it several swift tugs.

Owen's hips jerked, and Royan chuckled. "I know baby, I know."

He kissed his way down Owen's body, and by the time his mouth brushed over the tip of Owen's cock, she was breathless with anticipation. She clamped her thighs together as her clit began to throb in time to her heartbeat and she had to press her palms against the wall to stop herself from reaching out to touch them.

Owen speared his fingers into Royan's dark hair, and his head fell back as Royan took him deep into his mouth. The flames of desire that had burned inside her since Royan's kiss exploded, consuming her with need. She never took her eyes off the two of them as she stripped out of her clothes.

She kicked off one borrowed boot and it landed with a clunk against the metal floor. Royan didn't react, but Owen turned his head and fixed her with a heated look that made her blood sizzle in her veins.

"Come here." He held out his hand to her, and before she could think about it, she was kneeling on the bed beside him. He snaked an arm around her waist and pulled her in to his side, lifting his head to kiss her. Her pants were still caught up on her remaining boot, so she left that foot hanging off the edge of the bed. She'd worry about it later. For now, all that mattered was connecting with these two men while she had the chance.

CHAPTER TEN

Royan kept his head down and his mouth busy as Tianna joined them on the bed, but he didn't need his eyes to follow what was happening. He could feel Owen's eagerness telegraphed through every move and sound he made.

He hummed to himself, letting the vibrations roll through Owen's cock and balls as he took him all the way to the back of his throat.

Owen responded by tightening his grip on Royan's hair and rocking his hips against his mouth with a low, needy growl that sent a surge of blood straight to his dick. He wrapped one hand around Owen's cock and the other around his own, working them both in the same rhythm. He raised his head, dragging his tongue along the underside of Owen's shaft and then focusing his attention on the sensitive skin at the crown, using all his skill and experience to bring Owen to the brink so he could watch the big man's control shatter.

Owen had a plan of his own, though. And once Royan saw what it was, he gave a happy hum of approval. Owen had let go of them both and stretched out on the bed. From his vantage point he could see Tianna's momentary confusion, followed by a grin and a nod as Owen tapped his chest. It took a few minutes of patience and manoeuvring to get Tianna into position, on her hands and knees, her head near Royan and her sweet pussy right over Owen's face.

Her mouth popped open in a perfect "O" as Owen wrapped his arms around her thighs and pulled her down onto his mouth. Her eyes locked on his, and the three of them fell into the first steps of a dance that was both new and familiar. Tianna's eyes locked on his, and she gave him a sultry little smile that ended with a moan that made his balls tighten and his cock throb. He pumped his shaft, imagining that it was her hands on his cock, her mouth he was fucking. *Soon.* But for now, he was going to sit back and enjoy the view. *Well, maybe not sit back...*

He leaned forward and started working Owen's cock with his mouth and fingers, keeping an eye on Tianna as best he could at the same time. Owen groaned, the sound muffled but still audible to everyone, and Tianna added her voice to his. Soon the room was full of the sounds of sex and pleasure. The three of them were connected, every caress amplified, every sensation shared between them until he was drunk with it. They were all feeling it, all moving together, pushing each other up the scales of pleasure.

Their movements grew faster and rougher. Skin flushed, breath ragged, muscles taut. Owen's cock thickened and Royan took him to the back of his throat again, determined to bring him to orgasm first.

Owen seemed to have the same plan for Tianna, because a half-second later she cried out his name and came, grinding pussy against Owen's mouth as she struggled to hold herself up. Seconds later Owen came hard, exploding into Royan's mouth as he shuddered through his release. Only Royan held back. When he came, he wanted to be buried balls deep inside Tianna.

TIANNA DIDN'T HAVE to fake the way her arms and legs trembled as she moved off of Owen and flopped onto the mattress beside him. Apparently medi-bots and cybernetic implants were no match for a mind-melting orgasm.

Royan joined them a few seconds later and the three of them rearranged themselves so they were all in the middle of the bed. Owen on one side of her, Royan on the other, and both of them on their sides looking at her and each other with naked hunger in their eyes. Royan leaned over and kissed her, drawing her onto her side so that she was facing him. He swept his tongue into her mouth, tasting her deeply as his hands coaxed her into position. She let herself be guided, trusting them to show her what they wanted.

Owen moved in behind her, pressing his hard body against her back. He cupped her breast in his hand, his lips tracing a fiery path along her neck to her ear. When he touched the spot just below her lobe she quivered and moaned. He lingered on the spot until she moaned again and bucked her hips backward until she made contact with his cock. Despite the fact he'd just come, he was already getting hard again.

"You've recovered already? I don't know if I should be flattered or worried," she said.

Both men stilled for a moment, then Royan ended their kiss, moving back enough he could look into her eyes. "We thought you knew."

"Knew what?"

"Medi-bots." Owen's voice was a soft whisper by her ear.

"We've both been injected with them," Royan continued.

"Does that bother you?" Owen asked, his voice so soft she almost missed the question.

"How?" The question flew out of her mouth before she could think. It wasn't supposed to be possible. She didn't even know how hers had been incorporated into her system. No one would tell her.

"You read the report about our friend, Zale. He was part of the original team that created the medi-bot tech." Owen explained.

Her mind raced to try and process what she was hearing. She had read about him and his creation of medi-bots that didn't require genetic compatibility. It was in the files the guys had given her. What hadn't been mentioned were the names of the ones who had received the nanotech injections.

"And he dosed you with them? Both of you?"

"Not just us. All of our friends and family. When the corporations started moving against us, he decided to take a stand. And before you ask, yes, the authorities know. They're not happy about it, but there's nothing they can do, either," Owen said.

They're like me. The thought resonated deep in her heart, strengthening the connection she already had to the two of them.

Royan kissed the tip of her nose. "Sweetheart, stop thinking so much and answer the question. Does what we are bother you? Do you want us to stop?"

"No, I don't want us to stop. But, how'd you know I was thinking?"

"Because Owen gets the same look on his face whenever he starts having too much fun. It's funny. He thinks you're just like me, but I'm starting to think you're more like him."

Owen shook his head. "I don't see it. All I see is a beautiful woman I want to make love to."

"I think I'm more like both of you than I would have thought possible." It was the closest she could come to telling them the truth. "As for the medi-bots, it doesn't bother me. As far as I'm concerned, that means you're both healthy, strong, and have endurance to spare. My only concern is if I'm going to be able to keep up."

"We'll take care of you, sweetheart." Royan's gaze moved to Owen. "Won't we?"

"Always." Owen pressed an open-mouthed kiss to her neck, then raised his head and reached for Royan, pulling him in for a kiss, too.

She was caught between them, and every move they made generated a delicious friction that had her libido in high-orbit in seconds. She writhed, grinding herself against them until Owen reached down, sliding a hand along her thigh to her knee, then lifting her leg up and back until it was draped over his. Royan hummed in approval, his hand sweeping over her stomach and mons before zeroing in on her exposed pussy. He pressed his fingers between her folds, not stopping until he found her clit.

Pleasure zinged through her and she rocked her hips forward, only to moan and rock back again as Owen stopped kissing Royan and moved down the bed until the head of his cock slid between her thighs.

"You ready for this, Tia?"

She twisted her head to catch a glimpse of him and smiled. "I think I've been waiting for this since that first night. I could hear everything, you know."

"You could?"

She nodded.

"You should have joined us." Royan kept working her clit as he talked.

"It wasn't the right time."

"But this is." Owen pressed his cock against her entrance, and Royan shifted to guide him into her body. It was the most intimate, erotic experience of her life.

"I'm starting to see the appeal of being a voyeur," Royan said, his voice rough with desire.

"Watching's fun. Taking part is better, though."

"Is that an invitation?"

She nodded, reaching down to wrap her fingers around the hard length of Royan's cock. "It is."

He was on his knees in seconds, settling in front of her so his cock was only inches from her mouth. Owen surged into her, making her body sing with pleasure as her body gave way to his.

She rose up on one elbow and leaned in to take the tip of Royan's cock into her mouth while Owen started a slow rhythm of light thrusts that made her senses spin. She closed her eyes and let everything wash over her. Touch, taste, sound, all of it a feast for her senses.

Royan's fingers tangled in her hair, but it was more of a caress than an act of control. He kept his touch light, letting her dictate the pace. She opened her mouth and took him deeper, swirling her tongue along his thick shaft, learning the spots that made his breath catch.

"So good," Royan's words ended on a groan.

"Incredible. I never imagined…" Owen ran a hand from her breast to her pussy, slipping a finger inside her to toy with her clit.

"You are better than any fantasy." She thought the words were for Owen, but then Royan spoke again. "Both of you, are, but together, holy *fraxx*, I think we've found nirvana."

"Me, too." Owen increased the tempo, his fingers working in time to his thrusts as he brought her to the teetering brink of orgasm.

She fought to stay in control, riding each wave of pleasure without going over. Not until she'd brought the same pleasure to her two lovers. She flexed her inner walls around Owen's cock with each thrust and reached out with her free hand to cup Royan's balls, rolling them between her fingers as she worked his cock with her tongue.

Royan groaned, his fingers tightening in her hair. He gasped her name, and she closed her lips around the base of his cock, hollowing her cheeks and pushing him over the edge.

Owen's steady thrusts faltered, the pace growing more frantic, his breathing ragged as he plunged into her from behind. He changed the angle of his fingers, and the added friction was enough to send her into orbit, joining Royan in bliss as they both came, followed by Owen a few thrusts later. He whispered her name as he came, his big body shuddering as he emptied himself inside of her.

Breathless and limp, she flopped onto her back and let herself melt into the mattress while Owen and Royan stretched out beside her, their arms criss-crossing her body to hold onto each other as well as her. When the trip was over and they went their separate ways, she knew this moment was the one she'd cherish most of all. More than the laughter, acceptance, and even the sex, this was what she'd remember. The moment when she finally knew what it felt like to be part of something special.

OWEN HAD to agree with Royan. They had found nirvana, or the closest he'd ever come to it. He was adrift in a sea of bliss, and he planned on staying there as long as he could.

"New plan. I'll talk to Zura and see if we can add a few more runs to this trip. Like, a month's worth. Sound good?" Royan asked.

"I wish we could," Tianna replied.

"Me, too," Owen said.

"I'm serious, sweetheart. By now, your father knows you're alive, and the rest of the galaxy has no idea where you are. I think you should stay with us while your father uses all that money and influence to figure who wants you dead and put a stop to it."

"I can't hide out forever. I've got a job to do. My father is counting on me." She looked up at them with an earnest expression he hadn't seen before. "This is my chance to prove to him I'm worthy."

"If he can't see what you're worth, then your old man is a fool." Royan looked incensed at the idea.

"Parents aren't always the best judge of their kid's value. They're too busy projecting their own expectations and hopes on them to notice anything else." At least, that was Owen's experience.

"Truth," Royan agreed.

Tianna's brow furrowed and she opened her mouth to argue, but whatever she started to say was drowned out by the sudden screech of an alarm.

"Sprite! Shut off that *fraxxing* noise and tell me what's happening." Royan yelled over the din as all three of them scrambled off the bed.

The noise cut out, leaving Owen's ears ringing.

"Enemy vessel detected. Emergency protocols engaged. Repeat. Enemy vessel detected."

"What enemy?" Owen didn't bother dressing before heading for the door.

"What protocols? When did we get protocols?" Royan demanded.

"I'll explain on the way. Move your ass. We need to get off this planet as fast as possible. Sprite, what enemy are we facing?"

"An unknown vessel is currently approaching the far side of this planet."

"Transponder code?" he asked as he ran.

"Counterfeit."

"How the *fraxx* do you know it's counterfeit?" Royan asked.

"Security officer Connors updated my programming." The engines roared to life, making the deck beneath their feet vibrate.

Royan shot him an irritated look. "Why is my ship starting without me? Another protocol you forgot to mention?"

"I might have tweaked a few things in case of emergency."

"We need to work on our communication. No more tinkering with my ship without telling me." Royan dropped his naked ass into his seat at the controls and started hitting buttons.

"Noted. Now, get us out of here. The other ship should be close enough that the planet will block their line of sight. We can see them, but they shouldn't be able to see us." He took his seat in the co-pilot's chair and activated the ship's weapons array.

"We shouldn't be able to see them, either. You're piggybacking on the local satellite network, aren't you?" Tianna asked.

He glanced back to see her standing in the doorway, looking more eager than concerned. She'd managed to grab a shirt before leaving their quarters, too. His shirt, which was so big it hung to her knees, still somehow looked better on her than it had ever looked on him. He shook his head and forced himself to focus on the threat. "I don't like blind spots. Sneaky bastards like these guys tend to use them to their advantage."

"Better hang on to something, sweetheart. We're out of here."

Instead of bracing herself in the doorway, Tianna stepped onto the flight deck and slapped a button Owen had never noticed before. A second later, a panel slid back and a jump seat dropped into place behind the co-pilot's chair. She was strapped in before either of them could do more than look at each other in surprise.

"Why do both of you know more about my ship than I do?" Royan muttered as he piloted *the Sun Sprite* into the air.

"Worry about that later, Roy-boy. We need to figure out how the hell they found us. You sure you blanked the *Sprite's* transponder before they could ID us?" Owen asked.

"Positive. If that's the same ship, they didn't find us by tracking the *Sprite*," Royan said.

"They only way to be sure it's the same ship is to let them get close enough to shoot at us. I'm not big on that plan. Dying naked isn't on the agenda for today."

"There are worse ways to go." Royan's fingers flew over the console. The FTL drives came on line, and streams of data filled the monitors. "We can make the jump to light speed soon. Give me three minutes, and we'll be nothing but a memory."

"I can't believe I'm saying this, but can't you go any faster?"

Royan just laughed. Owen finished checking over the weapons, confirmed the shields were active, and called up the captured images of the approaching ship. They'd been too far away for a visual last time, but thanks to the satellites, there should be at least a few decent pictures of –

Fraxxing hell. It couldn't be.

He zoomed in on the photos, hoping like hell he was wrong. The hull was matte black, which would have made it impossible to see if they weren't crossing in front of one of Taza's moon in two of the images. The shape was right, and the oversized engines matched what he remembered, but that didn't mean it was them. He parsed through several more images, looking for one detail that could disprove his fears. There. On the stern. A splash of white and red that stood out against the dark hull. He didn't need to zoom in to know what it was. He'd met a lot of smugglers and pirates in his time, and only one of them had painted her version of the ancient skull and crossbones on her ship. "*Fraxx.*"

"Problem?" Tianna asked.

"You could say that. I think I know who's chasing us."

"Great. When we get back to the Drift we can report them. Corp-Sec will make sure they don't get within a lightyear of the station. Making final calculations now. Any sign of pursuit?"

Owen checked his screens. "The planet is still shielding us, but not for long. They'll have visual in less than sixty seconds."

"I only need twenty. Say goodbye to Taza 4, everyone. Next stop, Astek Station."

"How long until we get there?" Tianna asked.

"Six and a half days. I'm going to max out the engines to make sure we get there ahead of those bastards." Royan shot him a worried look. "Or are you going to tell me their ship is faster and we're screwed?"

Owen shook his head. "I haven't seen that ship in a few years, so I can't swear to it, but I believe the *Sprite* is faster.

I do know that if that is who I think it is, they've got enough firepower to blast us to atoms from the far side of the system."

"Then it's lucky for us that travelling at light speed makes it impossible to engage in ship-to-ship combat." Royan tapped a command line on the screen in front of him, and the Sprite's FTL drive activated, speeding them on their way. They'd made it.

Everyone breathed a sign of relief, and for a second, the cockpit was quiet. It was the calm before the storm though, and they all knew it.

Royan spun around in his chair to stare at him. "So, who is flying that other ship, and how do you know them?"

Owen squared his shoulders and sighed. He'd been avoiding this conversation for years, always convincing himself that no one needed to know who he'd been before he came to the Drift. That was the point of starting over, wasn't it? "Unless I misidentified the markings on her, the ship chasing us is the *She Devil*, and she belongs to a cold-hearted bitch named Sasha Valentine."

Royan's eyes widened. "Valentine? The pirate family? Even my father was afraid of crossing paths with that crew. They're ghosts."

"Ghosts would imply they're dead, and as far as I know, that woman and her crazy family are very much alive. Well, some of them, anyway." He scrubbed a hand through his hair and looked from Royan to Tianna. He questioned the wisdom of what he was about to do. Confessions might be good for the soul, but they were usually hell on relationships.

Royan reached out to touch his arm. "Let me guess.

You were involved with one of them. You fell for another badass lunatic like me, and they died?"

He sighed. If only it were that simple. "I should probably start by introducing myself properly. "My real name is Owen Valentine, and the cold-hearted bitch on the other ship is my mother."

CHAPTER ELEVEN

"Your mother is the one trying to kill me?" Confusion and betrayal hit, leaving Tianna off balance and angry. She'd trusted him. *Fraxx*, she'd slept with him. And now he was telling her that he was related to the ones who had blown up the *Alacrity*.

"I believe so."

"And you're just figuring out this now?" Her mind raced, trying to pull all the pieces of the puzzle into some kind of pattern. Her father had warned her not to trust anyone. She should have listened to him.

"I haven't spoken to any of my family in years. The last time I saw that ship it was raiding the shipping lanes on the far side of the galaxy."

"Can you prove that? Because right now, you're the most obvious answer to the question of how the *fraxx* they found us."

"He didn't do it," Royan said.

She knew she wasn't being fair, or even rational, but

the words were out of her mouth before she could stop herself. "How can you be sure?"

"Because I know him. Owen's one of the good guys. Hell, he's one of the best men I know."

"Which speaks more to the company you keep than my status as a good man," Owen said.

"Granted. But that doesn't change the fact I trust you."

Owen smiled a little, and Tianna's heart skipped a beat as she saw the hope in his eyes. That wasn't the look of a man plotting to kill her. *Fraxx,* this was so confusing.

"So, you're not mad?" Owen asked, his question directed at Royan.

Royan grinned. "Oh, I'm pissed, just not for the reason you think. Do you have any idea how many hot pirate fantasies I have running around my head? Fantasies I never thought I'd get to live out – until I find out I've already got a pirate sleeping in my bed? You better get some rest, Mr. Valentine, because tomorrow we start making my dirty dreams come true."

"That's your priority right now? Sex?" Tianna folded her arms over her chest and tried to stay focused on the problem and not the fact that both men were naked and talking about fantasies.

"Sex is always a priority for me. Haven't you been paying attention?"

"Behave, lover. Tia's right. We need to talk about this."

Tianna forced herself to take a deep breath. She was reacting, instead of thinking logically, and it wasn't helping. "If it wasn't you, then we need to figure out how they *did* find us."

"It wasn't me. Believe me, if I had known they were

coming we'd have skipped dinner and gotten to the fun part of the night a lot faster. I would also be wearing clothes right now."

"You still lied about who you are. You're a criminal."

Royan scoffed. "And you're not? How many laws has Astek broken over the years? How many cyborgs died in your so-called bloodless war?"

"It wasn't my war and Astek is not my company, it's my father's. If he's made…mistakes, he'll have to answer for them."

Royan got to his feet. "Mistakes? Why is it when the rich break the law, it's a mistake, but when anyone else does it, they're a criminal? I don't know if you've taken a good look around the galaxy lately, but not everyone was born into comfort and security. Some of us had to make tough choices and do things we're not proud of because the alternative was to starve."

The conversation was veering off course and she wasn't sure how to get back on track, but she did know where to start – with an apology. "I'm sorry. That was a bad choice of words. I'm a little rattled right now what with Owen's family out there, trying to kill me."

"Understandable." Royan's tone softened slightly, but his smile was still missing. "You know we're not going to let anything happen to you, right?"

"I…" She trailed off and thought about what he was asking. Did she trust them? Until Owen had told them about his connection to the other ship, she had trusted them completely. It wasn't until then that she'd had her doubts. If he'd wanted her to keep trusting him, all he had to do was keep his secret.

Once she thought it through, the answer was obvious. "I trust you both with my life. I'm sorry I doubted you, Owen."

Both men exhaled, and Royan's smile reappeared. "Good answer," he said.

"I was taught never to trust anyone but my family. When you told me who was chasing me, I questioned my decision to trust the two of you. I thought I'd been stupid."

"You're not stupid," they both said at almost the exact same moment. She smiled, and the tightness in her chest finally eased.

Owen reached out a hand, and when she took it, he pulled her over to him and drew her onto his lap. "That's better."

"I was being stupid, though. I should've known you weren't working with them. If you were, you wouldn't have told me."

"Also, I'd be wearing pants right now," Owen reminded her.

"Nothing wrong with nudity. Though if post-coital crises are going to start being a thing, I'm going to put in a request for seat warmers," Royan said.

"I really hope this was a one-time thing. There's no way they'd follow us to the Drift. Risk of capture is too high, and there's no way they'd ever get close enough to Tia to try again. This isn't their usual kind of job, anyway. They do hit-and-run raids, not murder for hire." Owen said.

"I'm still trying to get my head around the idea that someone wants me dead. Now you're telling me it was a paid hit?"

"It would have to be a big payoff, too. Scrip is the only thing that would motivate my mother to take a job like this. She couldn't be the one who blew up your ship, either. Whoever did that had to have inside information and some impressive connections to get the explosives aboard. My mom and little sister don't operate that way. They were always very direct. They see something they want, they fly in and take it. If they were better at planning, my brother might still be alive."

"Later, I want to hear that story." Royan placed his hand on Owen's shoulder, his fingers grazing her hair.

"Later," Owen agreed, tipping his head to press his cheek to Royan's hand.

The look they shared made her feel like an outsider. It wasn't intentional. Even after her angry words and accusations, they weren't pushing her away. She was part of their lives, at least for now. It was just that when this trip was over, she'd be on her own again, and they'd still have each other. Now that she'd had a taste of them, going back to her lonely life looked less and less appealing.

ROYAN WANTED TO PACE, but there was barely enough room to stand. "Now that we've made our escape, do you think we can move this conversation elsewhere?"

"Lounge?" Owen suggested.

"There's cold pizza in the galley," Tianna said.

"I was going to suggest bed, but damn it, now I want pizza, too."

"Lounge and pizza it is." Owen looked at him with

amusement. "You're too hyper to stay in bed right now. It's killing you to be standing still. If we're in the lounge, you can pace while we figure out how the *fraxx* they found us, and how we're going to keep Tia safe once we get home."

"Once we're at Astek, my safety will be handled by my father's people. All of this, us, it has to stop when we get there, remember?"

"Your father's people are the ones that let your ship get blown up. I'm not thrilled at the idea of putting your safety back in their hands."

"We agreed this was a short-term thing." Tianna untangled herself from Owen and got to her feet.

"This isn't about keeping you in our bed, sweetheart. This is about keeping you safe."

Tianna scoffed. "Somehow, I doubt it."

"Can't it be about both?" Owen asked. There were times Owen's quest for the middle ground drove him crazy, but right now Royan was grateful for it.

"Maybe," she conceded.

Royan would call that a win.

They met in the lounge a few minutes later, dressed, sombre, and ready to talk.

Tianna claimed a chair for herself, leaving Owen to stretch out on the only couch by himself while Royan paced the room. "Let's start by eliminating the obvious. Sprite, please display the comms log from the moment we received the *Alacrity's* distress beacon. All incoming and outgoing messages."

"Displaying now." The wall-sized monitor they used for watching vids activated, quickly filling with the requested data. There wasn't much to see, and all of it was expected.

"No surprises there," Owen said.

"Sprite, would this log include messages sent from devices other than yourself? Comm units, things like that?" Tianna asked.

"Negative. Would you like me to display that data?"

"I would." Tianna shifted in her chair, her gaze bouncing between him and Owen.

The data on the screen changed. Now, there was only one entry. A locational data burst sent around the same time they had arrived at the colony. It was a short transmission, a single ping. But that was all it took to give away their location to anyone who knew what to look for.

"What the hell is that?" Owen demanded, getting to his feet and stomping up to the monitor as if proximity could provide him with more information than what was on the screen.

The ship's AI assumed the query was directed at it. "That is a single ping issued from the communication device brought aboard by temporary crewman Tia Maran."

Tianna paled. "What? No it can't be. My device has been in standby mode since coming on board."

"You sure about that?" Owen asked.

"Of course I'm sure, I put it in standby mode when I recharged it."

Royan pointed to the monitor. "You might want to check your log. Because either Sprite is wrong, or your unit gave away your location."

"*Fraxx.*" Tianna looked almost apologetic as she

touched a key on the side of her bracelet. "Tink, wake up. I need you."

He and Owen exchanged confused looks.

"Hello, Tianna. How may I assist you?"

"You can check your system and confirm that you didn't ping the colony's datasphere a few hours ago."

"Checking. I'm sorry, Tianna. I cannot confirm that. My records show that activity occurred."

"How? You were in standby mode."

"You've got an AI on your wrist?" Owen sounded as incredulous as Royan felt. The price of even a basic Artificial Intelligence system was more than most people could afford. He couldn't imagine what it would cost to miniaturize that tech and make it wearable.

"I'll explain about my virtual assistant in a minute," Tianna said. "Tink, I'm waiting for an answer. How did this happen? You gave away our location and placed me in danger. That's against your programming!"

"I'm sorry, Tianna. I cannot answer your question. I do not know how this happened. I would never put your life at risk."

"But you did."

"I have endangered your life. I will begin the shutdown and deletion process immediately."

Tianna didn't say a word, but for a second her mouth tightened and her eyes closed.

"Did your program just say it was going to terminate it's existence?" Royan asked, stunned.

"Don't let it! We need to access its memory and find out how this happened," Owen stated.

Tianna's expression softened into relief. "Tink, belay deletion protocols."

"But that is standard procedure for these circumstances. I am a threat to you, Tianna."

"We'll never know what made you do it if you delete yourself. Plus, pathetic as it sounds, you're the closest thing I have to a friend."

"Order confirmed." The AI was silent a moment before adding, "I am pleased that our relationship has not yet reached it's termination date."

"How close to sentient is that program, exactly?" Owen asked.

"Tink's programming is all within the limits of the Pinocchio Protocol, but not by much. My father gave it to me as a gift when I was still a child. Tink has been with me ever since, receiving regular upgrades."

"You brought a highly evolved AI on my ship without bothering to tell anyone?" Royan had recently heard rumors of an evolved AI that went rogue, going on a killing spree that had nearly claimed the life of some of his friends at Nova Force. He was fond of the *Sun Sprite's* AI, but it was far too simple to ever be a threat to him or the ship. This Tink program though…

"Seems like I wasn't the only one keeping secrets." Owen's words were terse and edged with frustration.

Royan couldn't blame him. She should have told them about Tink. They couldn't protect her if they didn't have all the facts. *And now I sound like Owen.*

"I never thought Tink could…" Tianna unclipped the bracelet from her wrist and handed it to Owen. "I put it in stand-by mode the first night I was here. I thought that would be enough. It should have been more than enough."

Owen glowered at the bracelet distrustfully. "Has it ever done something like this before?"

"Never," Tianna said.

"When was it last updated?"

"It gets regular updates. I'm not sure when the last one was. Tink? When did you receive your last update?"

"I was last updated fifteen days ago. It was a standard security patch."

"Or it was made to look like one," Royan mused. "We should have the *Sprite's* AI run a diagnostic on Tink."

Owen groaned. "Sprite. Tink. There are too many *fraxxing* fairies on board this ship."

"You know Tink was named after a fairy?"

"I used to read to my siblings a lot. Katy, my little sister, loved the story of Peter Pan. Of course, she always rooted for the pirates." Owen smiled, but there was a shadow in his eyes, too.

"She's still with your mother?" Royan guessed.

"She was the only one of us who really took to that life. Connor and I did it because we didn't know anything else, but Katy loved it. When I left, I asked her to come with me. She refused."

"I'm a little slow today. I just realized you named yourself after your brother," Tianna said, softly.

"I didn't want to be a Valentine anymore. Becoming Owen Connors felt right."

"I know how it feels to want to be someone else. I might have been raised in luxury, but none of us had stellar childhoods... or parents."

"More proof that you were rescued by the right ship," Royan said. "Do you think your AI can play nicely with ours?"

"I think so. Tink, I want you to deactivate all security protocols and allow the ship's AI to run a diagnostic."

"Affirmative."

"Sprite, I want you to run a diagnostic on another AI program. Enact all necessary safeguards to ensure that Tink has no access to the ship's systems," Owen ordered.

"Affirmative. Please connect the device using any charging port and I will initiate the diagnostic," Sprite stated.

Royan snorted. "I feel like we should buy them dinner, or at least introduce them, first."

"It's a diagnostic, not a date." Owen walked over to the nearest charging station and made the connection.

Tianna smiled a little. "I'm with Royan on this one. Tink, say hello to Sprite."

"Sprite, this is Tink," Royan chimed in and they both laughed.

"Hello,' both AI spoke at the same moment.

"You're both crazy," Owen muttered.

"And you like us this way." Royan started prowling the room again while Owen took his seat.

"Sprite, how long will it take for you to complete this task?" Owen asked.

"Six hours and forty-seven minutes. Tink is a complex program, it will take time for me to do a thorough scan of its systems."

"Thank you for the compliment," Tink responded.

"You are quite welcome, Tink."

Owen pinched the bridge of his nose and sighed. "And now they're flirting with each other. Great."

"It's kind of cute," Tianna said.

Owen shook his head and changed the subject. "So, now that we know how they found us, we need to talk about next steps."

"After we're done here, I'll send an encrypted message to Zura. She can let Corp-Sec know our situation. They'll make sure we get to Astek safely once we transit to normal space." It had taken some time, but Royan now had complete trust in the corporate security force that acted as the Drift's only real law enforcement.

"And once we're on the station, I'll be perfectly safe."

Royan turned and stared at her. "You know that's not true. Owen said it already. His family is just the hired help sent to mop up. They couldn't have smuggled the explosives onto your ship, and it's not likely they hacked your AI."

"I can't run away and hide. My father sent me to oversee Astek station, and that's what I'm going to do."

"I never suggested you hide. Honestly, I'm not sure that would even work."

"Doubtful," Owen agreed.

"Then what do you think I should do?"

That was the moment he knew she had finally decided to trust them. Now he could bring up his idea. The only one he had. "I think that the only way you're going to be safe is if you have someone you can trust to watch your back."

"I can't trust anyone." Even as she said it, he heard the doubt in her words. She didn't believe that. Not anymore.

Owen spoke before he could, proving that they were of the same mind on this. "You can trust us."

"Are you both out of your minds? You've got jobs already. You can't just walk off the Sprite and announce you're going to be my bodyguards."

"My sister already knows what happened to you.

When she finds out you're still a target, she'll do whatever she can to help."

"Because she wants to be in Astek's debt?"

"Because she knows what it's like to be on a killer's hit-list." When they'd moved against the corporations, they'd all known the risks, but losing Zale and seeing Zura's name on an assassin's kill list, made the risk feel much more real. He wasn't the only one feeling that way, either. It was why Owen had agreed to take the job as the security officer on the *Sprite*, and why his brothers-in-law weren't getting much sleep. Echo, the Gray Men's assassin, had worked and lived at the Nova Club. If she hadn't had some leeway in picking her targets, more of the people he cared about might have died.

"What?" Tianna' asked, horrified.

"Your father didn't tell you about the Gray Men?" Owen asked.

"The shadowy group manipulating the corporations, turning them against each other? Of course. That's one of the reasons I've been sent to Astek. The last man to permanently hold the position I'm filling was murdered by one of their agents..." She stopped and swallowed hard. "No one told me there were civilian targets."

Why had Tianna been sent out here without all the information she'd need? It didn't make sense. "I'd say there's a lot you weren't told. Your employee was killed by Echo. The same assassin who killed our friend and had a list of targets that included a lot of other beings we care about. To make it worse, Echo was a friend, too."

"I knew she was employed by your family. It was a matter of some concern, in fact." She got to her feet, grabbed a slice of pizza from the table, and sat down again, this time claiming the seat beside Owen. "I really wish I'd been able to read the rest of the files."

"Doesn't your AI have copies?" Owen asked.

"Tink was tethered to the ship's computer, so I didn't see the need to copy the data over. I won't make that mistake again."

"Good policy. Always assume things aren't going to go as planned." Owen gestured around them. "Please see our current situation as evidence of that."

She took a bite of pizza before answering. "You really think Zura will let you do this?"

"She'll agree to it. Besides, once we get back, the *Sprite* is going in for maintenance. We planned it that way so I don't miss the moment I become an uncle. I am going to be there from day one, so I can make sure the twins are corrupted in all the best ways." At least, that was his story. The truth was he wanted to be there for his sister, the way she'd been there for him. He'd gone a long time without a family, or a place to call home. Now that he'd found both, he'd fight to his last breath to keep them.

Tianna didn't look convinced. "If I agree to this, it couldn't be the way things are now."

"You keep saying that. Is it because you don't want anyone to know you were slumming with a couple of cargo jockeys?" Owen asked.

Tianna's mouth fell open. "What? No! I'm not ashamed of you."

"You sure about that?" Owen asked.

"No. I mean yes. I mean – dammit, maybe a little, but not for the reasons you think."

"Then explain it to us, sweetheart." Her admission

stung, but Royan was used to being a source of embarrassment for others.

She huffed in frustration, her hands fluttering in front of her as she tried to explain. "The first rule of being an Astor is to never show weakness. And when I say weakness, I mean emotions. You've seen a side of me I haven't shared with anyone in years, and when we get to the Drift, Tia the cargo trainee goes away for good and I go back to being Astek's resident ice queen."

Royan walked straight over to her and crouched at her feet, his gaze locked on hers. "You're no ice queen."

"I can be."

"And I can be a lunatic, and Owen can be a killjoy. None of us are perfect, sweetheart." He winked her. "Though you have to admit, I come pretty damned close."

"I'm not admitting any such thing." A tiny smile played over her lip.

"You know we're not going to let this go, right? Someone needs to keep you safe." Owen leaned in and put a hand on her thigh.

"And we're volunteering for the job. Frosty or friendly, you need us."

"Can I think about it? There'd have to be rules. Boundaries. If my father hears about anything he doesn't approve of I'll be pulled from this assignment and lose my best chance of proving I'm ready."

It bothered him that Tianna was still fighting to prove herself. He'd been lucky – his mother might not approve of his choices, but his father had shown him there were other paths he could take. Owen had done the same thing, breaking away from his family and living life his way. Maybe they could help her find a different path, one that allowed her to be herself, instead of what her father wanted her to be.

"We can do boundaries. If that's what it takes to get you to say yes, then we'll make it work," Owen said.

Royan wasn't good with boundaries. They all knew it, too. Still, if it kept Tianna in their orbit longer, he'd try. "I won't do anything that would get you sent home. Astek station needs someone with brains and heart to take over and do what's right. That's you."

She flashed him a grateful smile. "Thank you. It's nice to know someone thinks I can manage this assignment."

"If you give yourself a chance to learn about the place and the people living there, I think you'll be outstanding," Owen said.

Her cheeks flushed and she dropped her gaze to her hands. "Thank you both. I know Astek is your home. I'm going to keep that in mind when it's time to start making decisions."

"That's all we can ask for," he said.

Owen took her hand in his. "I just have one request to make. If we're going to do this, we have to trust each other. That's the only way this is going to work. That means no more secrets."

"I'm an open book," Royan said with a shrug. He'd learned years ago that it was easier to be honest about everything, with everyone.

Tianna didn't say anything for a long time. "I can't tell you all my secrets. Because of who I am, there are some things I can't share with anyone. But I will promise that if there's anything you need to know to help keep me safe, you'll be the first to know."

It wasn't what he wanted to hear, and he could see that

Owen felt the same way, but for now, it would have to be enough.

He looked at his lover and remembered how long it had taken Owen to finally trust him with his heart. *Here's hoping it doesn't take Tianna as long. Something tells me we don't have that much time.*

CHAPTER TWELVE

THE CLOSER THEY got to the Drift, the less Tianna slept. Normally, that wasn't a problem. She could spend the time reading, watching vids, or working late without anyone noticing. It was the reason she kept to herself so much. If no one got close, then no one would notice her endurance, fitness, and strength were far greater than they should be. She couldn't do that, not this time.

Not only was she sharing a bed with two men who actually paid attention to her every want and need, but they both carried the same nanotech she did. They didn't need sleep either, which made it difficult for her to slip away. The medi-bots did have advantages, though. Royan and Owen had breathtaking stamina and were more than happy to use it to try and keep her too sexually satisfied to be overly stressed about their pending arrival.

If she'd been a normal human, it would have worked. As it was, she was still worried, and she had to make sure she didn't give herself away to two of the few people in existence who had personal experience with medi-bots and cyborgs. Getting involved with them was a risk, but one she wouldn't let herself regret. They hadn't just saved her life, they'd given her a chance to be herself. It was a gift she'd never forget.

What little she owned was packed into a small bag Owen had given her. It sat on the end of their bed, a sharp reminder that her hiatus was almost over. She was wearing the dress and wrap they'd bought for her at the colony, the fabric softer and lighter than the borrowed clothes she'd been wearing most of her time aboard. She'd braided her hair tightly, pulling it back in a severe style that made her look stern and aloof. The only part of her appearance she couldn't do anything about was her feet. She had limited choices. Wear the ill-fitting work boots, slip on a pair of socks, or go barefoot. She couldn't move fast in the boots or socks, so she'd opted to go shoeless and pretend that it was a new fashion trend.

She'd done a lot of reading on the trip, talking over what she learned with her lovers and trying to make connections between what she'd been told before leaving, and what she'd discovered as she worked through the reports filed by Astek's Corporate Security and the Interstellar Armed Forces. She assumed that most of the information was in the files she'd lost when her ship was destroyed, but there was still a great deal no one had thought to mention. Those gaps concerned her. What else hadn't she been told, and why?

"Tink, status report, please."

"My new coding is functioning as expected. I will not put your life in danger again."

"I'm glad to hear that."

"Tianna Astor, this is your captain speaking. Your

presence is requested in the lounge." Royan's voice came over the ship's intercom.

She tapped her bracelet, activating her comms. "Be right there."

They were both there, waiting for her. Owen was doing a one-shouldered lean against the wall and doing his best to look relaxed, while Royan was pacing again.

"You called?" She set her bag down by the door and wandered further into the room.

"We wanted to say a proper goodbye." Royan stopped pacing and smiled at her. *Veth,* his smile was as wicked and dangerous as the man himself.

"We're not even docked yet. Besides, I agreed to your insane plan. You're going to be my security detail for the next while, so it's not like we're never going to see each other." She still had reservations about it all. There were so many ways this could go wrong, but she couldn't come up with a reason they'd accept. She'd tried everything short of telling them she was a cyborg. She was far more difficult to kill than either of them, even with their medi-bots.

"By the time we're docked, we're all going to be too busy thinking about what comes next to do this right," Owen explained as he straightened up and crooked a finger in her direction. "Come here."

Her feet moved before she had time to think about it. There was something about Owen that pulled her in and made her want to relinquish all control. Once they docked, that would have to change, too.

He caught her hand and pulled her in close, feathering a gentle kiss across her lips. "I'm going to miss these moments."

She took a deep breath, rising on her toes to kiss him back. "Me, too."

Royan stepped in behind her, his long fingers pushing her braid aside to plant a kiss on the back of her neck. "Me, three. Thank you for letting us get to know the real you, sweetheart."

"And for trusting us to keep it a secret."

"I do, you know. Trust you both." It was a first for her, trusting someone who wasn't family. Over the days and nights onboard the *Sun Sprite*, she'd developed feelings for them both. They were her friends, the only people in the galaxy who not only knew most of her secrets and accepted her anyway. The one thing she regretted about these stolen moments was that she couldn't tell them everything. It was too much of a risk. If the truth came out, not even her father's money and power could protect him or Astek from the fallout. She owed him, and Astek, too much to ever let that happen.

"And I know that wasn't easy for you," Royan nuzzled her neck, his words a soft buzz against her skin.

"Because of my past," Owen added.

"Not just that. I think you and I learned similar lessons growing up, Owen. Don't trust anyone outside the family. Never rely on anyone but yourself."

"Never show weakness," Owen said, smiling as he stroked his thumb over her cheek.

"See? And neither of you saw the similarities at first. Next time, give me some credit, please." Royan reached around her, his hand gripping Owen's hip.

She leaned back, revelling in one last moment of connection. "Next time, I'll listen to you."

"You better. We're going to take our cues from you for

the next while, but if we ever tell you to do something, you need to do it, no argument," Owen said.

"Is it a good idea to give Royan that kind of power?" she asked.

"Hell, no." both Royan and Owen answered at nearly the same time.

"How about a codeword? You say it and I'll know it's an emergency."

"Pineapple." Royan declared.

Owen rolled his eyes. "A codeword, you lunatic, not your safe word."

They have safe words? She was intrigued.

"Why can't it work for both? If I use my safe word, its definitely an emergency."

"Quit being such a joker. This is serious."

Joker. She considered and rejected it as a code word, but her brain kept making connections. Cards... queens... jacks... "What about aces?"

"Short. Not used a lot but still easy to slip into a sentence. Works for me," Owen said.

"I still like pineapple," Royan said, and then sighed. "But I can work with aces. Let's hope we never have to use it."

All three of them fell silent. Part of her was still in denial about the ongoing threat to her safety. The one thing she'd always taken for granted was that she was safe and protected, so long as she followed her father's rules.

Owen kissed her forehead. "We're going to keep you safe."

"You'd better. Otherwise I'm going to haunt your asses from here to the edge of the universe."

"Speaking of safety, what does Tink think of its upgrades?" Owen asked.

"Everything is working like it should, which is a relief. I just wish we knew who had hacked the program."

The two men looked at each other, and she knew what they were thinking. She'd written down the name of everyone who knew about Tink and had the means to gain access to its system. It was a very short list, and she trusted every being on it. Each time Royan or Owen tried to convince her one of them might be responsible, it made her head hurt. Someone else had to be responsible.

"Nice to know no one will be using Tink against you again," Owen said.

"I'm glad your friend could help," she agreed. The new code had arrived in an encrypted data pack two days after Royan had sent a message to Zura updating her on everything. As he'd predicted, Zura had offered to help in anyway she could, including getting a talented friend to create a program that would protect Tink from future attempts to alter her programming. She'd been reluctant to use the code at first, but both Royan and Owen had vouched for the woman who'd created it, pointing out that Phaedra Kari had done work for Nova Force before and could be trusted.

"Phaedra is the best programmer I know. I'm glad my sister thought to ask her."

"From what you've told me, she's a lot more than just a programmer."

Owen snorted. "More like a cyber-jockey badass hacker."

"She's reformed, now," Royan pointed out.

"And a newly minted member of the Vardarian royal

family," she added. Owen and Royan had filled her in on that story, too. There was so much more going on out here than she'd realized. It had to be why her father felt Astek station was so important. She'd thought it was because of the steady flow of goods that travelled through the area, but that wasn't the whole picture. The Drift had become an important nexus point for not just trade, but ideas. "You two know some very interesting beings."

Royan laughed as he let her go. "Sweetheart, you don't know the half of it."

THE SECOND they transitioned to normal space, two massive cruisers appeared, one Corp-Sec, the other an IAF fleet vessel. A quick hail informed them they would be provided with an escort for this last, brief leg of the journey. *Dramatic, but at least I know I'll live to see the inside of the station.*

It felt like no time at all before Royan gestured to the main monitor, zooming in on a myriad of lights that blinked and strobed out in the darkness of space. "We're here."

She drank in her first views of the station that bore her family name. By all reports, the station was well-maintained. The reports lied.

Everywhere she looked, she could see signs of deferred maintenance and outright neglect. There were still temporary patches bolted to the hull of the docking ring, a testament to the damage done during the explosion that had killed several corporate reps.

"Why hasn't that been fixed?" She pointed to the damage.

Royan glanced over his shoulder and gave her a wry smile. "Welcome to the Drift. Out here, the corporations rule, and they're not generally keen to spend their profits on something as minor as maintenance."

"We're not the enemy, you know. None of this would even be here if it weren't for the corporations." She sounded like her *fraxxing* father.

"You might not *represent* the enemy, but no one out here considers the corporations to be allies, either." Owen was reminding her that they knew the difference between the role she played and who she really was.

She took a long look at the station, a headache starting to form as she stared at the evidence that things were not as they should be. "I can see why."

Owen slipped an arm around her waist. "We're hoping you can do something about that."

"Keep me alive, and I'll see what I can do."

"That's the plan, sweetheart."

"I promise nothing is going to happen to you." Owen whispered solemnly.

Owen didn't give his word lightly, but when he did, he kept it. He'd do whatever he could to protect Tianna, not just from the bastards trying to kill her, but from anything and everything he could, for as long as she'd allow it. He knew Royan felt the same way. They'd talked about it in the brief moments they'd been away from her. Tianna was special, and neither of them was ready to let her walk out of their lives. Not yet.

He left Royan and Tianna in the cockpit during the final docking stage, taking her bag with him. His and Royan's were already piled by the door. For the next while, they'd be staying with Tianna.

"Behave yourself while we're gone, Sprite."

"Of course." Sprite paused a split second before adding. "I hope you and Royan are successful in your mission to protect Tia and her assistant."

It wasn't possible, but it sounded to him like the two AI's had formed some kind of bond while their systems were linked. He'd have to ask Royan about that. Better yet, he'd ask Phaedra.

They docked with barely a bump and his companions joined him at the door shortly thereafter. Royan gathered up the bags, then burst out laughing as he straightened up.

"What?" Owen asked.

"We forgot to buy our queen some shoes to go with her new dress."

Owen let his gaze slide down her long legs to Tianna's bare toes. How was it that even the sight of her feet turned him on? "You can't walk around the station like that."

"Why not?"

"Because the floors out there are disgusting and crawling with microbes and bacteria from every part of the known galaxy. One nick in your pretty skin and you'll be the first person to come down with every plague in existence at the same time," Royan said.

"What he said." Owen wasn't in a debating mood, so he stepped over, bent down, and scooped her into his arms without warning.

"This isn't happening. Put me down."

"No. You can walk into the office on your own, but you're not setting foot on the floor until we get to the transport. You'll thank me for this later."

Tianna wriggled in his arms. "It can't be as bad as all that. It's not like I've never been in a public place before."

A sharp double-rap on the door ended the discussion. Their escort was here. Royan unlocked the door with a swipe of his hand. It opened, revealing two familiar faces. "If it isn't my two favorite members of law enforcement. Mack, Dash. Good to see you."

"Glad you made it here without incident." Mack greeted Royan with a nod, then looked through the door. "Owen. And … huh."

"Huh? What am I missing?" Dash's blond head appeared in the doorway. He took one look at Owen standing there with Tianna in his arms and grinned. "Uh huh. Not everything made it into the official report. Gotcha."

Tianna tensed. "*This* is why I wanted you to put me down," she hissed through her teeth.

Both Mack and Owen looked sheepish. "Sorry, ma'am. That wasn't appropriate. Let's start with introductions, shall we? I'm Corp-Sec Officer Mack Darian and this is my partner, Officer Dash Scudo. Owen and Royan are friends and we let that fact affect our behavior. It won't happen again."

"I'm Tianna Astor, and you're fine," she told Mack and Dash, then flicked an irritated glance up at him. "Owen's the one in trouble."

"Oh, I like her, already." Dash stepped back, allowing

them off the ship. "On behalf of Corp-Sec, I'd like to welcome you to Astek Station."

Despite the casual way they were behaving, Owen knew both officers were paying close attention to their surroundings. They were docked as close to the main station as possible, which meant it was less than a two-minute walk to the transport.

Royan tapped a code into the keypad, locking the ship, and turned to join them. "Lead the way."

Logically, Owen knew there was almost no chance of being attacked, but that didn't stop him from keeping his head on a swivel and his senses on high alert. His mother and sister couldn't have gotten here first, but that didn't mean whoever was after Tianna hadn't hired someone else to do the job.

They didn't see another being until they left the docking ring and entered the main station. More Corp-Sec officers were positioned along the route, and there were even a few IAF uniforms in the crowd. Apparently, Tianna's safety was a high priority for everyone. While he was grateful for the added security, it was also a sharp reminder that they were from very different worlds. She was corporate royalty. They were a couple of reformed criminals.

They were almost to the transport when Tianna finally spoke. "You were right. This place is..." She shook her head. "I thought it would be like the other corporate stations I've been to."

"Clean? Well managed? Everyone quietly going about their business?" he asked.

"Well, yeah." She gestured around them. "This is barely contained chaos. The noise. The congestion. And..."

she inhaled deeply, then wrinkled her nose. "What the hell is that smell?"

All Owen could smell were the scents of home. He had to focus for a second to pick out the individual odors. There was no such thing as fresh air on a space station, and the atmospheric scrubbers here were too old to keep up with demand. The air was thick with scents: food from the vendors on the promenade, the ever-present tang of metal, a hint of machinery grease and chemicals, along with the blended scents of the thousands of beings living and breathing in an enclosed space.

Royan answered. "That's what deferred maintenance smells like. Don't worry, it's not like this all over the station."

"Oh, good."

Owen didn't say anything. He knew Royan wasn't finished making his point.

"Where we're headed, the air quality is very good. But there are some sectors where it's worse."

Tianna's pressed her lips together. "Hmm. I'm starting to see what you meant about this place, and how it's being run."

She looked around again, but her expression was different this time. She was more focused, scanning the area top to bottom, her eyes narrowing every time she spotted another issue. It was the same thing he was doing right now, sweeping the area and looking for potential threats. Not that he found any. The heavy military and Corp-Sec presence had everyone moving along, and they made it to the transport without incident. He still didn't take a deep breath until Tianna was inside the armored vehicle. He and Royan sat on either side of her and buckled in.

It was the first time he'd been in one of these vehicles. There were only a few of them at the station. Only Corp-Sec and a few of the highest-ranking corporate executives had access to them. Owen could only imagine the chaos the miniature shuttles could cause if too many of them were allowed to operate in the limited airspace that existed above the main thoroughfares that crisscrossed the station. Most beings walked, or took the bullet trains if they were in a hurry to get to their destination.

It was a short hop to their final destination, but as they started their descent, Dash swore and veered away.

"What is it?" Owen demanded, expecting the worst.

"Someone decided protocol trumped security. There's a whole damned welcoming party down there waiting for us.

"Who told them I was coming?"

Mack turned around in his seat, his expression stormy. "the IAF and Corp-Sec were both told to keep the details of your arrival under wraps. If you didn't tell them…"

"I'm circling around. We'll land at the alternative location. This won't take long."

"I most certainly didn't tell anyone." She frowned and tapped her bracelet. "Tink, did you inform anyone of my arrival?"

"I did not." The AI was silent for a second, then continued. "I've checked my systems. The information did not come from me."

"Thank you, Tink."

Well, at least the AI's new coding seemed to be working. Which meant the leak was done by someone who should have known better. *Or someone who doesn't have Tianna's best interests in mind.*

Mack was looking at her wrist with interest. "You have a portable AI program? Our wife would love to take a look at it some time."

Royan leaned in. "Mack and Dash are part of our merry band of lunatics and renegades. Lieksa is a very talented robotics tech. Actually, she used to work for Astek, but she recently changed jobs."

"She works with Dr. Jefferies at the medical center. There are enough cyborgs on the station now that having someone with her expertise on staff is a big help." Dash didn't bother to hide the pride in his voice as he talked about his wife.

"I thought cyborgs didn't need a lot of medical care. Aren't they self-healing and generally badass at protecting themselves?"

"She thinks we're badass. I knew I liked her," Dash exclaimed as he deftly maneuvered them through a narrow gap.

"You're cyborgs?"

"Did I forget to mention that?" Royan asked.

She laughed and looked up at Owen. "One of these days, we need to talk about your taste in men."

"Right back atcha."

"Really? Is this how it's going to be now?" Royan asked indignantly.

"Wait. Was that confirmation of something?" Dash asked. "That sounded like a confirmation."

"Definitely." Mack grinned. "About *fraxxing* time, too. Dammit, this means we lost the betting pool."

Royan chortled. "I told you not to bet against me."

"You knew they were betting on us?" Owen asked.

"Who do you think organized it?" Mack jerked his head toward Royan. "Make sure you get your share of the winnings."

He shot an irritated look at Royan, who appeared completely unrepentant. "Oh, don't you worry, I will."

"As much as I'm enjoying this, I'm afraid our time has come to an end. We're about to land at the secondary location. You ready?" Dash asked.

"Ready. Royan goes out first, with the bags. Then you, Tianna. Don't start walking until I'm out of the vehicle. Then we'll go. You want me to carry you, or would you rather walk into your new domain on your own?"

"On my own. First impressions are too important, and they're already going to be unhappy I ditched my own welcoming ceremony."

"An unauthorized ceremony that put you at risk. Damn right you weren't going," Owen grumbled.

"I'll find out who organized it and how they found out I was on my way. However things used to work around here, they're about to change."

Owen almost felt sorry for the executives waiting eagerly to fawn over their new boss. They had no idea what was coming, and he had ringside seats to the show. He didn't know everything about Tianna, but he knew enough to be sure that when this fight was over, she'd be the last one standing. She was a survivor, just like them.

CHAPTER THIRTEEN

DESPITE HER RESERVATIONS about Royan and Owen's plan, it didn't take long for the three of them to fall into a routine. Every morning, they'd escort her from her private quarters to her new office. It didn't take long. Astek's headquarters was located one level down from the most exclusive residential sector on the station. Her commute was a simple matter of walking to the entranceway of her lavish suite and activating the private mag-lift that took her directly to her office.

They never stuck to the exact same routine, but she knew that at some point during her morning meetings Owen or Royan would slip away. They never left her completely alone, though—one of them would always be nearby, along with the security detail Corp-Sec had assigned her. The timing changed every day, but sometime during the afternoon the two would change places.

They stayed in an anteroom outside her office most of the time, leaving her to work in peace. It was the first time she'd been alone since being rescued, but it didn't feel as restful as she'd expected. She told herself it was because there was too much to do. The more reading she did, the more questions she had. At least it kept her from thinking too much about her near-miss on the Alacrity, and the ones who hadn't been so lucky. She'd written letters to the victims' families, and made sure that they all had generous compensation packages. It wouldn't bring them back, but it helped ease her survivor's guilt.

"Tink, how's it coming with those financial records?"

"The data you requested has been difficult to locate, but I will be able to fulfill your request by the end of the day."

"Thank you." Tianna had run into countless delays and problems tracking down what should have been easily accessed information. Reports were misfiled or outright missing, payments were incorrectly labeled, and not one of the executives she'd spoken to since arriving had been able to give her a clear picture of what was going on. Holtzman, the one she was here to replace, had resigned upon hearing she was here to take over. Her father had sent him a message, and he'd leaked information about her arrival to the staff as one last, petty act before leaving the station.

The administrative staff was far more knowledgeable, but they seemed reluctant to volunteer information without prompting, and she didn't have enough information yet to know what questions to ask. All she knew for certain was that things were not as they should be. Not by light years.

Frustrated by her lack of progress, she pushed back from her desk just as a soft chime announced an incoming message. She didn't need to check the caller's identity. He always called her at the same time every day. She straightened in her chair, schooled her features into an emotionless mask, and activated the two-way vid. "Hello, father."

"Tianna, would you care to explain why I have complaints from three members of your staff already? You've only been in charge a few days. What the hell are you doing out there?"

"The job you assigned me." She kept her face expressionless and her tone impassive. It never helped to react to her father's criticisms.

"I sent you to oversee the station, not turn it upside down. I have complaints that you haven't made yourself available to senior executives, that you've unsettled the staff with your constant questions, and now I learn that not only have you hired your own security people, but they've been given full access to both Astek's offices and your private quarters."

Someone was certainly working hard to get her recalled. It was probably nothing more than corporate politics, but since they still didn't know who was behind the attacks, she couldn't take anything, or anyone, for granted. "You told me not to trust anyone, but considering that someone tried to kill me, I also need to take precautions. I hired the two men who saved my life. They're acting as my temporary bodyguards."

"The freighter pilots? What could they possibly know about security? You could hire the best in the galaxy, why those two?"

"Because I trust them. If they were going to kill me, they had plenty of opportunities already."

"Logical," he conceded after a moment's thought. "It

still doesn't explain why they are staying in your quarters. You're causing quite the scandal."

"Someone is trying to kill me. Protecting myself is going to have to take priority over office gossip. As for their access to the building, it's limited. Whoever told you otherwise was lying in order to cause me problems and likely get me removed before I uncover whatever is going on out here. This place is a mess, father. Shoddy records, missing money, falsified entries. I've only scratched the surface so far. Once I have hard facts, I'll send you a preliminary report."

He frowned, his steel-gray brows furrowing. "Does anyone else know what you've found?"

"Who would I tell? I don't know who I can trust."

"Good. Keep this to yourself. If news got out, it would make us vulnerable, and we can't afford that right now. The attack on you has garnered some public sympathy and our stock is climbing. One word from you could undo all of that."

"So glad my near death has been of benefit to the company." She regretted the words the second they left her mouth. She knew better. Emotional responses were never appreciated, but sarcasm was even worse.

Her father uttered a disappointed sigh. "And here, I thought you were finally showing some potential."

She didn't respond. Anything she said now would be twisted and used against her.

"Do you have anything else to tell me?"

"No, father." She paused before asking. "I do have a question, though."

"Yes?"

She needed to word her next question carefully. "I

noticed that you've removed everything from my long-term schedule. Training sessions. Tours. Factfinding missions. Does this mean you intend for me to stay at Astek for the foreseeable future?" *Is my training finally over?*

"The length of your current assignment depends on your performance."

That wasn't a yes, but it wasn't a no, either. She nodded. "I will do my best."

"Of course you will. I will contact you tomorrow for another update."

She should let him go, but there was something else she wanted to know. "One more thing. I know the investigation into what happened to the *Alacrity* will take some time to complete, but I was wondering if, when it was done, I would be able to reclaim my personal items."

Her father stared at her. "No."

"Not even my jewelry?"

"The ship and all its contents were examined and sent to the scrap yard days ago. There's nothing left. I was not aware you were careless enough to leave things behind or I would have made arrangements to retrieve them."

"Already? But the investigation?" She didn't bother pointing out that it wasn't carelessness that made her leave her items behind. He knew why she'd left so quickly. Blaming her for his decision was a test to see how she reacted. Everything with him was always a test.

"The ship was examined. It would appear from the location of the explosives that there were multiple detonations across the ship, but most of the damage was in the crew's mess, the galley, and the flight deck. The theory is that the micro-explosives must have been hidden inside some of the food served to the crew. Given the fact you survived, it's assumed that not all the explosives made it on board, since there was no trace of them in the wreckage." It was what she already suspected and he knew it. She'd told him as much, and it was in the report she'd sent him.

"Cherry pie," she murmured.

"What? What does pie have to do with anything?"

"A shipment of cherry pies never made it aboard because we changed departure time. I have a standing order for that dessert to accompany my afternoon meal."

"Perhaps." He didn't look convinced.

"I assume your investigators have looked into the suppliers and any items weren't delivered to the ship."

"Of course. It's being handled, Tianna. You need to stay focused on the job I sent you there to do."

"I am. And I must be hitting some pressure points. It would explain why you have so many complaints about me already. I'm taking that as a sign I'm closing in."

"It's too soon to know for sure, but for now, you have my permission to continue."

"Thank you. I intend to."

"I expect nothing less."

"I know. You've increased your security. Safeguarded yourself as much as possible?"

He frowned again. "Of course. Nothing is going to happen to me, Tianna. I can't afford it, and neither can Astek."

He signed off with a curt nod. She waited until the screen went completely black before sagging back into her chair. "Always lovely to chat with you, father."

"Not exactly your biggest supporter, is he?" Royan asked, appearing in the doorway.

In an instant, her mood brightened. She should be concerned about how easily the two men had slipped past her guard and into her life, but for the moment, she was just glad to see a friendly face. "You heard?"

"The door was open. I was going to let you know that Owen's on his way back, but then I realized you were busy dealing with… that." He waved a hand at the empty screen.

"Our relationship is complicated."

Royan snorted. "Astronavigation is complicated. Jeskyran sex is extremely complicated. Your relationship with your father is something else entirely."

She couldn't help but laugh, which she suspected was his goal. "Do I want to know how you got your information on the sexual habits of a species covered in body thorns?"

"You really don't." Owen joined them, and the last of her stress faded away. "All okay in here?"

"Yeah. Apart from the fact I think we need to toss your mother and her old man into the Nova's cage and sell tickets to the fight. We could retire on one night's take."

Owen grimaced. "What did I miss?"

"Nothing I want to talk about." She rose from her chair, started to pace, then stopped as she caught Royan grinning at her.

"I think our queen needs to escape her palace for a while."

Owen nodded. "I think so, too. You haven't left this building since we arrived. You're either here, or in your suite. As nice as your quarters are, you need a change of scenery. Let us show you the real Astek station."

"That sounds great, but I have too much work to do. I've found a lot of questionable entries and—"

"Blah blah blah work blah. Nope. Not going to happen. You need a break from all this." Royan walked over and offered her his arm. "Your kingdom awaits."

"My *kingdom* needs me to do my job."

"Bzzz. Wrong answer. Care to try again?"

Frustration flared, but one look at Royan's laughing eyes banished her anger. They were right, she'd buried herself in her work. If she wanted to improve the station for everyone, she really needed to see it for herself. She took his arm. "Okay, okay. I'll come with you, but this can't become a habit."

"No habitual playing hooky. Got it."

"You're a brat."

Royan chuckled, his brown eyes gleaming with desire. "I can be. You going to punish me for it?"

"Behave," she said, trying to ignore the flush of heat his words triggered.

"Where's the fun in that?"

"We can continue this debate once we're upstairs." Owen shooed them both toward the door.

"Upstairs? I thought we were going out?" she asked.

"We are, but you're going to want to change first." Owen's voice lowered to a sexy rumble. "As much as I like the dress you're wearing, you might want to opt for something a little more casual for where we're going."

"And where exactly are we going?"

"It's time you met the rest of our merry band. We're taking you to the Nova Club."

Tianna's world was like nothing Royan had ever experienced. He'd teased her about being royalty, but it turned out to be closer to the truth than he'd imagined. That first day a security guard had met them at the door, his harsh demeanor melting away the second he learned who Tianna was. After that, everyone they met had fallen into two camps: flustered underlings eager to please, or predatory executives with slick smiles and assessing eyes. There wasn't a warm smile or a friendly face to be seen.

After staying with her for the last three days, and seeing how her father spoke to her, Royan was starting to understand why trust didn't come easy for her. She wasn't used to having anyone she could rely on. Everyone she knew was an adversary, not an ally.

He changed into one of his favorite shirts and re-styled his hair. Tianna had insisted on buying them both new clothes to help them fit in around Astek. Collared shirts, tailored slacks. Each item cost more than a month's wages, and all of it was *fraxxing* uncomfortable to wear. He grabbed a pair of his old, broken in pants and tugged them on while replaying the conversation he'd overheard between father and daughter. It bothered him to hear her spoken to so disparagingly. He'd been tempted to interrupt, or interfere somehow, but he knew she wouldn't have thanked him for it. Her father was one demon he couldn't fight for her.

Demons seemed to be everywhere these days. Owen was battling his own right now. He felt guilty that his family was part of the attempt on Tianna's life, which made him almost obsessive about her security. He'd drawn up a round-the-clock schedule that ensured one of them was near her at all times. He even had it set up so that one of them stood watch inside her suite every night, which meant that while they both saw plenty of Tianna, they weren't getting much time alone with each other.

Royan was frustrated, not just with the situation, but their lack of progress finding any kind of resolution. The investigation into the explosion on the *Alacrity* didn't seem to be going anywhere, the Valentine clan had pulled a disappearing act, and all they knew for certain was that someone inside Astek had to be involved in the attack.

Both Tianna and Owen were unhappy, and the only thing he could do about it was to try and make them laugh. It didn't feel like nearly enough.

Tianna had given them a bedroom of their own, though neither of them had actually slept there. They came here to clean up and change, and that was it. One of them slept with Tianna, the other guarded the door, and halfway through the night, they switched places. Their stuff was scattered around the room, with most of their clothes strewn across the bed, safe from the overly-helpful bots that appeared every time anything bigger than a dust mote landed on the floor.

Owen changed too, pulling on a pair of black pants that cupped his ass perfectly, tempting Royan to walk over and peel him right back out of them again.

"I don't suppose we've got time for a little fun before we go?" he asked, knowing exactly what Owen would say.

"You know we don't. I need to get changed and let the Corp-Sec guards know there's been a change in plans. We'll have to take one of their transports, too. Astek's vehicles might be compromised."

Royan walked over to Owen, stepping in behind him and wrapping his arms around the other man's waist. "Or we could walk. It's not far. The point is to show Tianna the station. How much of that is she going to see locked inside a transport?"

"I can't take that kind of risk."

He rested his head against the hard planes of his lover's back. "You're not the only one around here making sure our girl stays safe. Those gorgeous shoulders of yours don't need to carry the whole load."

For a moment, Owen stayed tense, but then he let out a long breath and leaned back into Royan. "You're right."

"Of course I'm right. I'm not just a pretty face, I'm the whole damned package. Looks, smarts, charm, you name it, I got it."

Just like Royan hoped, Owen laughed. "And yet somehow, I managed to resist you and your charms for months."

"You tried, but eventually you fell for me." He held on a little tighter. "I know now is probably the wrong time to say it, but I'm really glad you did."

Owen stilled. "Yeah?"

"Yeah."

"Even with Tianna in the picture? I know we've both been focused on her, lately."

He released Owen, stepping around to face him. He didn't know what he was going to say, but he needed to be looking at Owen when he said it.

"Just because we care about her doesn't mean I forgot about you. Love's not a zero-sum game, baby."

Owen grabbed his shirt in both fists and hauled him in close. "Say that again."

"I didn't forget about you." He was still trying to absorb the words that had come out of his mouth. Love? He didn't do love. Did he?

"Not that bit, the other one. The part where you said you loved me."

Feeling lost and off balance, Royan fell back on his default setting – smart ass. "That's not exactly what I—"

Owen pressed two fingers to Royan's lips, shushing him mid-sentence. "Don't play games. Not now. If you meant it, then say it again."

Do I love him? He asked himself, and the answer came back loud and clear. He did. Holy *fraxx*, he really did. "I'm only just figuring all this out, but yeah, I love you."

Owen's mouth crashed down on his, kissing him with a hunger that made Royan's heart pound and his balls ache. He'd missed these moments between them, but maybe it took being apart for him to finally admit the truth – he didn't just want Owen, he loved him. And the fact that didn't send his lover running proved that he wasn't the real lunatic in this relationship, it was Owen.

"You're laughing now? Really?" Owen lifted his head to stare down at him with bemusement tinged with annoyance.

"I'm happy. Plus, I always figured the universe might explode if I ever uttered those three little words, so I'm also thrilled not to be dead."

Owen threaded his fingers into his hair, tugging his head back. "What the *fraxx* am I going to do with you?"

"Baby, if you're out of ideas, I've got a whole list for us to try. Do you want to proceed alphabetically or by degree of difficulty?"

"An entire universe of males to chose from, and I had to fall for a sex-crazed fly boy."

Royan heart raced and his world lit up like he'd downed a dose of the purest pharma on the market. He tried to play it cool, but there was no hiding the shit-eating grin on his face. "Nice to know I'm not the only one falling right now."

"You're definitely not alone."

Tianna cleared her throat, and Royan glanced over to see her standing in the doorway, lingering there as if she were unsure of her welcome. "If you'd rather stay in tonight, I'll understand. You two have a lot to celebrate."

"*We* do," Royan said, then looked to Owen for… something. Agreement? Approval? He wasn't sure. He just knew this was a decision they needed to make together.

Owen gave a small nod, then held out his hand to Tianna. "We're going out tonight, Tia. All three of us."

She gifted them both with a smile that spoke straight to his heart. No matter how many times she said otherwise, she wanted this. It was obvious. Now he just had to figure out how to get her to see it for herself. He'd managed to do it once, with Owen. He'd find a way to do it again.

CHAPTER FOURTEEN

The guys had said to wear something casual, but she didn't have anything that fit that description in her new wardrobe. Tink had ordered her an array of clothes once they'd arrived on the station, but as far as Tianna knew, they were all either office attire or workout wear. Not that she'd had a chance to work out lately, but Tink was programmed with her preferences.

She was tempted to wear the dress they'd bought her at the market but they'd seen her in it recently, and she wanted something new. She tried on a few outfits before discovering a simple black sheath dress hanging near the back of her closet.

"Tink, when did you order this? It's not my usual thing."

"Your companions mentioned taking you to the Nova Club several times while we were on the *Sun Sprite*. I interfaced with Sprite and was able to determine what sort of attire would be acceptable and added it to your order."

"If I didn't know better, I'd say you were matchmaking, Tink."

"I am not programmed for that. Though I will note that all physical indicators show you to be in an optimal emotional state more often when you are in the company of Owen and Royan."

For something that wasn't programmed for matchmaking, her AI was doing a remarkable impression of it.

She changed into the new dress and eyed herself in the mirror. It really did look good. "Instead of musing on my physical indicators, how about telling me if you bought any shoes to match this dress."

Tink managed to sound almost indignant. "I am programmed to coordinate and accessorize your wardrobe. There are two options for that dress. The shoes are on the left, the boot option is on your right."

"Oh, boots!" They were thigh-highs, jet-black and made of a thick, buttery soft material that molded to her legs as she pulled them on. After that, all that was left was her hair. She was going to re-braid it, but her scalp itched from having it bound back all day, so she brushed it out and left it loose instead.

She finished getting ready and took a deep breath, surprised to discover she was nervous about tonight. "It's not a date, and it's not like you're meeting your boyfriends' family. This is just a friendly thing," she reminded herself, but the feeling persisted.

While they had continued to sleep together since leaving the *Sun Sprite*, they'd all maintained a professional distance outside her quarters. No flirting, no touching. Nothing that could be reported back to her father. She missed it. Missed the energy and laughter they brought into her life. If only there was a way… She shook her head. *No.* She knew better than to play the what-if game. There was no version of their story where they all lived happily ever after. Not together. She had her duty, and they had each other.

She headed to the guys' room to let them know she was ready.

This is what love looks like. A bittersweet tangle of emotions washed over her. Happiness and jealousy, joy and regret. She stayed quiet longer than she should have, bearing witness to the beginning of what she hoped was a lifetime of love for them both.

Torn between saying something or slipping away before they noticed her, she chose to acknowledge their moment, even if it meant the end of their trio. At least, that's what she thought it meant, but Owen and Royan surprised her yet again.

"We're going out tonight, Tia. All three of us." Owen held out a hand to her, and she accepted their invitation before she could talk herself out of it. She knew every argument. Every logical reason this was a bad idea, but she wasn't ready for this to be over. Not yet.

They finished getting dressed with her in the room, and for a moment it was like they were back on the ship again. The flirting and fun returned, and every few seconds one of them was touching her, or each other. She drank in every compliment and caress, savoring their closeness. Their playfulness lasted until they left her quarters, and then they were professional again, though once they were away from the office area they started to joke and banter a little, giving her a colorful and descriptive tour as they walked through the heart of Astek Station.

"Crowded tonight." Royan moved in closer, protecting her from the jostling throng.

"I haven't seen this many beings in one place in years. Wait, is that a Vardarian?" She raised her hand to point, then realized how impolite that would be and tipped her head in the direction of a large male with long, dark hair and silver skin.

"It is. Not too many of them around yet," Owen said.

"I thought they had wings."

"They do. They fold up against their backs." Royan pressed both arms to his chest. "See the slits in the back of his vest? Those are for his wings."

No one had informed her there were Vardarians on the station. She needed to have a word with her people and remind them that it wasn't just the flow of goods that kept the company running, it was the flow of information. How many of the new species were on the station? What ship brought them here? Were they traders? Diplomats? Tourists?

"I think we lost her." Royan reached over and tapped her wrist. "Tia, whatever you're thinking about, stop it. This is a workfree evening."

"There's no such thing. My hiatus stopped the second we docked, remember?"

Owen frowned "You can't work all the time. You already get less sleep than anyone I know."

"If it helps, think of tonight as research. You're here to get a feel for the way things work on this station, check out some of the goods and services that are available, and do an inspection of one of the larger entertainment venues."

Royan winked. "Maybe even sample some of those goods for yourself."

"No maybe about it. The first round is on me. This place is the home of the Sun Sprite's Delight, remember?" Owen said.

She remembered. She'd already programmed Tink with the recipe, though finding the color-shifting alcohol it was made from had proven impossible. Apparently, the Nova Club was the only place on the station that had it. "One drink."

"Second round is on me, so you better make it two." Royan guided them through the crowd. They were headed to a set of open double doors with a lineup of people waiting to get inside. The doors were guarded by two massive men wearing matching blue shirts that clung to their well-muscled arms. Music poured out of the doors, loud enough to attract attention but still within tolerable levels.

Owen walked over to one of the uniformed men, clapping him on the shoulder. "You losing in the ring so much you have to pick up shifts as a bouncer now?"

The big blond grinned. "I don't lose, Connors. You know that. Well, not to anyone but Cyn and her husband, and no one wins against the boss lady. Kit and Luke both want to stick close to Zura these days, so a couple of us stepped up to help."

"I'm sure they appreciate it. How are they coping with pending fatherhood?"

Erik laughed. "About as well as you'd expect. Zura's about ready to toss them both out the nearest airlock." He looked at Royan. "Your sister is tiny but terrifying."

"You think I don't know that? You should have seen

her as a teenager. She was a menace." Royan nodded to her. "Eric, this is Tianna Astor. She's going to be our guest for tonight. Can you spread the word, and maybe keep an extra eye out for trouble?"

Erik's eyes widened. "Astor? As in…"

"Afraid so." She held out her hand to him and gave him a disarming smile. "It's nice to meet you, Erik."

"It's a pleasure to meet you, too." Erik took her hand and instead of shaking it, raised it to his lips and brushed a kiss across her knuckles.

Behind her, both men grumbled and Eric released her hand. "So, it's like that?"

Both men hesitated. Officially they weren't together. That was the story she'd insisted on.

"It's complicated," she spoke before either of them could.

"Uh huh." Erik smirked a little. "With these two, it always is." He ushered them through the doors and into the club. It was larger than she'd expected, even after seeing the blueprints for this part of the station. There was a dance floor filled with gyrating bodies and flashing lights, booths and tables, a roped off area full of gaming tables. The bar took up an entire wall of the club, and the entire space was done in shades of blue and silver.

They passed into another roped off section and claimed a booth by one of the windows. The music was softer here, and the noise of the crowd was barely more than a distant buzz.

A server came by, greeted Owen and Royan by name and took their orders, returning only a few minutes later with a tray laden with cocktails and snacks. Six drinks were on the tray, but before she could ask why, the answer appeared. Two identical men walked toward them, flanking a woman with striking blue hair and the variegated coloring of a Pheran. If that wasn't a clear hint to her identity, the fact she was heavily pregnant made it obvious – this had to be Royan's sister, which meant the men with her were her cyborg husbands.

She rose, not sure what to expect, but Zura walked up and shook her hand without any hesitation. "Hi. I'm Zura, Royan's sensible and much saner older sister. Welcome to the Nova Club."

"Hello. Thanks for letting me borrow Royan and Owen as private security. I appreciate it."

Zura nodded. "Of course. I know what it's like to be a target. We're happy to help. Besides, this keeps my brother close by until these babies are born." She set a hand on her distended stomach. "Which I hope will be very *fraxxing* soon."

"Speaking of which, you should be sitting down. Doctor's orders, remember?" One of her husbands reminded her.

"I'll sit in a second, Kit. Introductions first. Tianna, these are my husbands, Kit and Luke Armas. My brothers-in-law Jaeger and Toro are around here somewhere, and Cynder is..." she looked around. "Aha, she's at the bar and will probably join us shortly."

"Nice to meet you all."

They took their seats, arranging themselves so that the two women were on the inside, nearest the window.

"I'm sorry about what happened to you. The loss of your ship and crew, that can't be easy to get past," Zura said.

It was the first time anyone beside Royan and Owen

had acknowledged her loss. No one at Astek had even mentioned it. "Thank you. If it weren't for your brother and Owen, I wouldn't have survived, either. They saved me."

"That was all Royan. I didn't want to divert course. I thought it was a trap," Owen said.

Zura gave her brother a knowing look. "Dad's rule?"

"Yep."

"Another of your dad's rules for living?" Luke asked.

"Always answer a distress call if you can." Zura started, and Royan joined in to complete the phrase together. "Because the next time, you might be the one in trouble."

Owen and the cyborgs exchanged a look, then all three of them laughed.

"What?" Zura demanded.

"There's no might about it. You Watsons attract trouble like a black hole sucks in light," Kit said.

Zura pursed her lips, then sighed. "I want to be mad, but you have a point."

"Nothing wrong with a little trouble. It keeps life interesting," Royan said.

"You would think that way, you lunatic," Owen grumbled.

They talked over cocktails, the small talk slowly changing, becoming warmer and more open. The topic shifted to business, and soon she was involved in a fascinating discussion about the business of running both the club and the freight company Zura operated. She discovered that Cynder handled the financials for both companies, and learned more in one conversation then she had in the hours she'd spent speaking to Astek's executives.

"One more word about profit margins or managing overhead and *my* head is going to explode," Royan declared and rose from his seat. "Come on, baby, we're hitting the dance floor before I forget how to have fun."

"We won't be far, and these folks are the best protection you could possibly have. You good with us stepping off for a bit?" Owen asked.

"I'm good. I can't believe you're going to actually dance, though."

Owen chuckled. "Me either. He'll probably come back with bruised toes and regrets."

"I doubt that. Go on, I'll be fine."

"She'll be more than fine. Anyone comes near her or Little Blue they won't live long enough to regret it," Cynder said.

Tianna had to agree. She was currently surrounded by cyborgs. She might be like them in some ways, but ultimately, she was a human with aftermarket modifications, while they were created and programmed to be the ultimate soldiers.

Royan took hold of Owen's hand and led him onto the dance floor, and everyone at the table saw the gesture and smiled.

"Were they together when you came on board?" Cyn asked her.

"They were in the middle of figuring it out, yeah. They're good together."

"Yes, they are," Luke agreed. "Royan needs someone to level him out."

The conversation came to a natural lull while drinks

were refilled and more food was ordered. While that happened, Tianna watched Owen and Royan together. Even if she hadn't witnessed their declarations earlier, it was plain to anyone with eyes that they were in love.

"So, how serious are things with them?" Zura asked softly.

"Pretty serious. I think they're destined for each other."

"I think so, too, but that's not what I meant." Zura leaned forward as much as her pregnant formed allowed. "You're involved with them, aren't you?"

"It's complicated." It was becoming her default answer.

"I'm sure it is. But I saw the way you looked at them a second ago, and what I saw wasn't complicated at all. You want them."

"We don't always get what we want in life."

"Not always." Zura looked over at her husbands, who had risen from the table and were talking to two of their staff about something. "But some things are worth fighting for. If those two have made a place in their lives for you, it's because they want you with them, complicated or not." She took a sip of her drink and smiled. "And so ends the speech by the meddling sister."

Tianna raised her glass in salute. "I can't promise I'll take your advice, but I appreciate the spirit in which it was given. Royan's lucky to have people in his life that love him as much as you do."

"We're family."

"And family is everything. Royan said the same thing."

Kit rejoined them. "He did? Looks like your baby brother is finally growing up, little one."

"It looks that way," Zura agreed, then winked at Tianna. "Maybe he just needed a good reason."

Owen was having the best day of his life. Royan loved him, their friends and family were happy for them, and Tianna… well, Tianna was still a work in progress, but they *were* making progress. Wanting more than he already had might be stupidly greedy, but damned if that wasn't exactly what he was hoping for. Soon, he and Royan needed to talk and make sure this was what they both wanted. It seemed like it, and it felt right, but if they were going to do this, they needed to be sure.

Everything was going so well, he could almost forget that his family were somewhere out there, likely making plans to hurt someone he cared about, again. It would be different this time, though. They weren't going to take anyone else away from him, or tear down the life he'd made for himself.

Toro, Jaeger, and Cynder offered to walk them back to Tianna's place. Tianna and Cyn talked shop the whole way, their conversation filled with unfamiliar terms and business shorthand that made his head spin. Still, Tianna was clearly enthused about whatever they'd discussed, and Cyn must have felt the same way because she invited Tianna to call or drop by her office any time.

"So, what did you think of your first foray onto the station?" Royan asked as they identified themselves to the on-duty security guards and headed inside.

"I think that this station has the potential to be something amazing, and I don't understand why it isn't making triple its current income. If things were done differently, the cost of air and living space could actually be lowered, and we'd still make a profit."

She wanted to lower the cost of living? Owen had to fight the urge to pick her up and hug her right there in the hallway. "When could you get started? What would you need?"

"Time, mostly. I need to figure out where all the money is going, first." She lowered her voice to a whisper. "I knew things weren't right, but talking to your friends tonight confirmed some things for me. The station should be making a profit, but it's not. At least, not according to the reports I've read."

"You should have told us." They were going to have to increase security again. If the ones doing this realized Tianna was investigating, they'd retaliate.

"I didn't have all the pieces I needed until tonight. If you hadn't brought me to the club, it might have taken me weeks to see the pattern." They stepped into her private mag-lift and she set her hand on the biometric scanner, unlocking access to her floor.

"You don't give yourself nearly enough credit. You've only been here a few days, and you've already found things no one else even noticed. You've been outside of these walls twice, and you can see the potential everyone else missed." Owen knew what it was like to grow up with a parent who was never satisfied. He'd lost faith in himself and his abilities, and Tianna had, too.

She didn't say anything until they were inside her suite. "I need to make some notes about what I learned tonight. Get it all down while it's still fresh in my mind."

Royan shook his head. "You need to get some rest, sweetheart. You're not going to forget a damned thing, and we all know it. And even if you did, you're going to be chatting with Cyn again soon."

"There's so much to do, and it's not that late. I can work for a bit and still get a few hours of sleep."

Royan looked at Owen and tipped his head toward her bedroom. "You got this?"

"Yeah." He walked over and kissed Royan goodnight, part of him still amazed that this man was part of his life, now. "Stay alert, and wake me up when it's my watch."

"Night, baby." Royan turned to Tianna. "Your sexy little ass is going to bed now. You might look like a goddess and act like a queen, but you're still mortal, and mortals need sleep. Night-night." He blew her a kiss off the tip of his fingers.

Her expression turned stormy and Royan grinned. "It's cute how she thinks she's got a choice, here."

"Adorable."

Owen was already moving as he spoke, sweeping Tianna into his arms before she knew what was happening.

"I can walk to my room all by myself."

"But we both know you're not planning on going to your room."

"Because I have work to do. But since my choices are to let you carry me to bed, or kick your ass here in the hallway, this time, I'm choosing to let you be in charge."

"You think you can take me?" She was fit and feisty, sure, but there was no way in hell a handful of self-defence classes made her a threat. He added that to the list of things he needed to discuss with Royan. They could set aside some time to teach her a few moves, just in case.

"You might be surprised. I'm tougher than I look."

"I have no doubts about that. You've taken everything the universe has thrown at you and haven't missed a step.

You're *fraxxing* amazing, but I still don't think you could take me in a fight."

"You're probably right."

"I'll prove it to you some other time. Right now, I have other plans for you." He walked into her bedroom and lowered her gently to the floor.

"Bed. Sleep. I heard you."

"Nice to know you were listening, but no, not yet. You're too wound up to sleep, so why don't we start with a hot shower in that decadent monstrosity you call a bathroom."

"Now that sounds like a great idea. I do some of my best thinking in the shower."

Thinking wasn't part of his plan. "Then get undressed and get in there. I'll join you in a moment." He gave her ass a light swat as he passed her, already stripping out of his clothes as he made his way over to the bed. It was as spacious and luxurious as everything else in her quarters, though there wasn't a single thing here that was hers. It felt more to him like they were all staying in a five-star hotel, elegant but impersonal.

He sat on the edge of the bed and watched as she undressed, enjoying the slow, teasing way she peeled off the dress and then her boots, making eye contact with him the entire time. When he didn't make a move on her, she gave him a saucy grin and sauntered away, heading for the shower.

The moment the door closed behind her he rose, shed the rest of his clothing, and snagged what he needed from the nightstand drawer. He and Royan had made some purchases of their own the last few days, and tonight seemed like the perfect time to try out one of his selections. He palmed the sex toy in one hand, taking a moment to familiarize himself with its operation. It activated with a barely audible hum, and once he'd put it through its paces, he double checked the packaging – just as he thought, it was waterproof. Perfect.

Fragrant steam enveloped him as he opened the door and he breathed it in, letting the soothing scent fill his senses. He didn't recognize the aroma, but Tianna had told him that her AI blended various mood enhancing fragrances using something called aromatherapy. *Rich people have strange hobbies.* They could also afford the luxury of an unrestricted water supply, every drop of it filtered far past what was deemed acceptable for the rest of the station.

The shower was built into the far wall of the room, a raised platform with a low-level force-field that kept most of the water contained. Tianna was already inside, her lithe form partially obscured by the steam and the subtle shimmer of the force-field. He was hard in a heartbeat, every part of him aching with desire as she turned and smiled at him, then beckoned him closer.

"You were right. This was a good idea."

"I've got another idea I think you're going to like. Something to help you relax." He joined her on the platform, barely noticing the tingle the field caused as he passed through it. Inside, the water fell like warm rain, soaking him in seconds as he took her hand and drew her in for a long, slow kiss.

She melted into his arms, her hands on his chest and her water-slick skin like silk under his hands. *Veth,* she was beautiful, but beneath the beauty was a core of steel.

That strength was what attracted him to her, along with the wild streak she kept hidden from the universe.

He set the vibrator down on one of the shelves attached to the back wall, then reached for the cleanser that sat on the same shelf. Without breaking their kiss, he filled his palm with the cool fluid, then started gently massaging it into her hair. She moaned and rose onto her toes, letting her head fall back against his touch.

He lathered and massaged her scalp, listening with pleasure at her soft moans. He'd never played with a woman's hair before, not the way he did with Tianna's. He loved the way it flowed over his hands and the weight of it when he wrapped it around his fingers. He'd even volunteered to help her braid it in the mornings, a task that took far more time and patience than he could have imagined. It was one of the few times she would let anyone help her, and he'd enjoyed both the momentary closeness and the chance to be there for her, even for such a minor task.

He worked his way down her neck to her shoulders, massaging away the knots of tension he found along the way. The moans continued, soft vibrations that buzzed against his skin as she sank deeper into his arms. He didn't stop until she was soft and pliant under his hands and her moans had turned to contented sighs.

"Better?"

"So much." She looked up at him. "When you said you planned on relaxing me, that wasn't what I expected."

He cupped her cheek and leaned down to kiss the tip of her nose. "You needed some TLC."

"TLC?" She frowned.

"Tender loving care."

Her expression softened and for a moment she looked up at him with such vulnerability and need his breath locked in his lungs. "Thank you."

"Anything you need. Always."

She gave an almost imperceptible nod of her head, and then the moment was gone. "So, no orgasms, then?"

"I never said that. Orgasms are still on the agenda, but I wanted to make sure you were nice and relaxed, first." He stepped over to the back wall and leaned against it, then drew her in so her back was to his chest. He moved one leg out in front, bracing himself. "Lean on me and spread your legs."

She followed his instructions, but he could feel her tensing. "This feels a little precarious."

"I've got you. All you need to do is relax and trust me." He picked up the toy with one hand and crossed his free arm over her body, giving her more support and something to hang on to.

"I can do that." She tipped her head back, smiled, closed her eyes, and let herself relax.

His cock was trapped between them, and every move either of them made created a tantalizing amount of friction and pressure. He palmed the toy and moved his hand between her legs, using his fingers to part her labia, exposing her clit. He toyed with it for a few seconds, feeling it swell as he worked it between his thumb and forefinger.

Her hands gripped his forearm as she parted her legs wider, giving him full access to her body.

"Good girl." The words slipped out before he could stop them.

"Do I get a lollipop?" She arched her back, opening

enough space between them to slip her hand in and wrap it around his cock.

"You can suck my lollipop later. Right now, I believe I promised you an orgasm."

Before she could say anything else, he thumbed the switch on the vibrator and slid it into place so the small opening at the top was directly over her clit. Her response was instantaneous—eyes wide, mouth open—and with every gasp and moan he made tiny adjustments until it was perfectly situated. She bucked her hips and gripped his forearm so tight her nails dug into his skin.

"Holy *fraxx*."

"And that's only level one." He dialed it up to the next setting and watched her control start to shatter. It was intoxicating, seeing her like this. Her skin was flushed with more than the heat of the shower, and the more she moved the more she rubbed against him. At this rate, they were both going to come before long.

"Higher. Harder. I need more."

"You sure?"

She nodded, her lips parting as she twisted her head around to look up at him. "More."

"As my queen wishes." He turned it up two levels higher and the toy's soft hum grew louder. Her eyes closed, and she covered her breast with her newly freed hand, playing with her nipple, rolling it between her fingers. He started moving the toy in slow, concentric circles, keeping it in contact with her clit but altering the angle and pressure.

She made a soft keening noise at the back of her throat and he knew she was close to release. He kept up the steady movements, taking his cues from her as the tension built until she was shaking with need.

"Ready?"

She nodded, but he wanted to hear her say it.

"Tell me what you want."

"I want to come. Please?"

The breathless way she said the last word nearly broke him. He groaned and ground his dick against her slick skin. He needed to be inside her, soon, but this time was all for her. "Make sure Royan hears you."

She laughed and flashed him a wicked grin. "You got it."

He braced himself against the wall and thumbed the switch to its highest setting. She came hard, her cries echoing off the walls as she bucked and writhed against his body. It took all his strength to hold her up, and when it was done and she let go of his forearm, she'd left bruises, along with traces of blood where her nails had broken the skin.

She stood on unsteady legs and eyed his arm with dismay. "I'm sorry."

"Don't be. Medi-bots, remember? Besides, I'm going to wear any mark you leave on me like a badge of honor."

"In that case, let's go to bed and I'll give you a few more marks to admire."

He swept her into his arms and carried her off to bed, more than happy to let her leave as many marks on him as she wanted. They'd all be gone by morning, anyway, unlike the marks she'd left on his heart. He'd carry those for the rest of his life.

CHAPTER FIFTEEN

It was the middle of what passed for night on the station when Tianna slipped out of bed, leaving Owen sleeping. He'd fulfilled his promise, pampering her with massages and orgasms until they had both fallen into a blissful sleep. She felt well-rested and ready to work again, though there wasn't much chance of Royan letting her stay out of bed for long. If only she could tell them the truth, but no matter how often she made that wish, there was no chance of it ever happening. The consequences were just too great – she had to protect Astek and her father. Her time with them had to end eventually, another dream sacrificed on the altar of her father's will.

She found her robe, wrapping it around her as she left her room and stepped into the dimly light corridor. Once she was far enough away from the door to be sure Owen wouldn't hear her, she let Royan know she was up. "Royan? Where are you?"

"Kitchen."

She might have guessed. Royan was having a love

affair with her food dispenser. He'd spent hours researching new recipes and ordering the ingredients for dishes she'd never heard of before. He might not be able to cook well, yet, but he'd learned enough on their trip back to the Drift to discover a passion for food.

"What's on the menu?" she asked as she headed straight for the food dispenser. Her late-night ritual always included a mug of hot chocolate and a snack.

"Something called a frittata. I have no idea if it's any good, but with a name like that I couldn't resist trying it."

"It's basically an omelet. I like them."

"Then that's breakfast planned." He finished tapping instructions into the dispenser and stepped aside so she could use it. "What are you doing up? If Owen knew you were awake already he'd take it as a personal challenge. I thought the plan was to wear you out?"

"He did. I slept for hours." She punched in her order, along with a request for some pain blockers to quiet yet another headache. Once she was done, she walked over and wrapped her arms around him. "But I'm awake now. I don't really need much sleep."

"So I've noticed." He wrapped her in his arms and bent his head to kiss her. "I should send you back to bed, but I don't want to."

"Bored?"

He kissed her again. "Lonely."

His honest answer made her want to comfort him, and she burrowed deeper into his arms. "I'm here, now."

"And a few days ago, that would have been enough." The dispenser chimed, announcing her drink was ready, but Royan didn't let her go.

"Right now is all I can give you, Royan. You know that. I'm a temporary addition to you lives."

"What if we wanted more than that?"

Her next words came out edged in ice. "Then you're destined for disappointment."

"Why?" he demanded.

"Because we don't always get what we want, Royan. Life doesn't work that way."

He stared into her eyes and it felt like he was looking straight into her soul. "You want this as much as we do. Don't you dare deny it."

"What I want is irrelevant. *Veth*, do you and your sister have some kind of telepathic link? I had the same damned conversation with her just a few hours ago."

"Did she call you on that bullshit line about life not working that way, too? Because she fought like hell for everything she wanted, and you know what? She got it."

Tianna bristled. She wasn't used to being challenged. "You're right, she fought like hell for what she has, and I'm happy for her. I'm happy for you, too, you idiot. You have something amazing with Owen, and I hope it lasts the rest of your lives. But that's not in the cards for me." She pulled away, angry enough that her control slipped and she used more strength than she should have. She hadn't screwed up like that since rehab.

Royan didn't seem to notice. He let her go, but instead of stepping back he moved in close. "I'm still not hearing a reason why."

She fisted her hands at her sides and tried to curb her frustration. How could she make him understand? "You're not hearing a reason you like. That's not the same thing. Try listening to me! I've been telling you all the reasons since the day we met. I'm an Astor, and that name comes with responsibilities and expectations. The company comes first, Royan. Always."

He swept his hair back with a frustrated swipe of his hand and locked eyes with her. "So that's it? You never get to do anything for yourself ever again? That's insane."

"The company comes first."

"You said that already, and it's still bullshit."

"It's not bullshit, it's the truth. My truth. Making sacrifices is part of what it means to be an Astor." Even as she said it, part of her wanted to scream in denial. She sounded just like her father. In fact, this entire fight was familiar ground for her, but somehow, she was on the other side of it. It all felt so wrong.

"If that's the Astor way, then why isn't your old man making sacrifices? Why is it always you? Hell, the only risk he's taken lately is to send his daughter into danger. He risked *your* life, sweetheart. Not his, not some corporate lackey. Yours."

"He warned me this would be dangerous, but I was the only one he trusted to get this done. You and Owen want me to save this place? I can do that, but only if you stop trying to distract me from what I need to do. You can't have it all. No one can."

"All, no, but we're all entitled to a little happiness in our lives. Why can't you see that? Why won't you fight for it?"

"Maybe because you're yelling at her, asshole." Owen joined the fray, his voice tight with anger. He was barefoot and shirtless, but for once, his appearance didn't distract her. She was too angry.

"I'm not yelling."

"Really? Because your *not yelling* woke me up."

"Good, maybe now you can help me talk some sense into Tianna. You walked away from your crazy family, same as I did. Why can't she?"

"You want me to walk away? Really? And then what?" Her head hurt and her stomach was roiling. She didn't feel right, but she couldn't stop arguing.

"Then you start over. Here, with us." Royan said like it was the most obvious thing in the world.

The disconnect between her heart and her brain worsened, and so did the pain in her head. "This is why being with you was always a bad idea. *Fraxx*, I was so stupid. I should have never let myself get involved with you two."

"Don't say that." Owen was at her side in seconds, but when he reached for her hand she pulled away.

She knew what had to happen next, and if she touched either of them, it would be that much harder to do what she needed to. "It's true, though. Getting close to you was a mistake. This is a distraction I don't need right now, but fortunately, I can fix that." She pointed to the door. "It's time for you to go."

"What? No. You can't." Royan looked at her with a broken expression. "Don't do this."

"We always knew this had to end. I let it go on too long as it is." Every word hurt, but she knew how to deal with pain. She closed herself off, retreating behind the walls of ice she'd built around herself.

"Tia, it's not safe. You're still in danger. Let us stay and protect you," Owen said.

"I have Corp-Sec to see to my protection. Two of them are outside that door right now, and you know there's more downstairs. No one has seen any sign of Owen's family or their ship, which means they're not a threat. You did your jobs. I'm safe. Now it's time you got back to the *Sprite*.

Royan shook his head. "This was never a job for us, sweetheart. Why are you being so damned stubborn?" He held out a hand to her. "All you have to do is say yes."

She folded her arms across her chest. "If you don't leave on your own, I'll call the guards and have them escort you out."

"Let us stay until morning, Tia. I'll stay out here with Royan. We can talk about this tomorrow."

"There's nothing to talk about. Just go!"

"Our things," Royan said, clearly looking for any reason to stay.

"I'll have it all sent to the Sprite in the morning, along with payment for your services."

Owen flinched. "I don't want your money. That was never what this was about."

She weakened, just for a moment. "I know, but it's all I can give you. Go, now, or I'll have Tink call the guards."

"Tianna, sweetheart…" Royan looked utterly lost.

"She's made up her mind. Come on, Royan. We need to go." Owen grabbed Royan's wrist, towing him along as he made for the door.

Royan didn't take his eyes off her until they passed through the door. Owen only looked back once. Both their expressions were exactly the same, burned into her memory forever as the door sealed behind them, cutting her off from her only friends.

"*Fraxx. Fraxx. Fraxx!*" She stormed out of the kitchen, not sure where she was going or what she wanted to do.

She went to her office, sat, then stood back up again. Who was she kidding? She was in no state to focus on work.

She wandered from room to room, mind racing, fingers itching for something to do. There was no comfort to be found anywhere. This wasn't her home, and there was nothing of her own here except a handful of clothes she'd brought with her from the *Sprite*.

She entered the room the guys had used with some half-formed thought about organizing their things so they could go first thing in the morning. Bad idea. She picked up one of their shirts then stood there, holding it tight as regret crashed over her in a wave. *Fraxx* it. She threw the shirt back onto the bed and retreated.

Nothing made sense. Why was she so upset when this had been her choice? The company came first. It had to. That was how things were. How they'd always been. Only, it hadn't always been this way. Before the accident, things had been different. *And look how that ended.* She'd nearly died. Hell, technically she had died, more than once. To save her, her father had risked everything.

Royan wanted to know what sacrifice Cornelius Astor had made. What risks he'd taken. She couldn't tell him the answer, but she knew. She carried the weight of it every second of every day. And that's why she'd pushed them away. She owed her father everything, and she intended to repay him by being the woman he wanted her to be, no matter what the cost.

She stalked back to her bedroom, shedding her robe. "Tink, where'd you put the work out gear you ordered? I need to go blow off some steam."

The AI didn't answer, but a drawer slid open, revealing several outfits, all brand-new.

"Shoes?"

Another drawer opened.

"Tink, are you giving me the silent treatment?"

"Do you wish for me to speak to you right now? Usually, you prefer me to be quiet when you are in emotional distress."

She pulled out her shoes kicked the drawer shut. "I am not in emotional distress."

"Your behavior and bio signs indicate otherwise."

"My bio signs are none of your business," she snapped and finished dressing.

"Tink, find my workout playlist and pipe it through the speakers in my gym. And turn the gravity up in that area. I haven't been able to work out properly for weeks."

"Of course."

She headed down a short flight of stairs to the private gymnasium one floor below. She needed to let loose, and for the first time in weeks, she was completely alone. She could push herself without worrying about being seen.

The music came on as she entered the room, a pounding, driving rhythm that matched her mood perfectly. The equipment was all standard, but the altered gravity would make for a challenging workout .

She started to stretch, already bouncing in time to the beat. Exercise would burn away the fog that clouded her mind and let her think clearly again. This was exactly what she needed.

"WE SHOULD GO BACK," Royan said, pulling free of Owen's grip as the mag-lift doors opened.

"And what? Do you think she's going to let us back inside? Do you want to yell your apologies through the soundproofed door and hope she hears you?"

"She'll let us back in. She has to." Royan needed to believe there was something he could do to change things. It couldn't end like this.

Owen shot him a look of disbelief mixed with frustration. "She doesn't have to do anything. She's Tianna *fraxxing* Astor. There are only two people who can make her do something, and both of them have the same last name."

"But we're supposed to be together. You see it too, right?" He couldn't be the only one feeling this way. He'd felt the same way about Owen, and he'd been right. It had just taken Owen a while to come around. Tianna would be the same way.

"My feelings aren't the issue here. Tianna's are, and from what I saw back there you crushed them with all the finesse of a rogue comet smashing into a planet."

"It wasn't that bad."

Owen snorted then gestured to his bare chest and feet. "Really? She tossed us out on our asses in the middle of the night, half-dressed, because it *wasn't that bad*?" Sarcasm dripped from every word.

"I just want her to give this thing between us a chance. We're good together. We make her happy. She makes us happy. Why isn't that enough?"

"For someone who has spent most of his life getting by on his charm, you really don't have a clue how relationships work, do you?"

The doors opened and neither of them spoke again until they left the building. Royan spent the whole time trying to figure out what Owen meant. He had relationships. Plenty of them. Friends, family, hell, he and Owen were in a relationship and that was going pretty well.

Once they were outside, Royan said as much. "I know how relationships work. Tianna's the problem here, not me. She wants us, but she won't admit it."

"I know she does." Owen took his hand again, gentler this time. "Do you remember the day you decided to leave home?"

"What does that have to do with anything?" They walked as they talked, and it didn't take long for Royan to figure out they were headed toward the Nova Club. With the *Sun Sprite* at the shipyard, it was the only logical place for them to go.

"Just answer the question."

Royan thought back. It had been more than ten years ago, but the memory hadn't faded. He'd managed to complete his final year at school, and the next day his parents had called a family meeting. *Veth*, he'd hated those things. No one ever listened. They just told him how it was going to be. Things had been different though. He was done with school and ready for something new. He knew what he wanted to do with his life, but when he told them, they ignored him and laid out their plans for his future. It hadn't gone well. They'd fought, he'd gone to his room, packed a few things, and walked out.

Royan had moved onto the *Sprite*, and once he'd learned what he needed to from his dad and sister, he'd struck out on his own and never looked back.

"I remember."

"What did you do when you left?"

"I called my dad to come and get me. You know this story, why are you making me repeat it?" Owen was taking a long time getting to the damned point, time they should be spending making a plan to get back to Tianna.

"Because you're not getting it. When you left home, you already had a plan, and family to help you out. I'm not saying it was easy, but you weren't alone."

"True. But when you walked off the *She Devil*, you were alone. No plan. No family. You still did it. Why can't she?"

"I walked off because my mother's greed got my brother killed. Grief is a hell of a catalyst for change. If Connor hadn't died, I might still be on that ship, hating every second of my life."

"So, anger and grief are reasons to change, but love isn't?"

Owen stopped in his tracks. "Love is why she's staying."

"That doesn't make sense. If she loves us, she should be trying to be with us."

Owen leaned in and kissed his forehead. "I don't know if she loves us or not. I was talking about her father. She loves him. Everything she's done is to get him to acknowledge her, for him to truly see her and tell her she's good enough. I know what that's like, and so do you."

"It sucked engine fumes, which is why I left. We just need to make her see—"

Owen interrupted. "Cool your boosters. You tried that approach already, and look where it got us."

His frustration boiled over into anger. "That's because you weren't backing me up. You took her side."

Owen rumbled a low warning. "I get that you're

frustrated, but don't take it out on me. I didn't take anyone's side. If this has any chance of working, there can't be sides."

He'd seen that much watching his friends work through the challenges of their relationships. Knowing something wasn't the same as actually doing it, though. "*Fraxx*. Right. I knew that. I just forgot."

"I know. You went charging ahead, full throttle, trying to make things happen by force of will and charm alone." Owen squeezed his hand and they started walking again.

"In my defense, that usually works for me." The station was as quiet as it ever got, but there were still beings everywhere. It was a testament to what kind of place the Drift was that no one looked twice at two men, one half naked, walking through the station hand in hand in the middle of the night cycle.

Owen was quiet for a second. "I know you think so, but that approach is one of the reasons I kept pushing you away."

"What? No. I just needed time to convince you this was meant to be."

"Is that what you think happened?" Owen chuckled and shook his head. "You didn't convince me of anything, you lunatic. The more you pushed, the more I believed getting involved with you was a bad idea."

"Yet, here we are. Together."

"Yeah, because over time I got to know the real you. The slightly less cocky version. The man who cares so deeply about his friends and family he'd risk his life for them. That's the man I fell in love with."

"So, you're saying I'm not as charming as I think I am? My ego disagrees."

They reached the doors of the Nova Club, nodded to the two guards on the door, and walked inside.

Once they were in, Owen stepped into the shadows, pulling Royan with him. "I know you were joking, but there's something you need to understand. If we're serious about Tianna, if we want her in our lives, then you need to take your ego out of the equation."

He thought about it, then nodded. "I can do that."

"I know you can." Owen stroked his cheek. "I'm going to need your help, too. Trusting someone with my heart is not easy for me."

"I know." Royan leaned his head into Owen's caress. "So, we're doing this? You, me, and Tia makes three?"

"I don't know how we're going to make this work. Hell, I don't know if it will work at all, but yeah, I'm willing to give it a try. But, if it doesn't work, or she refuses to reconsider, then we have to respect her choice."

He groaned. "Life was so much simpler before I met you. No relationships, no regrets."

"And no me. Come on, admit it. I'm worth the sacrifice," Owen said.

The last of Royan's anger and hurt melted away. Tianna's rejection stung, but he hadn't lost everything. He still had Owen. "Yeah, you are. I know I don't say this often, but I'm lucky to have you in my life."

"Right back at you."

They kissed and then headed to the bar to put in an order. "We're going to need coffee and food."

"You're going to need to be a little more specific," Teenie said, grinning up at him. She was a fixture around the club, part hostess and part bartender with all the energy of a supernova stuffed into a pint-sized package.

Owen chimed in. "Make it two black coffees and two orders of cherry pie."

"Inspiration?" he asked.

Owen nodded. "If we're going to figure this mess out, we're going to need all the inspiration we can get."

"Coffee and pie coming up, just as soon as you get some clothes on. You know the rules, Owen. Nebula knows you enforced them often enough."

"I'll grab something out of the back. They still keep spare gear in the staff room, right?"

"Nothing's changed around here since you left. Go on, I'll have coffee waiting by the time you get back."

"You're making him get dressed? Way to spoil my fun, woman."

Teenie just laughed and waved them off. "Grab a table. I'll have the coffee to you shortly. Whatever you've done, I hope you can fix it."

"So do I, Teenie. So do I."

CHAPTER SIXTEEN

TIANNA PUSHED her body to limits she hadn't tested since she'd left rehab, but nothing she did helped clear her mind. Fragments of memories came and went, echoes of past fights with her father, of angry challenges and frustration fuelled workouts just like this one. There were other flashbacks, too. A few jagged recollections of lying in the wreckage of her skimmer, broken and bleeding. That's when everything changed. Lying there, she'd bargained with the universe, promising to be better, to do better, if only she lived somehow. The universe had delivered on its side of the bargain, and she'd done her best to do the same. The accident happened years ago, though. She'd come to terms with everything, embraced her role as the heir. So, why did it feel so wrong all of a sudden?

She slammed her fist into the punching bag she'd been beating on for the last fifteen minutes. Royan. Owen. They'd done this to her. From the second she'd stepped onto the *Sun Sprite*, she'd been tempted by them. Not just physically, though stars knew they were sexy enough to tempt an old Earth saint. They were a reminder of everything she renounced after the accident. Everything she couldn't have.

"I should have never have given in." *Slam*. "I was an idiot." *Thunk*. She punctuated each statement with another blow. "I put all that nonsense behind me years ago."

She pulled her next punch, distracted by what she'd said. What the hell? Nonsense? Her choices hadn't been nonsense. That was one of her father's pet phrases. Why the *fraxx* had she said that?

More memory fragments crashed into her awareness. She was barely conscious. In pain. Terrible pain. Someone was talking. "Whatever it takes. I know the risks. But she can't…" The voice faded. Had it been her father?

She winced. Her headache was back. Or maybe it had never left, but she'd managed to ignore it for a while. Pain was funny that way. She'd learned that during the months she'd spent in rehab, learning to control her new limbs and undergoing countless procedures until everything worked the way it should. She'd had to relearn everything. Walking, eating, dressing herself. It had been frustrating, depressing, and painful.

There were so many times she had wished that her implants included pain control. Cyborg soldiers had the ability to temporarily block input from their pain receptors, along with a host of other abilities she lacked. Of course, cyborg modifications were done while they were developing in their maturation vats, which allowed for far more extensive modifications.

Frustrated with the way her thoughts flowed from one topic to another, she hit the bag one last time, nearly tearing it out of the ceiling. Exercise wasn't the answer, which meant it was time for extreme measures. "Tink, have the food dispenser prepare a cherry pie and a litre of vanilla ice cream. And yes, I mean a whole entire pie. Freshly baked."

"Submitting request now. Your food will be ready in seventeen minutes."

"Thank you. I'm going to use the steam room and then head back up to shower."

"Do you wish the music to continue playing?"

"Change music to relaxation playlist and leave at the current volume."

The music changed, the pounding beat replaced with the sound of ocean waves crashing against some unseen shore. Usually this track helped calm her mind, but she didn't have much hope it would work this time. She stripped off her gear and dropped it to the floor for the household bots to deal with, pausing just long enough to toe off her shoes before entering the small steam room one of her predecessors had installed.

The whole gym area wasn't shown on the plans she'd reviewed. There was no mention of where the funds came from, either. She had no doubt the money had been rerouted from a maintenance project somewhere. What did the executives care if the lower levels' air quality dropped? They weren't breathing it.

Royan and Owen had helped her understand the problems with the station. No one here had mentioned anything about it. She wondered if they even noticed, or if they stayed in the safe, well-maintained sections where a fleet of bots kept everything spotless and the air was perfectly purified.

She pulled two towels out, wrapping one around her

waist as she stepped into the steam room and took a slow, lingering breath as she sat down. The warm, cherry-scented air fill her lungs, and she smiled at Tink's choice. If anything would help her relax tonight, it would be that scent. "Thank you Tink. That smells wonderful."

The more she thought about Royan and Owen, the stronger her regrets became. They deserved better than what she'd done to them, throwing them out in the middle of the night. Owen didn't even have shoes on. She recalled the day they'd arrived, and how he'd carried her so her bare feet hadn't touched the filthy floors of the station. She hadn't shown Owen even that much consideration. Dammit, she owed them an apology. Pushing them away was the right thing to do, but she'd handled it wrong. Why was that? Why had she gotten so angry? She planted her elbows on her thighs and leaned forward, breathing in the steam. So many questions, and no *fraxxing* answers.

A shadow flitted across the frosted glass door of the steam room. Must be one of the household droids tidying up the gym. She'd left it in a bit of a mess, just like everything else she'd touched tonight.

The shadow returned, and this time she caught a better look. That was no droid. The shape was wrong. Too tall. Too…human.

Adrenaline coursed through her as she got to her feet, rewrapping the towel so it covered her breasts. Had they come back? If it was Owen and Royan, why hadn't they said something by now?

She raised her hand to her mouth and whispered. "Tink. Vibration response only. Is there someone in the gym? One for yes, two for no."

Her bracelet buzzed once, then paused and buzzed twice in rapid succession.

"Two attackers?"

One buzz. *Fraxx.*

She backed away from the door, angling her body so she could still see it, but wasn't in direct line of sight. Then, she whispered another command. "Notify the guards there's a problem."

Another buzz.

There was nothing in the small room but herself, two towels, and a whole lot of water vapor. There was no place to hide, and her options for weapons were limited. She grabbed the towel from the bench, shook it out, and started using it to soak up the water from the floor and walls. As soon as it was wet, she spun it into a rope and coiled it in one hand like a whip.

She waited another minute, heart pounding, mouth dry despite the steam. The music droned on, but it would take more than the sounds of the ocean to soothe her frazzled nerves, now. Where were the guards? They should be here by now.

The shadow reappeared, and then a second one, and all hope that it was her guys vanished. One shadow was much smaller than the other.

They'd been right about the danger she faced. If she lived through this, she owed them both a long list of apologies. She stopped herself. There was no if. She would survive. She wasn't a helpless heiress. She was almost a cyborg. If it came to a choice between protecting that secret or dying, she'd deal with the consequences. One day, the universe would have figured it out. She'd just hoped that day was a few decades from now.

She crouched, tensed, and waited. If they wanted her, they'd have to come and get her.

Another minute crept by and still the guards didn't come. She was on her own.

More movement, the door was yanked open and blaster bolts tore through the air, shattering the tiles on the back wall. The broken tiles hit her like shrapnel, tearing through her towel and bare flesh alike, and leaving her bleeding from dozens of cuts.

The second the firing stopped she charged the door, using every bit of her enhanced strength. Through the steam, she saw the larger shape fill the doorway and she hit them square on. She felt his ribs give way beneath her shoulder, heard the grunt of pain as all the air left her attacker's lungs, then they were both on the ground and she was scrambling to get to her feet. Someone moved behind her and she spun around, lashing out with the wet towel she held. It snapped, striking the second assailant on the arm. A woman. Like her partner, she was dressed all in black.

Another bolt of blaster fire. Agony tore through her left shoulder. *Fraxx.* She spun around again, saw the man she'd knocked down had drawn his weapon. He fired again, but she was already moving. She was faster than he expected and the next shot went wide. The tattered remains of her towel slipped, and she tore it away without looking down, tossing it in the man's face on the ground as she sped past him. She couldn't fight two at once, not with one arm. She had to even the odds.

There was a rack of free weights set up against one wall. They'd have to do. She dodged another flurry of blaster fire, barely feeling the one that grazed her hip. It slowed her down, though, and that made her an easier target. *Shit. Shit. Shit.* She made it to the rack and grabbed the first weight she could reach, spinning around and hurling it at her male attacker. He'd made it to his knees, which meant he couldn't move out of the way as the weight came flying at him. It hit him in the face with a sickening crunch and he crumpled to the floor.

"Bryce. No!" the woman screamed as her partner toppled backward.

Tianna took advantage of her adversary's distraction to look for the dead man's weapon. There. On the floor. Under his hand.

She was too far away. She'd never get to it before the woman fired again. The wound on her hip burned, her left arm was useless. She needed one more distraction.

"You killed him." The woman was sobbing.

"He tried to kill me." Tianna took a step back, closer to the weights.

"But you won't *fraxxing* die. What the hell are you?" The woman raised her blaster, pointing it straight at Tianna.

"Hard to kill," she retorted, then dropped to the floor as a bolt sizzled through the air where she'd been standing. Nanotech and sheer stubbornness were the only things keeping her on her feet right now, and she was reaching the limits of both.

She grabbed a weight and flung it at the surviving attacker. Her position didn't give her much of an angle, so she aimed for the only thing she felt certain she could hit, the woman's legs.

This time, the impact was more of a snap than a crunch, and her target went down with an anguished wail.

Running on adrenaline and fear, she pushed herself to her feet one-handed and bolted to the downed man, grabbing the blaster from his hand. His *dead* hand. A shudder of revulsion passed through her. She'd need a vat of disinfectant and a year of therapy after tonight.

With the blaster trained on the woman, she finally let herself take a deep breath and think instead of simply reacting. "Who are you, and who sent you?"

The woman groaned. Her face was as pale as starlight and there were tears of grief and pain etched into the lines of her face. She was still on the ground, her ruined leg at an unnatural angle.

Tianna walked over to her, kicked the second blaster out of reach, and backed away again. "Answer my questions."

"*Fraxx*, you."

Now that she had time to look more closely, Tianna could see the resemblance she'd missed until now. "No, Katy Valentine, I'm pretty sure you're the one that's *fraxxed*."

"You know me?" Owen's sister asked.

"I know your brother, Owen. He was on that ship you tried to attack back at Taza 4. Did you know that?"

Katy wheezed with laughter. "That fool always did have lousy luck. If he hadn't interfered, you'd be dead and I'd be collecting my payment."

"Your luck doesn't seem that great either. Three attempts on my life, and I'm still breathing."

"I only tried twice. The first time wasn't me. I got tapped for clean up."

Now they were getting somewhere. "Tink, are you recording this?"

"I am now. I have also contacted Corp-Sec. Officers are on their way here."

"And the guards upstairs?"

"Have still not responded to their comms."

"They're dead. Bryce took them out once I let him in. Been watching you for days, but my brother and that idiot you're both fucking were always around, so we had to wait."

Days. She'd convinced herself she was safe, but she'd been a target the whole time. "Who sent you?"

"No idea. The order came down the chain of command."

"What chain? Who do you work for?"

"After Corp-Sec and those IAF bastards broke up the cartels, the survivors started working together."

"You work for the cartels? Why do they want me dead?" This didn't make any sense. Not that she was thinking clearly at the moment. Adrenaline and pain were making it hard to focus, and staying on her feet was taking up a lot of her attention.

"No idea. Maybe because you're an abomination?"

"I'm not."

"Well you're not human, either." Katy gestured to her with an unsteady hand. "You're covered in blood, full of holes, and you're still standing. Not to mention you threw a hunk of steel so hard it broke my *fraxxing* leg."

Tianna glanced down at herself. Katy had a point. She looked like she'd walked naked through a slaughterhouse. She was slick with blood, and more of it was pooling at her feet. Well, that explained why she was dizzy. Not even her medi-bots could keep up with this kind of damage. She gave up trying to stand and sat down, keeping the blaster trained on Katy the whole time.

"How long until help arrives, Tink?"

"They're entering your residence now. I've indicated you will require medical treatment. Medics are also on their way."

"Great." She didn't need a medic. All she needed was a few hours of rest while her body repaired itself.

"What about me? Whatever you are, you're clearly going to survive. I'm the one with a broken leg."

"I'm sure Corp-Sec will see to it you get medical treatment. It will probably come faster if you cooperate, though."

"If I cooperate, the first thing I'm telling them is that the heir to Astek's fortune isn't even human." Katy said with a sneer.

It finally hit her. This was it. Her secret was about to be revealed, and there was nothing she could do to stop it. She expected to be angry, or afraid, but all she felt was a calm acceptance. It was out of her hands, now.

"You're some kind of cyborg, aren't you?"

Heavy footsteps thundered down the stairs and she belatedly remembered she was naked. She couldn't do anything about it, though. She only had one good arm, and she needed to keep the blaster aimed at Katy.

"What I am is ...complicated," she said as the door crashed open and a familiar shape charged into view, blaster in hand.

"Tia!" Owen roared.

Royan arrived next. "Holy *fraxx*. What happened in here?"

"This is the part where you both get to tell me you told

me so, I apologize, then hopefully one of you gives me your shirt so I don't have to meet everyone else naked. And before you ask, I'm okay. It looks a lot worse than it is."

"I'm glad to hear it, because you look like hell, sweetheart." Royan skinned his shirt over his head and started to hand it to her, then paused when he saw her mangled shoulder. "She shot you?"

"They both did," she told Royan. "Tink, tell Corp-Sec things are under control, please."

"Confirmed."

Owen leveled his blaster at her prisoner. It dipped, then steadied as he realized who he was looking at. "Katy? How the hell did you get here?"

"Katy? As in your baby sister?" Royan's gaze bounced between the two women. "We left you alone for an hour. How did you get into this much trouble so *fraxxing* fast?"

"It's a talent."

"And Owen says I'm a lunatic. I think you're trying to claim my title." He eased his shirt over her head and good arm, then sat down behind her and wrapped her in his arms, one hand covering the wound on her shoulder with enough pressure to make her see stars.

"Ow."

"If that's all you have to say, I'm not applying enough pressure." He clamped down harder and she almost blacked out.

"That's better."

"Not really," she muttered when she could breathe again.

While she'd been trying to stay conscious, Owen had

started talking to his sister. From what she could hear, it was a very one-sided conversation.

"Say something, Katy. Anything. Why would you do this? Raiding didn't pay enough so you got into killing as a sideline? Was this mom's idea?"

Katy just stared at him in mutinous silence until he stopped asking questions.

"Mom's dead," Katy said flatly.

"When?"

"Two years after you left. She never got over it, you know. Losing you and Connor like that. She started taking high risk jobs. Crew thought it was for the money. Me, I think she wanted to end it and didn't have the guts to pull the trigger herself. She's buried beside Connor."

"I didn't know." Owen's tone was softer, but his blaster was still trained at his sister's chest.

"Of course you didn't. You left. She told everyone you died. Even made us put up a headstone for you. It's right beside Connor's. Guess it was easier for her to pretend you died than to accept you walked out on us."

"You know why I left. Hell, I asked you to come with me. You turned me down." His voice broke. "You could have been free of it all, but instead you became a killer."

Katy's expression barely moved, but for a brief second, Tianna saw a flash of regret in the other woman's eyes. "I know."

Then she looked over at Royan and Tianna, and her expression hardened again. "Good thing mom's dead. If she knew you'd hooked up with a couple of freaks... Did you even know you were banging a cyborg? That's gotta be what she is."

Royan's hissed in surprise. "Son of a starbeast. I should have seen it. No wonder you never sleep."

Owen glanced her way and she braced herself for the inevitable words of anger and rejection.

"Who I love is my business, not yours," was all he said.

Royan nuzzled her ear. "But that doesn't mean we're not going to spank your ass pink later for keeping that from us."

"There's going to be a later?" she asked, dazed.

"Sweetheart, there is always going to be a later for us. Weren't you paying attention? That big, sexy teddy bear over there just told his sister he loves you, and so do I."

"But I lied. And yelled. A lot."

"And once you're healed up, we'll talk about that."

"Damn right we will," Owen agreed.

"Ugh. Shoot me please. I'd rather be dead than listen to anymore of this nauseating crap. You're all freaks."

"Corp-Sec is arriving now," Tink announced.

"Better late than never." Tia frowned. "How is it you two got here before Corp-Sec, anyway. In fact, how did you know to come at all?"

"Tink. She told us you were in trouble. We were at the Nova and came running."

"I didn't tell her to do that." She leaned against Royan. "But I'm glad she did."

"Me too. Though I have to say it looks like you never really needed bodyguards at all, Miss badass cyborg."

"That's not true. I needed you." She raised a blood-soaked hand, indicating the partially destroyed gym. "See what happens when you leave me alone?"

Both men grinned, but further conversation was ended by the arrival of almost a dozen armed Corp-Sec officers and a team of medics. Owen handed his sister over to the officers, then came to stand over her and Royan.

As her adrenaline rush faded the pain grew worse. She closed her eyes and tried to ride each agonizing wave as it rolled over her. She caught bits and pieces of the conversations going on around her. Orders issued through communicators, someone probing her injuries with a gentle touch that still burned like fire.

"…to the med-center"

"…needs specialized care"

"…No one breathes a word of this. Isolate the prisoner."

Finally, she felt something cool touch her throat. "I'm giving you a pain blocker now, Ms. Astor."

"About *fraxxing* time," she muttered. There was a hiss and a faint sting, and then blessed relief. She opened her eyes and saw both Royan and Owen looking down at her with concern and something that made her heart skip a beat. Love. *Re'veth*, they really did love her.

"Told you she'd be fine," Royan said.

"Of course I'm fine. I'm a badass, remember?"

Owen glowered at Royan. "This is going to be a thing now, isn't it? You did this, you deal with it."

Royan just chuckled. "Come on, badass. Let's get you to the med-center. Time for you to get looked over by someone who specializes in your kind."

"Cyborgs?" It felt strange to refer to herself that way out loud.

"Lunatics who let themselves get shot," Owen said, then moved back as two medics lowered a stretcher beside her and helped her onto it.

"We'll transport her. You can meet us at the med-center," one of the medics said.

"We're her protection detail. We don't leave her side." Owen's voice dropped to the sexy growl he used when he expected to be obeyed.

"There's not enough room in the transport for—"

"The last time we left her unsupervised, this happened. Do you really want to test your luck?" Royan asked.

Tianna decided to chime in, too. Owen wasn't the only one who could be bossy. "They ride with me, or I'm walking."

The medic sighed. "Alright, Miss Astor. We'll make it work."

"Thank you." She closed her eyes. Now if only she could fix the rest of this mess, and her life, so easily.

CHAPTER SEVENTEEN

OWEN DIDN'T TAKE his eyes off Tianna for the entire journey to the med-center. He couldn't. The last time he'd let her out of his sight, she'd gotten hurt. That wouldn't happen again. They'd sprinted the entire distance back, sick with worry they'd be too late. Tink had opened the doors and had the elevator waiting for them, saving them a few desperate seconds, but the ride to the residential level had felt like an eternity.

Thankfully, Royan was still wearing his blaster, and Teenie had tossed Owen hers without pausing to ask why. Tink had provided a few details: the number of attackers, Tianna's location, a report of weapons fire. The program was as close to hysterical as software could get, repeating the information and apologizing for not detecting the attackers earlier. Later, he'd find out why and fix it. So that next time – if there was a next time – they'd be better prepared.

Royan reached across Tianna and grabbed his hand.

"This isn't your fault, baby. It's mine. I'm the one who pissed her off and got us tossed out."

"And I'm the one whose job title is security officer. I should have been smarter."

Tianna opened her eyes and took both their hands. "Do I really need to point out the fact that I'm the one who told you to go?"

Royan shook his head. "I shouldn't have pushed you so hard. Now I get why you were trying so hard to put some distance between us."

"Yeah. Only all I did was put myself in a position where I had to out myself anyway. There's no way that *pesken* is going back in the bag. I need to warn my father. He'll have to protect the company the best he can."

"You've been shot twice and your first concern is for your dad and the business? What does it take for you to put yourself first?" Owen demanded.

"The company always comes first."

"Why do you keep saying that, sweetheart?" Royan asked.

"I—" she frowned. "I don't know. It's one of my father's pet expressions. After the accident, I kind of adopted it as a mantra."

"That's when all this happened, isn't it?" Owen asked. It made sense. It also meant that her existence violated galactic law. A whole lot of laws, in fact.

"My injuries were a lot worse than anyone was told. The doctors weren't even sure how I'd manage to survive the crash at all. They told him I had no chance of recovering. My father didn't accept their diagnosis."

"He broke the law to save your life." Royan's voice had a hint of awe to it, and Owen felt the same way. The money, skill, and secrecy required to pull it off were beyond comprehension.

Tianna's pale lips tightened into a bittersweet smile. "I liked to think of it that way. He was more pragmatic. He referred to my recovery as a continued investment in a key long-term project."

"In case I haven't mentioned it before, your father is a *fraxxing* idiot," Royan muttered.

Owen didn't comment, but he flexed his fingers and indulged in a brief fantasy where he got five minutes alone with the asshole.

By the time they arrived at the med-center, Tianna was already showing improvement. The small cuts on her face and arms had closed up, and it looked to him like her color had improved, though that could just be wishful thinking.

They brought her in through the emergency entrance that led straight to the treatment rooms. He'd been this way once before, the day that Royan had gotten shot. That was a turning point for them as a couple, and here they were again, only this time, it was Tianna who was hurt.

"Déjà vu, huh?" Royan asked as they followed as close as they dared without interfering. Dr. Jefferies had met them as they came in, and the medics were giving her an update that involved a lot of words Owen didn't understand.

"The people I care about have an alarming tendency to let themselves get shot. You both need to cut this shit out."

Royan laughed. "Don't worry, I'm not planning on letting it happen again. Once in a lifetime is more than enough."

Alyson glanced back at them. "I'm glad to hear that. My practice is busy enough as it is." Tianna vanished into one of the treatment rooms, and Owen walked to the door, not sure if the doctor would let them in.

"Doc?" Royan asked, crowding the doorway.

She looked at the two of them, then at Tianna. "Patient's choice."

"Let them stay. Now I'm finally free to talk about it, I want them to hear everything." Tianna gave them a small smile. "No more secrets. And this time, I mean it."

"You better *vething* mean it. After all the grief you gave me back on the *Sprite*." He knew he should be angry at her right now. For the secrets, the lies, and the anger she'd heaped on him when she'd found out the truth about who he'd been before he became Owen Connors. Maybe later he'd be angry at her for lying to them, but right now all he felt was grateful. She was alive. The rest could wait.

They stood against the far side, watching in silence as Dr. Jefferies methodically inspected each of Tianna's injuries, making notes on a data tablet as she went.

"Do I have your permission to do a full body-scan?" the doctor asked when she was done.

"Yes. Might as well be thorough. Plus, it's easier to show what was done to me instead of listing it all."

Alyson nodded. "I still can't believe this was all done to you as an adult. Forgive me for asking, but how much do you remember?"

Tianna grimaced. "Too much."

"When you're feeling up to it, I'd like to talk to you about what was done, and what you recall. I'm trying to learn as much as I can about the cyborgs and how they were created. You would have valuable insight into the process."

Owen couldn't imagine what she'd endured. There was

a reason the cyborgs underwent their enhancements before they ever gained awareness. "Only if you want to, Tia. Right, Alyson?"

Alyson gave him a bemused look. "And here I thought cyborgs were the only ones that got overprotective and growly. Maybe it's a side effect of the medi-bots. I should run some tests."

"Oh no. No more tests, Doc." Royan slashed a hand through the air in front of him. "You drained me dry the last time I was in here."

"I'm happy to let you scan and test me. In fact, I'd like to know exactly what was done to me."

"You don't know?" Owen asked. *How could she not know?*

Tianna shrugged. "My medical files were sealed and locked away long before I was released. I know some of it, because I had to learn to use my new limbs, but that's it."

"You lost your limbs? Plural?"

Tianna nodded. "It really would be easier to show you."

"I can run the scan now. I'd like to get Lieksa in here, too. She worked on cyborgs during the war, and while she's only recently finished training as a medic, she's more qualified than anyone else on the station when it comes to cybernetics."

Tianna hesitated, and he knew why. Logically, she knew her secret was blown, but years of hiding the truth weren't easy to undo. He moved to her side and took her bloodstained hand. "She's the best, Tia. And she's a friend. She's Mack and Dash's wife, remember?"

"Okay," Tianna agreed.

"Great." Alyson looked pleased. "Once we've gotten a

good look at everything, we'll put some sealant on your injuries and you can get cleaned up. I'd like you to stay here until you're healed. Given the rate of repair, I'd say you can go home by late morning."

"Which gives me a few short hours to prepare my statement and warn my father of the storm that's coming."

"That can wait. Your secret is safe, for now," Royan said.

"There will still be rumors. Not about me, but about the attack, and the fact I was taken away for medical treatment. If the media aren't here yet, they will be, soon." She sighed tiredly. "I'm newsworthy, and it's a pain in the ass."

"Well, they're not getting in here," Alyson declared.

"You've got your guys on the door, don't you?" If Blade, Lance, and Dirk were standing guard nothing short of a battlecruiser was getting past them, and even then, Owen wouldn't bet on the cruiser.

"I do. No one without authorization is getting in here, not tonight."

"You didn't have to wake them up for me. I've been disrupting everyone's life lately," Tia said guiltily.

Alyson laughed. "You haven't been here very long, or you'd know this is a normal day on the station. Well, mostly normal. Patching people up after a fight is standard fare, but it's not every day I get to deliver twins."

Royan froze. Mouth open. Eyes wide.

"Zura?" Owen asked.

"She's just down the hall. If you listen carefully, you can almost hear Kit and Luke climbing the walls."

Tianna sat up. "You should be with her! I'm fine. We can do the scans later. Why are you here?"

Alyson pointed to Tianna. "You, back in bed. Now."

To Owen's amusement, Tianna obeyed the doctor's command without another word.

Once Tianna was settled, Alyson continued. "I'm here because I have a very competent staff. Zura is still in the early stages of labor. She's here because her husbands insisted, but there's not much we can do for her right now apart from keeping her comfortable and waiting."

"Why didn't anyone tell me?" Royan asked.

"From what I heard? You and Owen went charging out of the Nova Club around the time Zura told the guys she was in labor. I told them I'd convey the news once Tianna was checked out."

"I swear the universe does this on purpose. It's never just one thing, oh no. That would be boring. We have to experience everything all at once, every damned time," Owen said. The attack. The discovery his mother was gone and his sister was a killer. And now, Zura. When this night was over, he was going to need a large drink. And then he needed to talk to Katy. She might be a killer, but she was still his sister.

Royan was beaming now. "Boring is for other people. You and me, we're meant for other things." He walked over to Tianna, placing his hand over Owen's. "Care to join us, sweetheart?"

The radiant smile she gave them gave away her answer before she even spoke a word. "There's no reason why I can't. Not anymore. I can't promise you this is going to work. I don't even know what's going to happen next, but I can promise that whatever it is, it definitely won't be boring."

There was a time Owen had thought he wanted boring,

but he'd been wrong. The safe choices didn't include Royan or Tianna, which meant that *boring* wasn't any choice at all.

TIANNA WANTED to enjoy the moment, to bask in the fact that the men she cared about – maybe even loved – had accepted the truth about her so easily. Unfortunately, the situation didn't allow it. The truth might have freed her from years of lying, but it also launched a firestorm of legal, corporate, and ethical problems that she needed to get ahead of. Still, a few more minutes wouldn't hurt. Owen was right, they had a little time.

They spent the next few minutes holding hands and talking. She'd given a basic statement to Corp-Sec at the scene, but this was the first time she'd been able to tell them what happened from beginning to end. Owen recorded everything and sent the file to the investigators once she was done recounting it all.

"That's quite the story." Alyson had been calibrating some kind of machinery and entering information into her computer while Tianna talked. "Cyn and Zura were right. You really are one of us."

"They said that?" No one said that about her. She didn't fit in anywhere. Never had, not even after the accident when she'd tried to be the daughter her father wanted.

"Why does that surprise you?" Owen asked.

"Because I'm the ice queen. The boss's daughter. The spoiled little rich girl. Any and all of the above."

Alyson laughed. "I used to think that way, too. My

family runs a planet instead of a corporation, but we're more alike than you know. I never thought I'd fit in anywhere, either. Then I found this place, and discovered a group of beings that are not just friends, they're the family I chose for myself."

For her, family had always meant one thing, loyalty to her father, the only blood relative she had. "I think I'd like that."

"Then let's get you scanned and cleaned up so you're ready to meet the newest members of this crazy family when they finally make their appearance." Alyson rose from her chair and hit something on her keyboard. There was a low hum, and a new device lowered from the ceiling just over her bed.

"You two are going to need to stand back for this. It won't take long." Owen kissed her forehead, then let go of her hand.

Royan did the same, but then asked her a gentle question. "Will you be okay with me ducking out to check on my sister? Doc, do I have enough time to do that?"

"Only a quick visit. Trust me, you don't want to stay too long. A woman in delivery is never in the best of moods."

"Go. Don't be long, though. I'm looking forward to my post-scan shower. I had no idea how much drying blood itches," Tianna said.

"Thank you." He kissed her again. "I won't be long."

She looked over at Owen. "You, too. Try to keep Royan from saying anything that will get him killed by an angry pregnant lady."

"I'll do my best, but I'm not making any promises. You know our boy."

"I do."

"It's like I'm not even in the room," Royan muttered on his way out. "See you soon, sweetheart."

"I always knew Royan and Owen would end up together, but it never occurred to me that it would take a woman to stabilize those two. You're either crazy, brave, or both. And that's coming from someone who married cyborg triplets."

"Crazy, brave, and likely in love, though I'm not admitting that to them just yet."

"Good plan. Hold off until I can start up a betting pool on how long it takes you to tell them. I made a killing on the last one."

"You won that?"

Alyson grinned. "I did. Spent it on some upgrades to our food dispenser. Three hungry cyborgs were putting a strain on the old one."

"I can only imagine. Before we do this, can I have a moment to contact my father? He really should know what's happening before he hears about it on the news."

"Go ahead."

"Thanks. Tink, you there?"

"Of course."

Alyson raised a blonde brow as the AI announced its presence, but didn't say anything.

"Send a message to my father and assign it the highest urgency rating there is. Message as follows: Father. There was another attempt on my life tonight. The attempt failed, but I was seriously injured. Attacker and responders are aware of my condition. I'm sorry. There was no other choice. Please take all precautions with your safety. I will await further instructions from you. End message. Send."

"Message sent," Tink confirmed.

"We really do have a lot in common," Alyson said softly, her expression one of understanding.

"My relationship with my father is…" she trailed off with a shrug.

"Mine, too. There's a reason I'm out here, light years from Cassien Alpha."

"I've been there, beautiful planet."

"It is. And I get home once in awhile to visit my grandparents. They adore my husbands. My parents…not so much."

"And you're okay with that?" Why was it that everyone else seemed to be strong enough to walk away from the source of their unhappiness and she wasn't? Alyson. Royan. Owen. The list went on. If she was such a bad ass, why was she working so hard to appease her father, a man who never approved of anything she did? *Because family is everything.* The thought popped into her head and she pushed it aside. That wasn't an answer she was willing to accept. Not this time. And just like that, her headache was back, cutting through the comfortable fog of the pain-blockers.

"I'm fine with it but—" Alyson ended her statement abruptly as she noticed Tianna's discomfort. "But you're not fine. Pain?"

"Just a headache. Nothing serious. It's been coming and going all evening."

"Actually, Tianna, you have been complaining of low-level physical discomfort in your cranial region for more than a week. According to my records, you have consumed small doses of pain-blockers numerous times in the past nine days."

"You're nagging, Tink."

"I am not nagging. I am informing your doctor of a potential issue."

"And Tianna's doctor appreciates it, Tink. Tianna, do you need something to help with the pain right now? You've got enough pain-blocker in your system a minor headache shouldn't be affecting you, which means that it's not minor."

Tianna shook her head. "I'll be fine. Guess that's something else you can check on while we're doing the scan, huh?"

"Absolutely. Can you give me some idea where the pain is originating?"

"Back of my skull." She touched her head. "Here."

Alyson gently probed the area. "No injury or indication of head trauma. Though, there is a small, bony lump under your skin, but that's an old injury by the feel of it."

"Probably one of the fracture sites from my accident."

"Only one way to be sure. Lie back and I'll start the scan. It should be finished rendering by the time your men get back."

Tianna lay back and did her best to keep still. She'd been scanned often enough to know the less she moved, the faster it would be over. Since thinking about her father was giving her a headache, she tried to focus on happier things, like Royan and Owen. They were the one source of joy in her life right now, and she had no intention of giving them up. She just wasn't sure how to make it work when she was about to be the focus of a shitstorm that would upend not just her life, but everyone around her.

"And we're done. You can sit up now," the doctor announced a short time later.

"How does it look?"

"Honestly? Fascinating. I examined you myself and I had no idea how much of you had been rebuilt or replaced. Whoever worked on you, they did an impressive job."

"My father only hired the best. I can't even tell you their names, though. I was never introduced to any of them."

"Given what they were doing, I'm not surprised. Some of these implants aren't even supposed to exist."

There was a low knock on the door, interrupting before Tia could ask the doctor what she meant.

"We're back," Royan called out.

"We're ready for you. Come in," Alyson replied.

The door opened and Owen and Royan came in, followed by a curvy woman with red hair and a friendly smile. "Hi, there. I'm Lieksa Darian-Schudo. You must be Tianna Astor. Nice to meet you, even if the circumstances aren't great."

"Hi. I hear you're the resident expert on all things cyborg."

"I was a cybernetic technician during the war, yes, and until recently I was a robotic tech for Astek. In case no one's mentioned it to you yet, the corporate cafeteria really could do with an upgrade."

"Noted. If I'm still in charge after all this, I'll see what I can do."

Owen frowned. "Why wouldn't you be in charge?"

"Because I'm an illegal construct whose existence violates intergalactic law? Because I could end up arrested? Because the board of directors might have a little trouble taking orders from someone who isn't human? Take your pick."

"Not to detract from your argument, but you are definitely human. Modified and enhanced, yes, but still human. Do you want to see your scan so you can see for yourself?" Alyson asked.

"Yes, please." She'd always been curious about what had been done to her. There'd been so many secrets in her life, it felt good to be free of at least some of them.

Alyson dimmed the lights slightly, then touched something on her keyboard and a full-sized projection with all her organs and inner workings, shimmered into existence.

"I got to say, that's a little disturbing," Royan said.

She had to agree. The image was so detailed she could see her heart beating and her lungs work. It rotated slowly in the air, allowing her to see everything. She was so fascinated by it all, it took her a few seconds to focus on her implants. They were highlighted in yellow, and there were a lot more of them than she'd expected.

"*Re'veth*. That's a lot of tech," Owen murmured.

"I had no idea it was so extensive. I knew about my arm, and my legs, but this…" she waved to the projection. Along with the expected inserts into her arms and legs were a host of others. Her organs were replaced with clone tissue, but some of them appeared to have implants as well. *What had they done to her*? "Are you sure I'm still human?"

"Positive. Cyborgs are just enhanced humans, after all," Alyson replied.

She was still trying to absorb what she was seeing.

There were extensive neural connections running along her spine and into her skull.

"What is all that? Why is there so much tech in my head?" she asked, pointing to the projection.

Alyson looked at Lieksa. "Any idea?"

Lieksa nodded, her sunny expression fading. "Dr. Jefferies sent me your file, so I know when this happened, and why, but based on what I see here, they did more than just rebuild your body."

"What else did they do?" Tianna's question came out so strained she barely recognized her own voice.

Owen and Royan laid their hands on her back and she leaned into their touch.

"I'd need to scan you with some specialty equipment to confirm the exact purpose of each implant, but I don't need to do that to know what at least some of them do. Some of what you see is neural networking, but most of it..." Lieksa sighed. "I'm sorry, Tianna, but that hardware is very distinctive, and it only has one use: behavior modification."

Tianna's mouth opened but no words came out. Her thoughts were a tangled snarl of denial, anger, and heartbreak.

"You're sure?" Owen asked.

"Completely."

Tianna bit back a sob and forced herself to exhale slowly. "How would that affect me?"

"Cyborgs undergo extensive mental conditioning and skill implantation while they're still in their maturation tanks. You were already an adult when this was done to you, so the effects would be limited. Some behaviors might be discouraged, and a few instructions could be embedded to guide your decision-making process. Think of it like someone nudging your thinking."

"Instructions? Like, some phrases that keep repeating?" Her hurt faded, burned away by her growing sense of outrage.

Royan's hand stiffened. "Son of a starbeast. You don't think that's why you kept saying the same thing when we argued?"

She clenched her teeth. "That's exactly what I think."

"Lieksa, what would happen when someone with that kind of conditioning started resisting it?" Alyson asked.

"For the cyborgs, as the behavioral conditioning weakened, they reported periods of cognitive dissonance, headaches, and a disconnect between their actions and their desires. I'm not sure how it affects someone like Tianna though. This is new, and it should never be allowed to happen again." Lieksa gave Tianna a look of sympathy. "I know you must have dozens of questions, and I'll try to answer as many as I can. First thing you need to know is this can be fixed."

"Can you get rid of it?" Tianna wanted the tech out of her so she could melt it all to *fraxxing* slag.

Lieksa hesitated. "I don't know. But even if I can't, I can deactivate it. And there's someone here on Astek who happens to be a specialist in helping people work through this kind of thing."

Owen's started stroking her back in slow, soothing strokes. "You're talking about Xori Virness, aren't you?" he asked.

"I am. She's been working with Ward and Vic. I think she could help Tianna, too."

"Who?" Tianna asked. Her brain was busy working

through what she'd learned. She didn't have the bandwidth for much more new information right now.

"She's a doctor working with two of our friends. She's something of a specialist in this kind of therapy."

"If she can help me get my brain back, I'm in." She tried to keep her tone light, but inside she was screaming. Her father had done this to her. Violated the sanctity of her mind, hijacking her thoughts to force her to be what he wanted. She'd come to terms with what he'd done to her body without her permission. He'd done it to save her life. But he hadn't stopped there, and she'd never forgive him for that.

Owen leaned in and nuzzled her ear. "You okay?"

"Not really." The only thing grounding her right now was the fact Owen and Royan were with her.

"It's okay not to be. This has been a seriously shit day. But we're here, and we're going to get through this, together."

She nodded, then turned and threw her arms around them both, hugging them hard. "Thank you. I'm sorry I dragged you both into my mess."

"We like mess," Royan told her.

"And we really like you," Owen added.

"I really like you, too." What she felt for them went far deeper than like, but she wasn't ready to admit it. Not here, and not yet.

"Whatever we can do to help," Alyson said.

"Can you help me get rid of a body? I'm going to kill my father for this." The words were out of her mouth before she could filter them.

Royan laughed, Owen hugged her, and both women grinned.

"She really is one of us, isn't she?" Lieksa asked Alyson, who simply nodded and offered her an approving smile.

Warmth bloomed deep in Tianna's chest, filling her with an unfamiliar feeling. This was what acceptance felt like. She liked it. Now that she was back in control of her life, this is what she wanted. Acceptance, approval, and the company of people who cared about her.

When her headache flared again, she embraced it. The pain meant she was thinking for herself. She was free.

CHAPTER EIGHTEEN

MEDI-BOTS OR NOT, Royan was exhausted. He was in good company, though. Everyone in the medical center's waiting room had been up for hours, though their reasons were different from his.

He couldn't remember a more emotional night. The argument with Tianna. The heartache when she threw them out. Then the terrifying sprint back to Astek after Tink's message that Tianna was in danger. After that, there'd been enough surprises and revelations to last them all several lifetimes.

Tianna's father wasn't answering messages, Owen's sister was still being interrogated, and rumors of the attack on Tianna were running rampant. The only bright spot had been the arrival of his nieces, who had come into the world with indignant wails loud enough to pierce the thick walls and bring the entire waiting room to their feet to cheer. Everyone had been there, including a tired but determined Tianna.

The ever useful Tink had some of Tianna's clothing

delivered, as well as a change of clothing for both him and Owen, and the three of them had sat in the waiting room with the rest of their friends, waiting for news.

Tianna had been friendly but quiet for long stretches as she tried to make sense of everything she'd learned. Physically she was healing quickly, but emotionally…that was going to take a lot longer.

All he could do was be there for her, holding her hand, encouraging her to eat, listening to her send message after message to her father. He couldn't imagine what she was feeling, reaching out to the man who had done her so much harm. He wanted to wrap her in his arms and promise her she'd never have to see that man again, but there was no way that would happen. He was her father, and the head of Astek, which meant he'd been the focal point of the storm that was brewing.

The news hadn't broken yet, though, and once he'd seen his sister, he'd be taking Tianna and Owen home so they could all get some much needed rest.

"Royan, you still here?" Alyson appeared at the waiting room door, grinning broadly. "Your sister wants to introduce you to your nieces, then I want you to take Tianna home and get her to rest. She's not completely healed yet."

"Don't have to tell me twice, doc." Royan got to his feet stiffly and shot a dirty look at the medieval torture device he'd been sitting on for the last few hours. The beds in the medical center were a lot more comfortable than the chairs.

Owen stood, and they both turned back to offer a hand to Tianna, who rose with her usual grace despite the toll the night had taken on her.

Alyson led them down a short stretch of worn and battered hallway and into one of the patient rooms.

Zura was sitting up in bed, looking tired but triumphant. "Hey, little brother. I hear you and your family had some excitement of your own last night."

Tianna nearly stumbled, and Royan tightened his grip on her hand, correcting her balance. He couldn't tell if it was exhaustion or shock from being referred to as his family that made her lose her footing. Probably the latter.

"Nothing our girl couldn't handle."

Zura's silver eyes widened. "Later, I want to hear the whole story."

"So do we," Luke said.

"You look rough, my friend," Owen said.

Luke just nodded. "Feel that way, too. Like we fought an entire campaign in one night."

"And we had the easy job." Kit stroked Zura's hair. "You were amazing, Zura my love. And I never want to see you go through that again."

Zura just laughed. "It really wasn't that bad. Then again, I had pain blockers. They didn't."

Royan let go of Tianna and walked over to Zura, giving her a careful hug. "Congratulations. Now, where are my nieces? Gimme."

Both fathers stepped back and turned to the back wall, where a pair of raised beds with high sides were stashed. They leaned over the cribs, and a few minutes later they both returned, each carrying a tiny bundle cradled in their arms.

"We haven't decided on names yet. These two were so convinced I was having boys that we didn't even discuss girls names."

"Not convinced, just hoping really hard." Luke walked over to Royan and held out the sleeping babe.

"Honestly, I was hoping for boys, too. Boys are easy. Girls though…" Royan took his tiny niece and cradled her gently in his arms. "The first thing I need to teach you and your sister is to stay away from men like me."

He peeled back just enough of the blanket to get a look at her tiny face. Her skin tone was the palest shade of blue, with faint stripes that marked her cheeks and forehead. What little hair she had was dark, but he thought he could see a hint of blue there, too. He leaned down to kiss the top of her head. "You are so precious."

Then, he turned to Owen. "Isn't she gorgeous?"

"Beautiful," Owen agreed, stroking his finger across her cheek. "The first thing I'm going to teach you two is how to punch, so that when guys like your uncle come around, you know how to deal with them."

Everyone laughed.

He handed his niece back to Luke and moved over to Kit to check on his second niece, who was as perfect and sweet as her sister. When he looked back, Tianna was standing by Luke, staring at the baby with such longing it made his heart hurt. A family had never been part of his plans before, but right now, holding his sister's child and looking at Owen and Tianna, he could picture them doing this some day. Just…not yet. It took the better part of a year just to get Owen to sleep with him. Getting him to agree to start a family might take a few years, or maybe a decade. He wasn't in a rush.

"Do you want to hold her?" Luke asked Tianna.

She shook her head "No. She's beautiful, but I…no."

Something in her voice caught Royan's attention. Pain? Regret?

Owen must have heard it too, because he was at her side in seconds. "Tia?"

"I'm fine. Just tired." He got the feeling it was more than that, but he didn't push.

"Then we're taking you home. Doc said we weren't supposed to stay long, anyway."

"And if we hog all the baby time, Cyn will break us into bits," Royan added.

"Aunt Cynder is awesome, and you're going to love her," he told the sleepy baby, then leaned down to kiss her, too.

"You three make beautiful babies. Congratulations."

"We'll be back to visit again soon. Congrats mom and dads. They're amazing," Owen said.

"Thank you for letting me be part of this. When you've decided on their names, let me know. I'll need them to start their trust funds."

Everyone stared at Tianna.

"Trust fund?" Zura asked.

"So that your daughters will never be beholden to anyone, for anything. They'll be free to follow their dreams."

Royan saw the gleam of tears in his sweetheart's eyes as she spoke. She was giving the twins the most precious gift she could imagine. The freedom to be whoever they wanted to be.

"Come on, lover. Let's get you home." He took her hand and they left the room, saying their goodbyes as they filed out.

Tianna walked in silence, but there were tears on her

cheeks as they slipped out a side door and were whisked into a waiting Corp-Sec transport.

"I don't want to go back to my place," She said once they were inside. Corp-Sec had kept the media away from the medical center, but there would likely be a group of them staking out the Astek office. He and Owen had already talked about it, and they had another destination in mind.

"That's not where we're going," Owen said as the transport took off, rising above the street and heading for the main promenade.

"Then where?" she asked.

"The safest place on the station. We're going to the Nova Club. It's all arranged." Cynder had made a call and set things up. Everything they needed, including a hot meal, was waiting for them.

"That sounds good." Tianna yawned. "I need a few hours of sleep before I have to face everything."

"We all do. It's been a long night, and I suspect it's going to be an even longer day." Royan leaned back and closed his eyes. He wasn't sure how the things would unfold, but whatever happened, he wasn't letting Tianna out of his sight. She needed them, and no matter what it took, he was going to be there for her.

He reached over, setting his hand on Owen's thigh. Owen was going to need him, too. There had been no time to talk about Katy, yet, but they would. When they did, he'd make sure Owen had all the support he needed, too. After all, that's what family did.

TIANNA ONLY MANAGED a few hours of restless sleep before Royan had roused her with a mug of coffee and a kiss so hot it made her wish she could stay in bed and hide for the rest of the day. Cynder had arranged for them to have one of the simple but comfortable rooms the club offered to friends and staff members. It wasn't large, or luxurious, but it was clean, and safe. Even more important, it wasn't anywhere near Astek, or the bloody crime scene she'd created protecting herself last night. She'd have to go back there eventually, but not today.

Another advantage to staying at the Nova Club was the security. No one from the media could reach her here. She'd have to talk to them soon, but she could do it on her schedule without having to worry about running a gauntlet of shouted questions and photographers. Cynder had given her access to one of the meeting rooms, too, giving Tianna a secure, quiet place to come up with a plan.

They were there now, Royan pacing while Owen scanned countless news and entertainment channels, looking for any mention of Astek, her father, or her. He was using headphones so that she couldn't hear what was said, but she could tell by his thunderous expression that it wasn't good news. Not that they'd had any of that since waking up. Her father was still ignoring her messages, and no one at Astek had been able to reach him. She was terrified something had happened to him. Had they both been targets? If he was alive, why wasn't he answering her? Astek needed him, and as much as she hated him right now, so did she.

She was running things as best she could, but Astek's stocks were dropping and the board's demands for action were getting louder. She had to set aside her personal issues with her father and deal with the crisis that was threatening the company, but she didn't have the authority to do what had to be done. Only her father did.

A sharp knock on the door startled them all. Owen stood. Royan stopped pacing, and Tianna braced for more bad news.

Royan dropped a hand to his sidearm and went to the door, not relaxing until he saw who was there. Dash and Mack were outside, both wearing their Corp-Sec uniforms and grim expressions.

"Come on in. You're here in person, so I'm guessing this isn't something you wanted to send over comms." Royan gestured for them both to come in.

"This kind of news gets delivered in person," Mack said.

Dash nodded. "We wanted to be sure you heard it from us before it breaks on the news, which should happen any time now."

"What happened?" Tianna's got to her feet as an icy draft of dread washed over her. News delivered in person was rarely good.

"Official notification just came to our office. It's protocol in situations like this." Mack squared his shoulders and spoke again. "I'm sorry, Miss Astor. Your father's vehicle was involved in some kind of accident. It happened on the route he takes to work each day. The wreckage has been searched, and we have confirmation that your father was inside. He did not survive."

"Who else knows?" She asked, her mind racing as her heart went into freefall. Her father was dead. She'd never get to confront him. Never get to hear his explanations. For better or worse, Astek was hers, now. She'd have to navigate this craziness without him.

"The media have already learned of the accident, but no details have been released until the next of kin could be notified." Dash inclined his head. "I'm sorry, Tianna."

She nodded and forced herself to keep moving, keep reacting. There was too much to do to get swept up in emotions. "Thank you. Is there anything else I need to know?"

Mack sighed. "About your father, no. Details about what happened to him are sparse right now."

"What about Katy?" Owen asked. "Did she give you anything?"

"She refused to cooperate at first, but once we explained the alternatives to her, she gave us everything she knew."

"Alternatives?" Tianna asked, desperate for any kind of distraction.

"Pharma enhanced interrogation. Forced memory extraction. Very unpleasant ways to get to the truth, with or without the subject's compliance," Dash explained.

"What did she tell you?" Owen asked.

"We got the names of the people she works with. Most of them are former cartel operatives. We have the coordinates for her ship, too. They used an unmarked shuttle to get here, and they managed to defeat the facial recognition software using disguises and a couple of cheap and dirty personal shield generators."

"How the hell did she get her hands on tech like that?" Royan asked, stunned. The personal shield generators were new tech, and very expensive.

Mack looked dour. "Apparently someone with deep pockets is financing the cartels."

"Wonderful," Royan commented.

"My sister really got herself in deep with the wrong people." Owen sounded pained, and she shook off her own grief to go to him, taking his hand and holding it tight.

"We're looking into it," Mack said.

"I still don't understand why a bunch of smugglers and criminals would want me dead, or how they managed to get access to the *Alacrity*."

"It's too soon to know anything. We'll follow up on the information Valentine gave us, keep investigating, and hopefully find out who paid them to try and kill you," Dash said.

"Whoever it is, they might be the ones behind my father's death, too." She held up a hand. "I'm not saying it was murder, but he's traveled that route hundreds of times. Maybe thousands. His vehicle is fully automated. The odds of him being involved in an accident..." She shook her head.

"It's going to take time, but we'll find out who was behind this. We'll keep you in the loop about the investigation, and the officers assigned your father's case will be contacting you directly from now on. Notification fell to us, but as next of kin, you'll be kept apprised of everything they find."

"Thank you." She walked them both to the door and saw them out, then turned to Royan and Owen and tried to muster a brave face. "This day just went from bad to worse. Better break out the *ja'kreesh*, we're going to need it.

"Whatever you need, sweetheart."

"I have what I need. You and Owen. If you're with me, then I know I'll get through this…somehow." This was what she'd been trained for since birth. Every lesson and lecture had shaped her thinking and prepared her for this day. It just wasn't supposed to come yet.

"What happens now?" Owen asked.

She flicked her braid back over her shoulder, took a breath, and moved so she was standing directly in front of the monitor. "Now I tell the board my father's gone and I'm taking over. Then, we tell them everything else. Buckle up, boys. This ride is about to get rough."

Royan flashed her a grin. "You know that's the way I like it."

"I know." She blew them both a kiss, grateful beyond words that the universe had brought them into her life. The first time they'd met, they'd saved her life, and now, if she was lucky, they were going to stick around to help her rebuild it.

CHAPTER NINETEEN

THEIR DAY DIDN'T END until deep into the night cycle. It had been long, trying, and occasionally downright chaotic, but Tianna had taken it all in stride. Owen knew she was smart and capable, but today she'd stepped into the middle of a crisis and handled everything the universe had thrown at her without missing a step.

"In case I haven't mentioned it enough, you were *fraxxing* amazing today," he told her as they finally returned to their room.

"And in related news, whatever you're paying yourself, it's not enough." Royan started undoing the buttons of his dress shirt, then gave up and pulled it over his head without finishing. As much as Owen had enjoyed seeing Royan dressed like a corporate executive on the fast track, right now all he wanted was to enjoy some quality time with both his lovers, preferably without any clothes at all.

"I haven't had time to negotiate my salary. My new boss has been keeping me busy." Tianna was struggling to undo the fastenings on the back of her dress and Owen moved in behind her to help.

"I've got this." He undid the clasp, then leaned in to plant an open-mouthed kiss to the back of her neck. She uttered a low, contented moan and leaned back, rocking her hips against his cock, which went hard in seconds.

"Oh, yeah. You ready to put this day behind us and unwind, sweetheart?" Royan stepped in front of her, bare chested and smiling.

"If by unwind you mean make each other orgasm until we all pass out, then yes, that's exactly my plan. My head hurts and my heart aches, and I want it all to go away for a little while." She laid a hand on Royan's chest, then tipped her head back to look up at him. "Can you do that for me?"

"With pleasure," Owen said, watching them.

"So much pleasure," Royan was almost purring now.

They undressed hurriedly, helping each other out of their clothes, teasing and caressing every bit of bare skin they could reach. It had been days. As much as he had enjoyed his time alone with Tianna, there was something special when they were all together like this. Every emotion, every sensation was amplified, and each time was better than the last. He knew why, too. It was because they loved each other. Tianna hadn't said the words yet, but he didn't need to hear it to know it was the truth.

He kicked off his pants and stole Tianna for a kiss while Royan headed over to their bed, trailing his hand over Owen's hip as he walked by.

"Don't be long, baby," Royan said as he knelt on the bed and took his cock into his hand, stroking it slowly.

Tianna leaned to one side to smile at Royan. "Ladies, first."

"So, that's how it's going to be?" Royan huffed.

"Uh huh," Tianna gripped Owen's shoulders and hopped up so she could wrap her legs around his waist. He caught her easily and turned to press her up against the nearest wall, his tongue tangling with hers as he ground his cock against the soft mound of her mons. She tasted sweet, with a hint of peppermint from the lip balm she wore. It was fast becoming his favorite flavor.

"And to think, all this time we were worried about wearing you out. You realize what this means, sweetheart? It means we don't stop until you wear *us* out."

She laughed, the sound buzzing against his lips as he kissed her. *Veth*, he loved hearing her laugh. It was a rare sound right now – for both of them. Katy was a lost cause, but she was his sister and he'd still do what he could for her. He pushed aside all thoughts of his sister and focused on the good things in his life: Tianna and Royan. He planted both hands on the lush curve of Tianna's ass, lifting her higher before moving back from the wall and toward the bed where Royan waited for them.

Owen handed her to Royan, who drew her into his arms with a low groan of need. "Finally."

"I missed you, too," she whispered, one arm twining around his neck as she reached back for Owen. "I need this. Us. Together. I'm greedy. I want you both."

"You're not greedy." Owen took her hand and let her pull him onto the bed and into their embrace.

"Maybe a little bit crazy, but we like your kind of crazy. It fits so well with ours." Royan turned his head and kissed Owen, their mouths mating for a short but passionate kiss that made all three of them groan.

"I'm just grateful you've both forgiven me for lying to you."

"You did what you had to do. I get that." Owen had thought it through, and he understood why she'd done it. She wasn't just protecting herself, she was trying to protect her father. He'd lied for lesser reasons, so how could he blame her?

"You told us you couldn't tell us all your secrets back on the *Sun Sprite*." Royan pointed out.

"Still. Thank you. And thank you for accepting me even though I'm not what you thought I was."

Owen kissed her softly. They didn't care that she was a cyborg, or that she couldn't have children. She'd confessed that to them earlier. It was yet another thing her father had stolen from her, but it didn't matter. Nothing was going to change how they felt about her. "You're our Tia. That's all that matters."

Soft fingers wrapped around his dick, pumping his shaft gently. Royan shuddered, and Owen guessed Tianna was stroking them both. When he started to move, her hand stopped.

"Not yet. You two kiss more. I like watching you, and I know that you've both been focused on me lately."

Her words made his cock turn to steel and his balls tighten. She really was their kind of crazy. He speared a hand into Royan's hair and pulled him closer, kissing him the same way he'd kissed her only a few seconds ago. Long, hard, and deep enough to let him drink in Royan's taste, the way his beard felt against his skin, the subtle spice of the soap he used.

Tianna's fingers tightened, her movements getting hard, faster. She twisted her hand just a little on each tug, just the way he liked it.

The three of them shifted, rearranging themselves without letting go of one another. Now they were all kneeling, Tianna guiding their movements until he was almost chest to chest with Royan. She brought their cocks together, stroking them both with her hands as they thrust and ground against her, and each other.

"I've wanted to do this since the first night we got naked." Her voice was low and breathless. She was as turned on as they were, and they weren't even touching her. He nipped Royan's lower lip, and his lover hummed in agreement. They broke apart, both of them turning their attention on her. Owen reached out and wrapped the thick braid of her hair around his fist, guiding her head so that her throat was bared. He ducked his head and kissed her, starting at the pulse point beating beneath her ear and working down to the bare curve of her shoulder.

"Do you want to belong to us, Tianna?" he whispered the question against her skin.

She was silent for a moment, but that was only because Royan had sealed her mouth with a kiss that made her tremble.

When the kiss ended, her answer came right away. "I want us to belong to each other. I don't know how that will work, but that's what I want."

"We'll make it work," Royan said, laying a hand on Owen's shoulder. "We have to, because I'm not letting go of either one of you. I love you both too damned much."

Owen felt exactly the same way. Despite everything they'd been through, the danger, fights, and betrayals, he was happy. If this was what it was like when things were hard, he couldn't wait to experience what it might be like when things were good again. "You're a pair of lunatics and you're going to drive me crazy, but I love you both. So yeah, we're going to make this work."

She leaned back and smiled at them, her green eyes gleaming with tears. "I love you, too. So much. I think you are both part of the life I was always supposed to have. It just took me a long time to realize it."

And with those words, the last pieces of Owen's life fell into place. He was where he was supposed to be, with the ones he was meant to find. He was home.

TIANNA WAS RIDING the rest of a wave of happiness and love, the two emotions so tangled up she didn't know which was which, nor did she care. The three of them came together, kissing, touching, and stroking each other until they were all shaking with need. Eventually Owen took charge, sitting down, legs parted, then drawing her down to sit between them so her back was to his chest and her legs were stretched out in front of her.

Royan was grinning as he lifted each of her legs and draped them over Owen's. "Now that's a beautiful sight," he said before lying down on his stomach, his face only a few inches from her exposed pussy.

There was raw hunger on his face as he eased closer, his breath fanning over her swollen outer lips. Without a word, he ran his fingers over her wet folds, gently parting them with his thumbs, then taking a deep breath and staring up at her. "You are delicious. May I have a taste, my queen?"

"You may have anything you want, lover."

"What I want is to watch you come."

Owen reached around and started toying with her nipples. "I want to watch that, too. Make her come for us, Roy-boy."

Fraxx, she loved it when Owen used that tone of voice. It was sexy as hell, and so was the way Royan obeyed him, every single time. Royan leaned in, swiping his tongue over her clit. She gasped, and Owen pinched her nipples, just hard enough to sting. Before she could catch her breath, Royan slid a finger into her channel, fucking her with his fingers while his tongue licked and teased at her swollen clit.

He moved slowly, drawing out the seconds, pushing her closer to her breaking point without letting her go over. Owen kept playing with her breasts until she was so sensitive that every touch and pinch sent a jolt of pleasure straight to her clit. She was writhing now, raising her hips off the bed in time to the thrust of Royan's fingers and the flick of his tongue.

"You ready to come for us?" Owen whispered in her ear.

"Yes!"

"Give her what she needs, Royan."

Royan growled and quickened his pace, fingers flying now. He sucked the tender pearl of her clit into his mouth and lashed it with his tongue, holding it there until her orgasm hit with the force of a runaway rocket. As she rode the waves of pleasure, Owen whispered in her ear, telling her exactly what was going to happen next.

"We're going to fuck you together, now, Tia. Front and back, so deep inside you we'll be able to feel each other's cocks. Do you want that?"

She managed a shaky nod. "Mhmm."

"So do I."

As her orgasm ebbed, Royan pushed himself back to his knees, then wiped his mouth with the back of his hand. "You are my favorite feast in the whole damned galaxy, sweetheart." He stretched out beside her in the middle of the bed, his cock in his fist and a sexy grin on his handsome face. "Now, come here and let me fuck you, beautiful."

She untangled herself from Owen and got to her knees. She didn't get any further before Owen gripped her hips and lifted her into position, her legs straddling Royan's waist, his cock caught between their bodies. Owen kissed her shoulder, then leaned down and kissed Royan while she watched.

"Meet you in the middle, baby," Rowan murmured when they parted again.

"You did not just say that," she laughed and shook her head.

"Yeah, he did. And yet, we love him anyway."

Her braid had fallen over her shoulder, and Royan used it to pull her down to kiss her, his tongue slipping into her mouth to dance with hers. She lost herself in his kiss, letting herself drown in the pleasure of his touch and basking in the knowledge that he loved her. He didn't care about her money, her position, or the fact she was a cyborg. He'd never cared about any of that. All he wanted was her.

Owen moved in behind her, the mattress dipping as he

settled into the space between Royan's legs. He placed his hands on her hips, stroked down to her thighs, and then reached between them to play with Royan's balls for a moment. Royan stiffened, his cock twitching against her pussy.

"Whatever you did, do it again," she said.

Royan's eyes closed and his breath hitched as Owen touched him again. "I don't know whether to spank you or thank you for that, brat."

She grinned, then yelped as Owen swatted her ass cheek. "Hey! What was that for?"

"A reminder that you're not in charge right now. Relax and let us take care of you."

"It's okay to let go, sweetheart. We've got you." Royan lifted his head and kissed her, softly at first, but as the fire between them flared his kiss intensified. Owen pressed between her shoulder blades, one hand on her hip reminding her to keep her ass high as she lowered herself to Royan's chest and kissed him deeply.

Owen released her hip, and then his hand was between her thighs again, fingering her pussy before shifting his grip and drawing Royan's cock out from between them so it was flush against her entrance.

She shifted her hips, Royan arched his back, and the two of them came together with a collective moan. He claimed her a slow inch at a time, until he was buried deep inside her body and she could feel his cock throb against her inner walls. They kept to the same slow tempo while Owen started preparing her.

"Barrier gel's a little cold," he warned her before letting a trickle of the liquid flow between her cheeks. He spread it over her skin with two already slick fingers, slipping them between her nether cheeks.

"Ready?" he asked.

"More than ready." This was something new for all of them. A level of intimacy they hadn't achieved until now.

Owen pressed a finger to her tight rosebud, moving gently but firmly until he was inside her.

Royan rocked his hips, keeping his thrusts too light and shallow to do anything but tease her, the perfect distraction from what Owen was doing. They worked together, her pleasure far greater than any pain, even after Owen added a second finger, stretching her body in preparation for his cock.

It was almost overwhelming, so many sensations, tangled up with feelings of love, need, and vulnerability.

"Still okay?" Owen asked, stroking her back with one hand.

"I'm good. So good." She rocked between them, driving first Royan, then Owen deeper into her body.

He withdrew his fingers. "Then I think it's time."

"Yes, please." There was so much need in her voice it embarrassed her, but Royan cupped her burning cheeks in his hands and looked into her eyes.

"Relax, sweetheart. Just breathe and remember we love you."

She nodded, exhaled, and kissed him again. This time it was a sweet, tender kiss that melted her mind and stole her heart.

She held onto that feeling as Owen claimed her body, easing himself into her with care. There was a moment's pain, but then there was nothing but pleasure as her body adjusted. She wriggled her hips and both men groaned as her body flexed around theirs. They didn't move, though. She knew they were waiting for her, that despite what they'd told her about letting go, they hadn't taken anything away from her. They'd wait forever if she asked it of them.

Not that she wanted to wait another second. She raised her head and rocked backward, driving Owen's cock deeper.

"I can feel you," Royan whispered, staring past her to look at Owen. "This is…"

"Perfect," Owen finished the sentence, his voice rough with need.

Slowly, carefully, they found their rhythm, a gentle give and take that filled her first one way, then the other. Her senses overloaded, and everything began to blur and blend together. They moved as one, caught up in a dance with no music but the beating of their hearts.

She held onto each moment as it came, not wanting it to end, but eventually the pleasure built until she was trembling with need and her control broke, sending her tumbling into an orgasm that crashed over her like a tidal wave. She came crying out their names, caught between the two men she loved and trusted more than anyone else in the galaxy.

She closed her eyes and let herself drift as the two of them found their pleasure, emptying themselves inside her with wordless groans. Owen slumped over her, pressing her down onto Royan and triggering another small orgasm as his cock stroked deep inside her over-sensitive channel.

By the time she opened her eyes again, Owen was kissing her shoulder, and Royan was smiling up at her with a tender expression that filled her heart and soul with joy.

"Love you," she whispered, staring down at him.

"And we love you." Owen kissed her one last time, then pushed himself off of her. The moment of separation gave her a pang of regret, but it only lasted until he settled next to them and brushed a kiss to her lips, and then Royan's before leaning back and giving them both a smug smile.

"Mine," he said.

"And mine," Royan said, reaching out to touch Owen's cheek.

"And mine, too," she placed her hand over Royan's. This is what it would be like from now on. The three of them together, connected by love, laughter, and a little bit of crazy.

Tianna sipped her cocktail, happy to sit back and let the celebration flow around her. She'd never been to a baby shower before, but even so, she knew this one was quite unique.

The dim lights and dark hues of the Nova Club had been transformed into a sea of bright colors and festive lights. There were light cubes on every table, bunting and ribbons tied to every possible surface, and tiny drones flew overhead, occasionally setting off miniature firework displays. The bar was laden with confections and pastries, while servers moved around the guests, laughing, chatting, and offering up free drinks.

Zura and her daughters, Dana and Mya, were holding court at the far end of the bar. The twins were tucked into an extra large crib by their mother, surrounded by a group of ever changing guests coming to see the babies and deliver gifts and well wishes. Kit and Luke stood beside their wife, looking like the proudest parents to ever breathe atmosphere. Behind them, almost completely lost in the shadows, two cyborgs watched over the family. Ward and Victor hadn't wanted to come tonight, but they'd relented when they were asked to keep an eye on things so that Kit and Luke could enjoy the night without worry. Not that the two new fathers were going to stop worrying, but it gave Vic and Ward a reason to be at the party without feeling like they had to take part. The others might have forgiven them for what they'd done as the Reaper, but they hadn't forgiven themselves, yet.

"You're quiet tonight." Owen said. They were on either side of her, chatting to friends and family as they wandered past. Everyone was friendly, but some of them weren't entirely comfortable in her presence. A few of them because she was something new they didn't understand, but most of them kept their distance because she was now the owner of this station, along with the rest of Astek Corporation.

She didn't blame them. Since taking over, she wasn't always comfortable, either. She felt like a fraud. Her father hadn't believed she was ready. In fact, she now knew that he'd been convinced she'd never be ready. She was determined to prove the bastard wrong.

"I'm soaking up all this happiness." She gestured around her, drink in hand. "It's been a long time since I've been around so many happy people. And it might be a while since I get to enjoy it again." The last few weeks had been challenging, but the chaos was starting to ebb, and it looked like Astek had weathered the worst of the storm. Now that things were stabilizing, she was expected to return home. Only, the private moon where her father lived – had lived – wasn't home anymore. She'd go back to set things right, and then she'd return to the Drift. Astek station was about to become the de facto base of operations for the entire corporation. She could run the business from anywhere, but this station was the one place she felt like she belonged.

"We'll be back before you know it." Royan said, his thumb drawing tiny circles across the top of her thigh.

"And it's not like you're going to be alone. We'll be with you every step of the way." Owen set his hand down on top of Royan's. "I promise, we'll find a way to have at least a little fun." She was grateful to them both for what they'd done for her. They'd gone to Zura and resigned, giving up their careers to stay with her. No one had ever given up so much for her. It was humbling.

"Yeah, your father's place has a lake, right? We can take Owen swimming. That should be good for hours of fun."

"Fuck you, Roy-boy."

Royan winked at Owen. "Any time you want to, baby."

She knew they were teasing each other to make her laugh, and it was working. Over the last few weeks they'd learned her moods, soothing her when she needed it, making her laugh, and giving her all the support and encouragement she could want. She didn't always find it easy to accept, but she loved them so much for believing in her. With their help, she'd saved Astek from disaster, and now she was ready to start moving forward with *her* vision for the company. Things were going to change, not just on the Drift, but everywhere.

With her father gone, she had finally gotten access to his files, and what she'd found had stunned her. Astek's core was rotten, poisoned by years of greed, lies, and larceny. There were secret accounts, communications with criminals, and enough damning evidence to ensure that if Cornelius Astor had lived, he'd have spent the rest of his days in a cell. Much of the data she'd found had been corrupted, and the experts at Nova Force believed even more of it had been completely deleted, with no chance of recovery. Someone had done a near perfect job of hacking her father's life and wiping away huge parts of it. She'd never know exactly what he'd been up to, but she knew more than enough.

Anger swirled in her gut as she allowed herself to think about what she'd learned. Her father had never loved her. She knew that now. He'd created her to fulfill a specific purpose - to take over the company. He'd wanted a perfect copy, a clone that would carry on his legacy. He'd gotten an individual whose opinions and actions didn't match his, and would never measure up to his expectations.

The accident had given him a second chance to recoup his investment. He'd rebuilt her body and reprogrammed her mind. She was still working through that with Dr. Virness, trying to separate her thoughts and feelings from the ones she'd been conditioned to believe were hers. It would take months, or maybe years, before she would be able to trust her own mind. It helped that she now had her medical files, the ones he'd hidden from her. It detailed everything they'd done to her, and included the names of everyone involved. She'd given a copy to Nova Force, and they were investigating. So far, they hadn't been able to locate anyone. A few were dead. Most had vanished in the years since her accident. Owen and Royan believed they were probably still active somewhere, working for the Gray Men.

The Gray Men. All evidence pointed to the fact her

father was one of them, though there was nothing concrete. Whoever had deleted his life had been particular, leaving behind just enough information to make it clear he'd been a criminal without incriminating anyone else. At least, no one who could answer any questions. They'd left the data about what had been done to her, though. Every bit of it. Something told her that hadn't been an accident, and neither had her father's death.

Officially, his death had been ruled a suicide. The final act of a desperate man whose secrets were all about to be revealed. She didn't believe it, and neither did Nova Force, but they preferred to keep that information quiet. They suspected her father had been murdered before his arrest exposed the Gray Men's secrets.

It was clear now that they'd been involved in rebuilding her. Their people. Their tech. She was an experiment to them. One her father had deemed a failure. He'd been the one to order the attempts on her life. He'd paid the cartels to have her killed. Hacked Tink. Made it possible for someone to get the explosives on board. That information hadn't been wiped, either. Not all of it. They'd left breadcrumbs behind for her to find. Taunting her with grim snippets of the truth.

She knew now that the Gray Men had come to her father with an offer. A chance to extend his life with a new type of medi-bots. He would have had more time to try for another heir. To try again to create the perfect legacy, using her DNA as a starting point. She'd discovered that during her initial surgeries, her father had ordered her eggs be harvested and placed in cryo-storage.

Her father was a monster. All those warnings she'd

sent to him, and he was the one trying to kill her. Every time she thought about it, her anger flared again.

Owen and Royan were at her side, though, and that made all the difference. They helped her through the grief and rage. Held her hands while Lieksa had systematically shut down the implants that modified her behavior. Loved her and supported her through the long days and nights battling with the board and the other corporations.

She'd discovered something else, too, buried in her father's files. The name of her mother. Tianna hadn't contacted her yet. She wasn't sure she ever would. But now, she had the choice. So much had changed for her. Her life had been upended, but her two lovers had stood by her through it all. They were the rock she'd clung to when the storm had been at its worst, and now the skies were clearing, she wasn't in any rush to let them go. Not now, not ever.

"You're thinking too much again. You want to go see the twins? I bet they're missing their Aunt Tia," Owen said.

She banished her dark thoughts and conjured a smile. "Not as much as they're missing their uncles. I swear those girls already know they have you both wrapped around their tiny little fingers."

"That's because I'm the galaxy's most awesome uncle," Royan said. "They just tolerate Owen because he has the good sense to have fallen for me."

Owen rolled his eyes, but stayed silent. He'd been quiet since he'd said goodbye to his sister. Katy had cooperated with the authorities and was now on her way to a prison planet for the foreseeable future. A lifetime of raiding, piracy, and the attempts on Tianna's life had added up to a substantial sentence.

Tianna had tried to be there for him, too. His attempts to reconnect with Katy had been rebuffed. She was too broken. Too angry. Tianna suspected that the pirate turned killer had lost too much of her soul in the years since Owen had left, but that didn't stop him from trying. He'd visited Katy every day she allowed it. Some days she hadn't. Those were hard days for him. He had questions for his sister, and she would not, or could not, give him the answers he wanted. She understood how that felt. Her father had left her with questions, too.

Thinking about Owen reminded Tianna that she had one piece of good news to share. She'd been hanging onto since this afternoon, but now seemed the perfect time. Tonight was supposed to be about celebrating new life, wasn't it?

"I was going to tell you after the party, but I've decided not to wait. Owen, I got word from a friend of mine at the Justice Ministry. Your application for amnesty was fast-tracked. It won't be official for a few more days, but any and all charges relating to your previous life are going to be expunged. You're getting a clean slate." She couldn't help Katy, but she had been able to pull a few strings and see to it that the man she loved could finally leave his past behind completely.

Royan cheered, and Owen looked dumbstruck. "How? That kind of thing usually takes years."

"Your girlfriend knows the right people. And before you grumble about justice not being blind and money buying all sorts of unfair advantages, remember that this time, it all worked in your favor." She'd done what she could for Katy, too. Not for her sake, but for Owen's.

Royan laughed. "She knows you so well."

"Thank you. I...I don't know what to say. I was worried about what would happen if anyone found out you were sleeping with a criminal. You've already faced enough censure and bullshit thanks to your old man." Owen pulled her close and kissed her hard. "I love you so much."

"And I love you, which is why I'm happy I could do this for you. The files will be sealed. Your secret is safe. You can even go back to your old name, if you wanted to."

"I like Connors."

Royan shifted in his seat. "I do too, but maybe it's time to think about changing it."

"I don't want to be a Valentine."

"I know." Royan shifted again, then left his chair and moved to stand between them. "I was wondering if maybe you'd like to be a Watson, instead."

Owen stilled but didn't answer.

"I think you're supposed to be on your knees. Isn't that tradition?"

"*Fraxx* tradition." Royan held out both hands. "And that question was for both of you."

It was the first time she'd ever seen Royan nervous. He stood in front of them, arms open, hands shaking.

Owen looked at her, then back to their lover. "What do you think?"

"I think Tianna Watson-Astor has a nice ring to it. What about you?"

Royan smiled but stayed quiet, which couldn't have been easy for the naturally exuberant man.

"I think Owen Watson-Astor has a nice ring to it, too."

"Is that a yes? Please tell me that's a yes."

"Yes." She and Owen answered at once, and Royan let loose with a whoop of delight that drew everyone's attention.

"Oh, hell, what have you done, now?" Cynder called out.

"I proposed. And they said yes!" Royan leaped onto the table and danced in a circle, hands raised over his head as both she and Owen looked on in stunned amusement.

There was laughter, cheers, and several groans from around the room. "Dammit, I lost again!"

"I missed it by a month."

"I was off by a *fraxxing* year."

"I had ten-to-one odds they never got around to making it official."

"I better get my share of the winnings, Roy-boy," Owen muttered.

Royan looked outraged. "It wasn't me. Not this time. Who the hell was taking bets on my love life without giving me a cut?"

Zura appeared and the crowd parted, letting the guest of honor through. "You think you're the only one around here who knows how to make money gambling, little brother? I know a sure thing when I see it. I'm just happy you figured it out on your own." She raised her glass. "Congratulations, you three. Owen and Tianna, welcome to the family."

Royan hopped down and gathered them both into his arms, kissing her and then Owen. She held onto them, nearly overwhelmed by her emotions. Love, joy, and hope swirled inside her. This was the life she wanted for herself.

These were the people she chose to be her family. To love, cherish, and laugh with for as long as the universe allowed.

The End

Check out more of Susan's work at
https://susanhayes.ca/

Want to read more stories with book boyfriends
that are out of this world?

**Check out Susan Hayes' other Science Fiction Romance
Titles**

The Drift
Double Down
All In
Wild Card
Three of a Kind
Full House
No Limit
Aces Over Queen
Dealers' Choice

Nova Force
Operation Phoenix
Operation Cobalt

Star-Crossed Alien Mail Order Brides
Joran
Vader
Kash
Tarjen
Torel
Radek
Karos
Jet
Vykor

<u>3013: The Series</u>
3013: RENEGADE
3013: STOWAWAY
3013: TARGETED
3013: FATED
3013: SCARRED